Quartet  Qrime

THE WATER WIDOW

Also by Ella Griffiths

Murder on Page Three

ELLA GRIFFITHS

The Water Widow

Translated from the Norwegian by
J. BASIL COWLISHAW

Quartet Qrime

English translation first published by Quartet Books Limited 1986
A member of the Namara Group
27/29 Goodge Street, London W1P 1FD
First published in Norway by Grondahl & Son A/S, Oslo, 1977

British Library Cataloguing in Publication Data

Griffiths, Ella
The water widow.
I. Title
839.8'2374[F]   PT8951.17.R5

ISBN 0-7043-2559-4

Typeset by M.C. Typeset, Chatham, Kent
Printed and bound in Great Britain by
Nene Litho and Woolnough Bookbinding
both of Wellingborough, Northants

1

On the last day of his life Georg Brandt was awakened at five in the morning by an agonizing toothache. He tried to alleviate the pain with camphor drops, which he rubbed into the offending molar and inflamed gum with the tip of his finger. When that didn't help he dissolved three Disprils in a glass of water, gulped down the cloudy mixture that resulted, and crept back under the bedclothes to await the expected miracle. When that too failed to materialize he climbed despairingly out of bed, put on his brand-new dressing-gown (last year's Christmas present to himself from himself), and began to pace to and fro across the room like an angry bear disturbed in its winter slumber.

At that moment, compared with the pain of the toothache, the fact that Harts the Clothiers were in difficulties and that there was talk of lay-offs seemed of little consequence – despite the fact that, although he had been there the longest, he was the oldest member of the staff and, unjust though it seemed, would very likely be the first to go. Nor did it appear so important as it had the day before that Johansen, his landlord, wanted the flat back because his nephew was nearing the end of his studies in Trondheim and would be needing somewhere to live in Oslo. 'You realize how painful this is for me, I'm sure, Georg,' Johansen had said.

After having played chess with him twice a week for the five years or more he'd lived there, Georg Brandt felt he knew

Johansen sufficiently well to know that it wasn't painful to him at all. But he'd held his peace.

Only yesterday evening he had been worried sick about the future. What would he do if he did lose his job? And where would he move to? He'd felt so settled, and his meagre savings were by no means enough to enable him to buy a flat of his own. But just now he was in such pain that he would have found it difficult to respond even if someone had burst in and shouted 'Fire!' And it didn't help any when he let his fingers do the walking and found in the yellow pages the cheerless entry: Dental Service, Municipal, Emergency, Biskop Gunnerus Gate 11/13, entrance Skipper Gate. Daily 2000–2300, Sat., Sun., public holidays 1100–1400.

He couldn't possibly hold out till eight in the evening, but his regular dentist had sold up and gone to live in Spain, and he'd never got around to finding a new one. A name suddenly floated into his mind: Peter Brenner. Where'd he got that from? he wondered. Oh, now he remembered. He'd heard Iversen, one of his fellow shop assistants, recommending him to another member of the staff. 'Best thing about him,' Iversen had said, 'is that he starts so early. Opens at seven, so you can get your teeth done without having to ask for time off. He's not all that expensive, either. Real good sort, too.'

Iversen, like Brandt himself, wasn't given to exaggeration. He hadn't said one could just turn up for treatment on spec, however. But if he rang and the dentist said no? It didn't bear thinking about. Better to take a chance and tackle him face to face in the waiting-room. Brandt had a vague idea that dentists in private practice occasionally took pity on suffering mortals like himself and slipped them in among their regular patients. The municipal service, on the other hand, stuck strictly to the first-come-first-served principle. People who went there were *all* urgent cases.

He was pleased to discover from the directory that Brenner's surgery was quite close, but was less pleased to see that his hours were down as 0900 to 1400 daily, Saturdays closed. It had been some time ago that he had heard Iversen mention the dentist, but he earnestly hoped that Brenner hadn't changed his routine. Perhaps it was only special patients he took so early?

2

Regulars. Well, there was only one way to find out: he'd have to go and see. One thing he knew for certain: he wouldn't be able to serve any customers until the tooth had been dealt with. His eyes were full of tears and his face was white and drawn. Harts wasn't Savile Row exactly, but even so he couldn't go about looking as though he'd been on a bender for the last couple of weeks. He neither drank nor smoked, but who was to know that? In all the years he'd been in the shop, twenty, nearly twenty-one, he'd had only nine days off through illness, so he felt entitled to take a few hours off now, the whole day, in fact, with a clear conscience. But did he dare? Those rumours . . .

It was a Friday, the fifth of March. In ten days it would be his birthday. He hadn't planned to do anything special, only visit his mother at the old people's home where she'd been for the last few years. The fifteenth fell on a Monday, and that was one of the days he was accustomed to visit her. Monday, Wednesday, Saturday, year in, year out. She was eighty-six; sharp as a needle still, but her legs had started to let her down, and in the end she'd had to give up her flat. His own was on the third floor and there was no lift, so there had been no question of her moving in with him. Besides, she was wise enough to realize that he had a right to live his own life.

He'd been doing it for so long, alone, that his innate sense of order and neatness was in danger of becoming an obsession. His toothache notwithstanding, almost without realizing that he was doing it, he made the bed and carefully smoothed out the coverlet. He couldn't face the thought of food, but he downed two cups of coffee. Afterwards he rinsed the cup, saucer and teaspoon under the hot-water tap, dried them, returned the cup and saucer to the cupboard, and replaced the spoon in the drawer. He put the half-full cream-jug back in the fridge and meticulously wiped the surround of the sink. Although he always slept with the window open and the bedroom door was always left ajar to allow fresh air to circulate through the rest of the flat, he aired the living-room well before putting on his outdoor clothes and stepping out into the dark of the winter morning.

No one gave him a second glance; he was just one more

3

anonymous figure among all the others, muffled up against the icy wind. Thin, stooping, with the beginnings of a pot belly. Five feet ten inches in height, with a pale face, now drawn with pain, and grey eyes so close-set as to give him a seemingly perpetual scowl. Restless hands in fleece-lined grey gloves. A grey overcoat with a herring-bone pattern. Tucked well inside his coat was a grey scarf. Covering his greying hair, which he wore combed to his skull, was a grey sheepskin hat. Georg Brandt was a study in grey, an undistinguished-looking man who would have gone on living his dull, undistinguished life for many years to come had he not that morning been awakened by toothache.

He scanned the numbers of the buildings as he walked. There it was! A dingy-looking pre-war block of flats with shops on the ground floor, badly in need of restoration. On the frosted lower halves of three windows on the second floor were the words PETER BRENNER – DENTIST in plain black letters. To his dismay there were no lights on, but he could make out the outline of a dentist's lamp just inside the middle window.

He took up his stance in front of one of the shops, gazing at the glass and china on display without really seeing it. It was five to seven. Should he wait till the lights came on? From where he stood he would see it as soon as they were switched on. Or should he go up straight away and wait outside the door? At least it would be warmer.

Although he had covered the distance from his home to the dentist's in no time at all, it took him at least five minutes to come to a decision. Would the tooth have to come out? Or would the dentist recommend a root filling? In any case it would mean an anaesthetic, an injection. Brandt felt his stomach muscles contract. All his life he'd been terrified of hypodermic needles. Twice he'd fainted when he was having an inoculation. A sudden twinge of pain decided him. Sweat beading his forehead, he strode to the entrance door, wrenched it open, and hastened up the stairs. On the landing he stopped, overcome by a new fear. What if Brenner didn't turn up? He might be ill, anything. Then he'd be left with his pain till the evening. He couldn't bear the thought of going to work, but at

4

the same time he was afraid to stay at home.

Staff cuts . . . Johansen wanting the flat . . . The whole of his once so stable but oh-so-fragile world seemed to be coming apart before his eyes. Needle or no needle he had to get his tooth attended to. Until he did he would be unable to fight for either his job or his flat. He closed his eyes for a moment to collect himself, then raised his hand to ring the bell. As he rang, the door opened. Who was the more taken aback, he or the person inside, it was impossible to say.

'Er . . . er . . .' he stammered, staring at the black-clad figure framed in the doorway. He couldn't remember when he'd last seen a woman in full widow's weeds. Although a black veil covered her features, he caught a glimpse of white curls peeping out from beneath her black hat. She was wearing a long black coat, black stockings, black shoes, black gloves, and carrying a black handbag. 'I . . . I . . .' he spluttered.

'Have you an appointment?' the woman asked in a voice so low that Brandt had to strain to catch what she said.

'Er, no . . . that is . . .' he mumbled. His voice trailed helplessly away.

'My son's not here yet, but you can come in and wait if you like.'

'Thank you,' he replied automatically, stepping into a long, dark hallway. He thought it strange that the light wasn't on.

It was almost his last conscious thought.

2

Detective Sergeant Rudolf Nilsen was still on top of the world over his promotion, although it was now three months old. It had certainly been a long time coming. Had he had to wait much longer, he reflected, he'd have started to lose some of his zeal. It was no fun slaving away day and night when no one in authority seemed to notice it. That had rankled, the fact that no one appeared to realize what a good copper he really was.

Rudolf was tall and powerfully built – so powerfully, in fact, that malicious tongues were inclined to call him fat. His mother's pet name for him when he was small had been Roly. All right when he was a wiry young lad at school, but now that middle-age spread was making its presence felt he was beginning to curse it. From Roly to Roly-Poly was but a step, one that some of his more facetious colleagues had already taken. He'd started tightening his belt and walking more erect than ever, but to no avail; he had a paunch, and it seemed to have come to stay.

'You're a disgrace to the Force,' his younger brother was fond of chiding him. 'Eating too much is as bad as drinking too much. Worse, in fact.'

'You only say that because you're so fond of bending your elbow yourself,' he'd retort. Such exchanges were always very lighthearted, but Rudolf was secretly quite worried about Karsten's drinking. Not that he drank to excess; it was just that he seemed to have stepped it up in the last year or so – ever

6

since his wife had left him.

Rudolf munched abstractedly away at a large Californian apple. It was nearly eight o'clock in the evening, time to think about calling it a day. He ought by rights to have packed up long ago, but of late he never seemed to be able to get away on time, and this evening had been no exception. He was actually on the Murder Squad, but since the theft of a lot of dangerous drugs from Ulleval Hospital a week earlier he had been on loan to Narcotics. That's how he came to be in the office at such a late hour – he was writing a lengthy report on the case.

In broad daylight, some time between one and two in the afternoon, a whole containerful of drugs had disappeared from the Surgical Department. Two trusted employees had carried the grey metal case, which came from the hospital's own dispensary, into the department. Two days earlier the dispensary had been broken into – also in the middle of the day. The brazenness of the attempt suggested that someone in the drugs racket, a supplier or an addict, was getting pretty desperate, either because supplies had run out or because they were short of cash to buy more. The police assumed that whoever it was was familiar with the procedure employed for such drug transfers.

Raoul Hansen and Jon Valberg had been delivering to the Surgical Department for the last five years. Hansen was thirty-five and his sister was married to Valberg, who was thirty-seven. Quiet, ordinary, respectable men, both of them. Everything had been as usual, they'd explained. Valberg's wife had been away at the time, staying with a friend in the country who was expecting her first baby. A local policeman had had a word with her, something she'd evidently found hard to stomach. Over and over again she had reiterated that her husband would never dream of getting mixed up in anything underhand, and as for her brother, quite apart from anything else he was too shy and retiring to become involved with anyone outside his own small circle. Approaching middle age and still unmarried, he'd never even been engaged; hardly been out with a girl, in fact, she'd said. He seemed to be perfectly content with his woodcarving. He carved all sorts of things, lovely they were, Mrs Valberg had declared proudly, and gave

7

them away to friends and relatives. It might not be art, she added defensively, but there was no harm in making with one's own hands things that one liked and giving them away. Her brother didn't ask much of life, any more than she did, or her husband. Far better, she insisted, to live a quiet life on a fixed wage than to live beyond one's means and have to turn to crime to make ends meet. The policeman who had questioned her had had his work cut out reassuring her that his visit was purely routine.

Every member of the staff, both at the dispensary and in the Surgical Department, had, of course, been interviewed, but without result. They all had alibis, and all their alibis had held up under examination.

Drugs . . . Rudolf Nilsen shuddered involuntarily at the thought that there were twelve- and thirteen-year-olds who not only knew all about them, but who were also addicts. Kids who were obsessed with where their next fix was coming from when they should by rights have been collecting stamps or kicking a football about. Youngsters who'd already 'graduated' running the gamut from grass to heroin, which was just about the end of the road. And there seemed to be no stopping it. For every haul the police and customs made, a dozen consignments came in undetected. More. And each was carefully weighed and portioned out and sold to all those poor devils who were already hooked. Or given away as bait to hook other potential customers. God, how he hated the whole dirty business! The big boys behind it, the chemists, the smugglers, the pushers, the lot. He felt a measure of sympathy for the victims, the end-users, but when he thought of the misery they caused, the wanton destruction that followed in the wake of their never-ending hunt for money to sustain their vice, his heart hardened. He'd seen too much, he and his colleagues, he reflected.

He put down his pen. To hell with it! With all this musing and philosophizing he'd lost the thread. Time to think about getting home. His wife Magda had promised him steak and onions for dinner and he was more than ready for it. She was pretty plump herself and blessed with a healthy appetite, like her husband. 'We're a right pair,' he used to tease her at the end of a particularly good meal. 'Like Jack Sprat and his wife. See –

between the two of us we've licked the platter clean!' He finished the apple, tossed the core into the wastepaper basket, and was just about to close the file in front of him when the phone rang. 'Blast!' he said to himself. He glanced at the clock. Ten past eight. Ten past eight on a Saturday night and still they couldn't leave him in peace. He fervently hoped it was only the sergeant at the desk in the hall downstairs wanting help with his crossword.

Sergeant Walther Antonsen was a crossword fiend and he was always phoning his colleagues to ask if they knew an Egyptian goddess in three letters or an alloy in six, the fourth one 'K'. 'I've a Miss Borg on the line,' Antonsen said briskly. 'I know you're not here, not officially, I mean, but I think you ought to have a word with her even so. She runs an old people's home and the son of one of the ladies in it seems to have disappeared. She said something about drugs, so I thought seeing as you're . . .'

'Put her on,' said Rudolf, suddenly wide awake again.

'Good evening,' said a woman's voice. It sounded to Rudolf as though she was somewhere in her sixties. 'My name's Johanna Borg. I'm in charge of an old people's home. "Rosemullion" – perhaps you know it?'

Mechanically, Rudolf noted down the address she gave him.

'You must pardon my troubling you,' the woman went on. 'For all I know I'm making a mountain out of a molehill. Only Mrs Brandt wouldn't give me a moment's peace till I'd phoned the police. She's one of our oldest – er, residents. She was expecting her son, you see. He comes to see her every Saturday afternoon and every Monday and Wednesday evening. Only today he neither came nor phoned. I've tried phoning his flat, but no one takes the phone. I've even phoned his landlord, but he says he hasn't seen him since Wednesday evening, when they played chess together. They play regularly, apparently, a couple of times a week. And he never said anything about going away then. Johansen – that's the landlord's name – Johansen had a key and he went and had a look at Brandt's flat while I waited. But there was no one there. That made Mrs Brandt more worried than ever. She insisted on sitting beside me when I phoned, so she overheard it all. She was too het up

9

to phone herself, though she does normally if someone helps her over to the phone. She's in a wheelchair, you see. Johansen even had a look through the cupboards. He said Brandt's suitcase was still there. Seems he only has the one. Mrs Brandt keeps on about drugs, only I can't quite get the hang of it. As I said, perhaps it's not right of me to bother the police as late as this on a Saturday, but she'd've been at me all night if I hadn't.'

'That's all right,' Rudolf assured her. 'I'll be round in about twenty minutes.' He rang off, then phoned his wife to say that he'd be a little late. 'Sorry dear, only this thing just came up and – well, I'd better go and see what it's all about. I'll be home as soon as I can. Don't start without me, will you?'

A few minutes later Rudolf closed the door of the office behind him, leaving his desk in its customary disorder, and left the building, only stopping on his way to tell Sergeant Antonsen where he could be found.

3

'Rosemullion' stood back from the road in the midst of a large garden. It was maintained by the local council, helped out from government funds. Some of the twenty residents contributed to their keep, but most of them were without private means. The men were housed in the west wing, the women in the east. Each wing had its own lounge and there was a common room where the two sexes could meet and watch television together or simply chat.

Rudolf found himself disliking the place from the start, partly because of the incongruity of the name (there wasn't a rosebush to be seen, at least not at the front or sides), but more especially because he felt he'd been called out on what would probably prove to be a wild goose chase when by rights he should have been at home sitting down to a plate of steak and onions. It was always the same: whenever he and Magda decided to splash out a bit and have a good dinner with wine and all the trimmings, Saturday, Sunday, it made no difference, something was sure to crop up and spoil it.

He parked his car in front of the wrought-iron gates, which were closed, and after observing the 'Beware of the Dog' plate on the gatepost, glanced warily around and went in. As a child he had been bitten by an Alsatian, and ever since he'd had a healthy respect for watchdogs; but he could see none. At home they had an Airedale terrier which they spoiled silly. When they'd adopted her six years earlier she'd been so thin that

11

without a moment's hesitation they'd named her Twiggy. After a few years of good living, however, she'd grown so fat that Magda had started calling her Roly-Poly instead. Had it been anyone else he'd have suspected them of doing it on purpose to take the mickey out of him, but he knew his wife well enough to know that it had never entered her mind. Besides, as far as he knew she wasn't even aware that some of his colleagues had begun calling him by the same name.

Miss Borg opened the door as soon as he rang, giving him the impression that she'd been standing in the hall waiting ever since she phoned.

'I'm so glad you could come so quickly,' she said effusively when he'd introduced himself. 'Mrs Brandt's beside herself with worry. I've given her some valium to calm her down, but it doesn't seem to help. Maybe she never took it, only pretended to, just to fool me. Has all her buttons on, she has, just you wait and see.'

Rudolf put Miss Borg down as being somewhere in her mid-fifties; she was certainly younger than he'd guessed from her voice. She was small – dumpy, in fact – with short, stout legs, chubby arms and hands, and a round face almost totally devoid of wrinkles. Her dark-brown hair had started to grey, something she clearly made no effort to conceal. She was wearing a grey two-piece costume he was prepared to bet she had knitted herself. She probably sat there, he thought, evening after evening, making small talk and knitting to pass the time. The house was bright and pleasant enough and bore signs of having recently been done up. It was far nicer inside than out, Rudolf decided. Still, most places were at the tail-end of winter, with dirty snow caked hard in all the shady corners and a keen wind whistling about one's ears.

He followed Miss Borg through a tiny reception area and up the staircase. He noticed that although there were only three floors the house had a lift; he supposed a lot of the residents couldn't make the stairs.

'It's just here,' the matron said as they reached the first landing. Rudolf was breathing heavily and he realized that she must have noticed. Embarrassed, he mumbled something about the after-effects of a cold and determined once again to

12

set about getting his weight down. And this time he really would, he told himself. He had a brief vision of his wife's steak and onions waiting for him at home and resolved not to start till next day. 'It wouldn't be fair on Magda' was the excuse he gave himself.

Mrs Brandt was sitting in a wheelchair near the window. The small room was crowded with furniture and bric-à-brac, the relics of her former home, Rudolf assumed. Beside her stood a low table on which was a beige cloth. A small lamp stood in the centre of the table, which it shared with a vase of tulips, three red, two yellow, their heads drooping. They look as tired as I feel, Rudolf thought wrily. Within the circle of light cast by the lamp lay an open bible, with an ornate bookmark alongside it. The door took up practically the whole of the corridor wall. One side wall was occupied by a bed, on which the coverlet had been turned neatly back. A bookcase crammed with books filled most of the opposite wall. There was a portable radio on the top shelf and a row of photographs, clearly amateur snapshots, in cheap plastic frames. What most caught Rudolf's eye, however, was a pack of cards next to the radio. Good for her, he smiled to himself, thinking of the open bible. God and Mammon all in one. The walls were adorned with pictures in old-fashioned oval frames. Most of them Rudolf took to be of the old lady's son at different stages of his life, from when he was a babe in arms right up to quite recently. A picture of a smiling clergyman in full vestments hung above the radio. Mrs Brandt's husband?

'This gentleman's a policeman,' Miss Borg said, patting the old lady on her bony shoulder. 'He's going to help you find your son. He's a sergeant, Detective Sergeant Rudolf Nilsen.'

Mrs Brandt studied Rudolf intently for a few moments with her dark eyes; they were exceptionally dark, Rudolf thought. Then, apparently satisfied with what she saw, she extended a frail hand. 'Something's happened to Georg,' she said. 'I *know* it has.'

'Now now,' Miss Borg admonished her, 'we mustn't go jumping to conclusions.'

Mrs Brandt gave her a withering look. 'You mustn't, perhaps, Miss Borg, but I can. I'm his mother.'

Miss Borg smiled serenely, seemingly unperturbed by the old lady's put-down. 'I think the sergeant would like to ask you a few questions, Mrs Brandt,' she said.

'I understand that the last time your son came to visit you was Wednesday evening,' said Rudolf. 'That right?'

The old lady nodded. Her white hair was so thin that the pink of her scalp was clearly visible through it.

'Yes, he was here from six to seven,' Miss Borg put in.

Mrs Brandt nodded in affirmation, but gave the matron an annoyed glance.

'Can you tell me a bit about what you talked about?'

'The usual things.'

'The usual things?' Rudolf repeated. He gave her an enquiring look. 'What, for example?'

'Oh, he asked how I was. He always does. I've had cancer, you see. That's why I'm so thin. But it was nearly ten years ago now. They took away half of my stomach. Georg thought I was for it that time. So did I, come to that. There's only him and me – my husband died fifteen years ago. Georg's never married and . . .'

Rudolf sat patiently, waiting for her to continue, but she didn't.

'He didn't say anything about going away, then?' he prompted at last.

Mrs Brandt shook her head emphatically.

'He neither said nor did anything . . . unusual?'

'No, he was just the way he always was. He wasn't very much looking forward to the next day. He didn't like the shop being open till seven on Thursdays. It disturbed his routine, he said. He usually eats dinner at six, so he always gets hungry about that time on Thursdays. Only then he can't eat till getting on for half-past eight, and then he finds it hard to get to sleep because he's eaten so late. My flowers were starting to droop and he promised he'd bring me some new ones today.'

'You're quite sure he said he'd come today?' Anticipating her scornful 'I've told you he always does', Rudolf hurriedly added: 'As usual.'

'Yes, most certainly.' After a moment the old lady continued: 'We talked a bit about the last lot of books he'd

14

borrowed for me from the library. Deichmann. In the end we agreed on which he should bring me today. Can't *buy* books nowadays, you know; they're far too expensive.' Mrs Brandt gave Rudolf such a severe look as she said this that he felt she was holding him personally responsible.

'No, no you can't,' he hastened to agree.

'And then we talked about Monday – the fifteenth. He'll be fifty-five. I asked him whether he was thinking of doing anything special as it was, well, sort of a halfway mark between fifty and sixty, but he said he wasn't. I didn't say anything, but I decided I'd order something good for the two of us. Splash out a bit. Bring it in from outside.' She shot a sideways glance at Miss Borg. 'I thought I'd order something from the Caravelle. They do it so nicely there and it would make a pleasant change.'

Another dig at Miss Borg, thought Rudolf. Aloud he said: 'The Caravelle? You really know your way around, don't you, Mrs Brandt? I think it's wonderful at your age.'

'It's only my legs that have gone, you know, not my brain,' the old lady replied tartly.

Rudolf saw the flicker of a smile cross the matron's face. His eyes on the pack of cards, he said: 'You mentioned something about drugs, I believe.' Then, looking Mrs Brandt full in the face, he asked: 'What made you say that? Did your son ever say anything . . .?'

The old lady hesitated. 'No-o . . .' A moment later she went on: 'But you know, down there where he works, between the East Station and the West – and then there's the Underground. He's with Harts, Harts the Clothiers, and it's right by the station. One reads so much, and it's all down there.'

'Yes, but has he actually mentioned drugs?'

'Yes . . . that is . . . we've only talked about articles we've read and agreed on how terrible it all is. He told me all about how it's done. They have a contact, don't they, I think that's what they call it, a contact, somewhere – Eger Square's the usual place, he said, and the sellers rake the streets round about. They're all pedestrian-precincts now, aren't they, only I've never been there since they were closed to cars. It was after my legs packed up. The buyers deal with the contact. He stays

15

put and the others keep on the move. The sellers. Pushers they call them, don't they? Pushers.'

She's really clued up on it all, Rudolf mused, but what it had to do with her son's alleged disappearance was beyond him.

'Was your son very, er – interested in the drugs traffic, would you say?'

'Yes, he was. Very.' She gave Rudolf a sharp look. 'In the problems. He wasn't involved in any way. Not Georg.'

It seemed strange to Rudolf, experienced though he was, to be sitting discussing drugs with a highly respectable old lady of eighty-six who knew all the jargon. 'Then what made you bring up drugs?' he asked in bewilderment. 'Perhaps he has a girlfriend and suddenly decided to go somewhere with her instead. Could be as simple as that.'

'He wouldn't do that without telling me first,' Mrs Brandt said, as though she were talking to a child. 'Anyway, I know my son, and he doesn't have a girlfriend. A woman friend, that is. No, I'm sure something dreadful's happened to him.'

It proved impossible to get any more out of the old lady, apart from a photograph of Georg Brandt and his address and telephone number, plus Johansen's. Georg had given his mother the landlord's number in case she needed to phone him during the working day. He didn't like taking private calls at the shop, and as Johansen was nearly always at home he was able to take messages.

When he had taken his leave and they were out of the room, Rudolf turned to Miss Borg: 'Nothing to it, is there, being old, when you're as with it as she is?'

'No, she's certainly perky enough,' Miss Borg agreed fervently. 'I was right, by the way. She never took the valium I gave her. Dropped it in with the tulips, I'll be bound. I was in there only a couple of hours ago and they were standing up like ramrods. It was all eyewash, that about her son bringing fresh flowers today. He brought the tulips himself on Wednesday. She just made it up on the spot. I don't think you need take all that talk about drugs very seriously, either. She probably brought drugs in just to make sure the police'll do something. She's a wily old bird, my word she is, as you no doubt gathered.'

16

Rudolf refused to be drawn. 'What about this son of hers? How's he strike you?'

The matron screwed up her features in disgust. 'To tell you the truth, I'm not awfully fond of him. Real mummy's darling he is, never got loose from the apron-strings. Probably still asks his mother if he may leave the room. Doesn't drink, doesn't smoke. Doesn't like anyone else smoking, either. Would you believe it, he threatened to have "Rosemullion" closed down if we didn't ban smoking in the public rooms. I told him where to get off, believe you me.' She paused to gather breath. 'And as for a girlfriend, nobody in their right mind would have him.'

'So you don't think he's gone away for the weekend with a woman friend, then? Or a man?'

Miss Borg gave a snort. 'Gone away? Him? He'd never dare!'

4

At a quarter-past eight on Sunday morning the telephone rang in Detective Constable Karsten Nilsen's flat.

Karsten was two years younger than his brother and so different from him that no one who didn't know would have believed that they were brothers. Unlike Rudolf, who was practically bald, Karsten had thick black hair that was a source of both pride and increasing vexation – the latter because the price of a haircut was going up by leaps and bounds. He had thick black eyebrows, too, whereas his brother's were fair and downy and almost invisible. Rudolf's eyes were blue, Karsten's brown. The brothers were about the same height, but Karsten was lean, almost scrawny by comparison with Rudolf, and far fitter, despite the fact that he'd let himself go badly over the last year or so. When Wendy had left him for another man it seemed as if life had lost all meaning for him.

'Yes?' he said softly into the mouthpiece, casting a quick glance at the girl fast asleep in what had once been Wendy's place.

'I didn't wake you, I hope,' said Rudolf innocently, knowing full well that that was precisely what he had done. He was sure, too, that his brother wasn't alone and that because of that he couldn't have rung him at a more inopportune moment.

'Wake me? No, of course not.' Karsten's voice came thickly down the line and Rudolf guessed that he was holding the receiver under the bedclothes to avoid waking his companion.

'I was just having a work-out with my chest expander. You ought to try it, Rudolf. Get rid of some of that flab.'

'Huh,' said his brother, unimpressed. 'Well, leave your chest expander to sleep it off and pin your ears back. You've got work to do, real work.'

Quickly Rudolf recounted the story of his visit to 'Rose-mullion', going on to say that he had talked things over with their immediate superior, Chief Inspector Albrektsen, who had been sufficiently intrigued by Georg Brandt's disappearance to okay Rudolf's plan of action without a murmur. 'It's not very probable,' Rudolf told his brother, 'but there's just a chance that this Brandt chap can have had something to do with those missing drugs I'm working on. So we're going to get cracking. We're not saying anything about drugs, though.'

'But it's my day off,' Karsten protested.

'Policemen don't have days off,' his brother replied unfeelingly.

'This one does. Did. Besides, I didn't get to bed until Lord knows when. Why'd you have to pick on me, anyway?'

'Because if we're in luck and there is a tie-in, then I want you to be in on it.'

'Want me to be in on it? Why don't you come right out and say what you mean? You're afraid there might be something left over from last night, aren't you, and that I'll start all over again.'

'Cut it out, Karsten, there's a good chap,' Rudolf implored. He felt embarrassed, because he knew Karsten was right: it had been a ploy to get him out and about, so that he wouldn't be tempted to fall back on a hair of the dog that Rudolf guessed had bitten him and report for duty Monday morning with a hangover.

Reluctantly Karsten dragged himself out of bed and dressed, moving quietly in order not to wake Ada, who was shifting uneasily in her sleep, muttering unintelligibly beneath her breath. The taste of last night's whisky lay thick on his tongue, and neither toothpaste nor a mouthwash seemed to help. The flat looked like a battlefield. No wonder, he thought to himself. Ever since Wendy had left he'd been invaded by an army of friends and acquaintances, all intent on consoling him and

19

making sure that he didn't feel lonely. He wasn't so stupid, however, as not to realize that what really brought them, although they would have been loath to admit it, even to themselves, was the prospect of a large, wifeless flat, a refuge where they could kick off their shoes and relax; or bring their girlfriends when their wives thought they were working overtime or out entertaining fellow businessmen. This gave them the best of both worlds: the company of their cronies and girlfriends, with no need for the furtiveness associated with being together in a public place; and the sympathy of wives who feared they might be overworking. Karsten's rambling flat had become a home from home for all and sundry, with people dropping in whenever they saw a light there or knew he was off duty. Most of them had the decency to bring food and a bottle, but by the time they left there wasn't much left of either. Last night there'd been about ten of them, and they'd stuck it out till four in the morning. If one of them hadn't happened to be a grass widower that weekend and carted them off to his place they'd have stayed even longer. And all the time he'd been itching for them to take themselves off so that he could be alone with Ada.

He'd lost count of how many girls there'd been since Wendy left. At the time he'd promised himself: never again. He'd determined that from then on he'd use girls, women, the way he felt Wendy for years had used him. But last night he'd felt for Ada the stirrings of something more than the fleeting emotions of a casual encounter. His resolution was beginning to waver. Karsten shook his head; it ached, and his tongue still had a furry coating. He cursed his brother for not leaving him in peace on his Sunday off. Rudolf had been getting to be a bit of a bind ever since his promotion, he thought.

But I'm after promotion myself, he reflected. His eyes fell on a row of empty bottles and two that were still half-full. If I don't muck it up by drinking, he thought bitterly. It was all Wendy's fault. If she hadn't deserted him for that creep, things would have been far different. 'But what kind of a marriage did I ever have, Karsten?' she'd complained. 'You were never at home.' That was when she left, but she'd asked the same question several times before over the years. He had to be fair: she had tried to warn him. But what could he have done? He was a policeman. It was his job, his life, in fact, and she'd known it when she'd married him.

If only they'd had children! But Wendy had insisted on completing her studies the first three years of their marriage. Had she not done so, she'd maintained, she would spend the rest of her life feeling that she'd failed to live up to her potentialities as a human being. Whatever that might mean, he thought sourly. And when she was through and had passed her exams it had been that she had to work for a while before starting a family. It would be a shame to waste all that hard work and not make use of her qualifications, now that she had them, had been the argument. So she'd started teaching.

'Now listen,' he remembered saying. 'I agreed you should finish your studies and get your degree. I never stood in your way, did I?'

'That's because it suited you. It kept me happy, gave me something to do, and everything in the garden was lovely. You knew as well as I did what it was leading up to. Surely you haven't the heart to stop me having a try? It's only for a year – just to see whether I'm really cut out to be a teacher.'

But after that first year there had been another. And another. In the end she was doing so well that she couldn't dream of throwing in her hand and settling down to raise a family.

'When we married you said you wanted children, Wendy,' he'd protested.

'I did, then. But now I realize that not all women are made to be mothers. And lots of those who are should never have had children at all. As far as I'm concerned I'm better off teaching other people's children.'

'So you've decided we're not going to have any?' It was more of a statement than a question.

'Think about it a bit, Karsten. What sort of home would it be for them? You're hardly ever there, and I . . . I'd always be longing to be back at school, along with my colleagues and the kids. No, Karsten, let's forget it. Anyway, I feel a bit too old now to start washing nappies.'

He'd been wise enough not to point out that hardly anyone

21

washed nappies these days, that they were mostly disposable. He knew when he was defeated. If he'd not been so stupidly fond of her he'd have left her on the spot. Instead he'd started having a drink to cheer himself up when he got home in the evenings, no matter how late it was. After a while the one had become two, and his consumption of alcohol had begun to creep upwards. In the end he found he couldn't get to sleep without what he euphemistically called a nightcap.

'Do you realize you're well on the way to becoming an alcoholic?' Wendy had challenged him one day, a chill in her voice.

'And if I am, whose fault's that?' he'd answered.

'Don't give me that,' his wife had responded. 'Where would we be if I wasn't out earning, and earning well at that?'

That had been before she left. It was only afterwards that he'd started to drink really heavily. Wendy had been gone almost a year. As he bent over the kitchen table, writing a note for Ada, he wondered if he'd ever manage to forget her. At the thought of her married to that chap Hollis he felt his stomach contract.

'So all those parents' meetings and staff meetings were just a blind,' he'd flung at her. 'Just so's you could have it off with that two-faced bastard Hollis.'

'Don't try to tell me you're so dumb you don't know that schools don't have meetings like that twice a week.'

The truth was that it had never even crossed his mind – because he'd been so busy working himself that he had never paused to wonder. And a policeman was paid to be suspicious! How could he have been so blind? He cast a last wistful glance at the dregs of whisky still in the bottles before tip-toeing into the bedroom and propping up the note on the dressing-table. Then he went out to his car. There he came to halt. He couldn't drive, not with all that alcohol still in his blood. How would it look if he, a police officer, were to be stopped for a breathalyzer test? That would be goodbye to his career, never mind to promotion. Resignedly, he turned away and hurried off to the tram stop.

5

There were people on duty in most of the offices at Victoria Terrasse, headquarters of the Oslo City Police, but the peace of Sunday morning hung heavily in the air. Rudolf bade a cheerful good morning to the duty sergeant at the reception desk, who stifled a yawn and nodded in return. Then he made his way to Records and asked them if they had anything on a man called Georg Brandt. He also made arrangements for Brandt's picture to be blown up and copied as quickly as possible. Only then did he take the lift up to his office. The same Sunday quiet reigned on this floor, too, but Rudolf knew that it was deceptive. More than the other departments, the Murder Squad always seemed to be working against the clock and in an air of suppressed excitement. All departments had their sudden flurries of activity, of course, and they were all equally indispensable, but there was something about the Murder Squad that set it apart, even within the Force itself. It seemed to be expected of its members that they should be just that little better than their fellows. They had acquired an elite image that Rudolf, for one, found a bit of a burden. 'If you only knew,' he was fond of telling people, 'how much time I spend at my desk. Sometimes I think I should have been a clerk instead – there'd have been less paperwork to do.' But in his heart he knew that that was all a façade: he loved every minute of his job, however humdrum it might be at times. As was the case with his brother, it was his life.

In his in-tray there was a memo to say that two young men had died last night at Ulleval Hospital 'shortly after admission'. That meant that they must have been too far gone to be saved when they were found. Drugs. Rudolf swore under his breath. Two young lives thrown away almost before they'd begun. He studied the report attached to the memo. They'd been students. Holidayed on the Continent the previous summer – Inter-railing – and had bought some drug or other without knowing for sure what it was. Fools! Rudolf thought bitterly. The package had been left lying in a drawer until last night. The two had been drinking and in a fit of alcoholic bravado had decided to try whatever it was they'd bought. One of the students was in a coma on admission and never recovered consciousness. It was the other who had gasped out the story shortly before he died. It didn't have to be true, Rudolf realized, but it was unlikely that a youngster on the point of death like that would have made it all up.

Both were from well-to-do families. Fathers in good positions, mothers active in social work. And now . . . In his mind's eye Rudolf saw the rings spreading out, engulfing first and foremost the immediate families, but also touching more distant relatives, friends, colleagues, business associates. Two homes that would never be the same again. And for what? It was senseless. Accidents were bad enough, but things like this were totally unnecessary. Yet they happened all too often. He cursed again.

It was rarely that Rudolf envied his counterparts in the other Scandinavian countries – and decidedly not those in Germany, who were up against terrorism and large-scale organized crime. But there was one thing he did envy them: their easier access to wire-tapping. In Rudolf's opinion the Norwegian authorities were far too restrictive in giving permission for telephone taps. It was terribly frustrating at times. The dice were loaded much too heavily on the side of the criminals it was. The customs and the police were badly undermanned. Why, the entire Narcotics Department numbered only thirty, and what was that when the frontiers were as good as wide open? After the haul at the hospital the department had been reinforced on a temporary basis by the addition of a few extra personnel, himself included, but they were nowhere near enough. He sighed. It was a depressing and unrewarding task, as there was so little hope of blocking all the supply channels. When other European countries with far greater resources had failed to staunch the flow, what chance had Norway?

Although people were constantly being cautioned not to do so, not only by the media but also by travel-agency couriers on the spot, far too many were returning from abroad with prohibited drugs and tablets in their pockets and handbags – always allegedly bought for slimming or for a headache. But there was no need to travel abroad. There were laboratories turning out illicit drugs in Norway, too – in Kristiansand, Stavanger, even in tiny hamlets where one would never have thought it possible to conceal such activities. And the police had a strong suspicion that there was at least one 'factory' in the country making amphetamines.

Rudolf had hardly slept all night, being unable to get his mind off Mrs Brandt. She'd seemed so bright, so clear in her mind, that she must have had a purpose in mentioning drugs in connection with her son's disappearance. But why only a hint? Why hadn't she been more explicit?

He was already beginning to feel hungry, having decided that the time had now definitely come to put his good intentions into practice. He had started by renouncing the previous evening's steak, despite his decision a few hours earlier to postpone his change of diet one more day. True to form, Magda had protested and urged him to wait till Monday, but the memory of Miss Borg's condescending smile had strength-ened his resolve. Now his gastric juices were threatening to burn a hole in the lining of his stomach. In desperation he popped a piece of sugar-free chewing-gum into his mouth and began to chomp it vigorously. He tried to visualize himself ten kilos lighter, but found it impossible.

There was a knock at the door and Karsten entered. He looked a bit under the weather and annoyed into the bargain, but Rudolf pretended not to notice. Instead he filled him in on the details of the case and instructed him to go and have a word with the manager of Harts, Gustav Lessner. He himself planned to visit Johansen and to get him to let him into

Brandt's flat.

'I take it you didn't bring your car?' he said, looking meaningfully at his brother as the thought struck him. Karsten shook his head in reply.

'Good. Take Haraldsen along. He loves driving. Don't breathe on him, though, otherwise he'll pass out!'

'Does it have to be the Scout?' Karsten groaned. 'Isn't there somebody else?'

But Rudolf had already picked up the phone and was asking Haraldsen to come in.

'Now that I'm going to be promoted . . .'

'If the recommendation isn't withdrawn.'

A cold hand clutched at Karsten's heart. 'Have you heard anything to suggest that it might be?'

Rudolf hesitated. He hadn't heard anything definite, but he knew full well that unless his brother pulled himself together, he'd never rise above his present rank. 'No-o,' he said finally. 'No, I haven't. Only – well, I'm fond of a drink myself, but I take good care never to show up for duty smelling of booze.'

'It's your fault,' Karsten shot back. 'We had quite a binge last night. You never gave me chance to sleep it off.'

'That's just it, you're always having a binge, and if you go on . . .'

Rudolf's homily was interrupted by a knock at the door, which opened to admit Detective Constable Haraldsen. Haraldsen had been with the Murder Squad only one month and had already earned himself the nickname of the Scout. The men on the beat had reportedly breathed such a sigh of relief to be rid of him that some of them had thrown a party to celebrate, a party which had turned into such a riot that the unfortunate fellow in whose rooms it had been held had been given notice by his landlord.

Haraldsen was tall, with fair hair, cut short, blue eyes, rosy cheeks, a plain, open face that seemed never to have needed a razor ('Face as smooth as a baby's bottom', had been one colleague's uncharitable comment on Haraldsen's first day), and a pleasant, melodious voice.

Rudolf had been a keen Scout himself in his boyhood, and he had tried, unsuccessfully, to transfer his enthusiasm to his son

26

Lars. So it was perhaps for that reason that he, as much as anybody and despite himself, was able to understand why the young constable should have been dubbed the Scout. He was the very archetype of the public's idea of a Boy Scout.

'You and Karsten are going to a place called Sneballveien, number 11. It's just off the main road, near Ekre Station. You're going to talk to a chap called Lessner, Gustav Lessner. Manager of Harts, the clothing people. Karsten'll tell you all about it on the way.'

As soon as he was alone Rudolf opened all three windows to get rid of the tobacco smoke with which his brother had filled the room. He wasn't normally troubled by other people's smoking, but just now, starving as he was, he found it unbearable. After a while he rose heavily to his feet, closed the window, and set off to interview Johansen.

6

Sneballveien proved to be a short road lined with detached houses. Number 11 was one of six identical brown villas, all with white-painted verandahs running across the front and with large picture windows, their frames also white. Espaliers on the side walls, crazy paving in the garden, a gravel drive, and what was evidently a two-car garage. 'Comfortably off, whoever he is,' Karsten remarked.

Haraldsen parked the car in the drive and the two policemen got out. There was a cold wind blowing, but Haraldsen didn't seem to notice it, although he wasn't even wearing a scarf. Karsten, on the other hand, was shivering. He muttered under his breath something about 'this blasted weather', but in some perverse way he was glad of it. The cold had a kind of purifying effect, purging his body of the taste and smell of stale whisky. Perhaps if he stayed out in the wind for a while his hangover would disappear altogether, he thought, but he had no chance to put his theory to the test. Eager beaver that he was, Haraldsen was already striding purposefully towards the front door. Reluctantly, Karsten hastened after him.

Some time elapsed before the door opened. When at last it did, it was to reveal a flabby-looking, smallish figure of a man, eyes screwed up against the light, with tousled hair and a pale, unhealthy complexion. He was clad in a crimson silk dressing-gown which one hand was clutching to his ample stomach.

'We should like to speak to Mr Lessner,' said Karsten.

'Gustav Lessner. We're police officers,' he added by way of explanation, proffering his identity card. Haraldsen did the same.

'That's me,' said the man, a puzzled look on his face. 'What can I do for you?'

Karsten explained that it was about one of his staff and asked if they could come in. After hesitating for a moment the man stepped aside and ushered them into a large hall. The floor was covered with linoleum of a pattern designed to give the impression of shells and pebbles. Haraldsen, with his healthy approach to such things, immediately dismissed it as ostentatious and vulgar, an affront to his puritan instincts.

'One of my staff?' Lessner queried, preceding them into a lounge that reeked of stale cigarette smoke and alcohol. The room bore clear signs of having been the scene of a party, a party after which no one had made any attempt to clear up. He must have realized how thick the air was, as he quickly flung open a window before asking them to sit down. When all three were seated he looked at them and asked if it was Brandt they had come about.

'He didn't come in on Friday or Saturday,' he said. 'Iversen, he's one of the other assistants, phoned him, but no one answered. It's most unlike Brandt. For one thing he's hardly ever away from work, and if he has to be because he's ill or something, he always lets us know.'

'His mother's reported him missing,' Karsten explained. 'I gather that he used to go and see her every Saturday, only yesterday he didn't turn up. He didn't phone her, either.'

'D'you think something can have happened to him?' Lessner asked.

'That's what we're trying to find out,' Karsten replied.

'Afraid I can't help you there,' said Lessner, casting a wistful glance at the rest of the whisky in a decanter on the table. By chance Karsten had recently admired an identical decanter in a shop window, and he knew exactly what it cost. He thought it surprising that the manager of a small shop like Harts should be able to live in such a house and to surround himself with such relative luxury. Because it was clear that neither furnishings nor ornaments came from chain stores. Everything in the room

29

bespoke quality. He didn't think much of the many paintings that covered the walls, but even to his untrained eye it was obvious that they weren't mass-produced reproductions. Probably from galleries, he concluded.

'I know it's early, but may I offer you a drink? Just a small one, perhaps? After all, it's Sunday. To tell you the truth, I've only had about three hours' sleep. It was my wife's birthday yesterday, and we had a little celebration, as you can see. It was all very nice, only no one wanted to go home.'

'I'm driving,' said Haraldsen before Karsten could answer. 'But there's no reason why you shouldn't have one, Karsten,' he added.

Karsten's brain raced. Of course it was too early for a drink, no matter who one was or what; and he oughtn't to drink on duty – and most certainly not in the presence of Haraldsen, the Boy Scout watchdog his brother had lumbered him with. On the other hand his whole being was crying out for a drink. He knew it wouldn't be long before the last of what he had consumed the night before released its grip on his body, and he was afraid his hands might begin to shake. Besides, it was better to smell of a recent whisky – just the one! – than of the accumulated staleness of many. It was possible that Haraldsen hadn't yet noticed the smell that exuded from his mouth, but he would; it was merely a matter of time. In that case it would be far better if he could attribute it to the one drink he'd had at Lessner's rather than to the excesses of the night before.

'Well, yes, thank you, I will,' Karsten said at last. 'Make it a weak one though, won't you,' he added, hoping that his host hadn't heard the rider. Lessner poured a generous quantity of whisky into each glass, but a moment later he had to apologize because there was no soda left.

'I can get you some water if you like,' he said, but Karsten brushed his offer aside.

'No, don't bother,' he replied, 'I'll have it as it is, neat.' He hated himself for it, but he knew that that was actually the way he needed it at the moment. 'What can you tell us about Brandt?' he asked Lessner, taking a couple of good pulls at his glass.

'Not much, I'm afraid. He's been with me for about twenty

years, give or take a year or so. I'm not sure exactly how long it is. And all that time he's kept himself pretty much to himself, so none of us really knows much about him. He's always cool, calm and collected. Good with the customers, never gets ruffled, you know. Gets on well with the rest of the staff, too. Good chap all round. Can't think of a single thing to his discredit, to tell you the truth, except that he's so withdrawn.'

'Has he been acting differently lately in any way?'

'No.' Then, after a moment's pause, Lessner went on: 'Well, if he has, I've not noticed it. I'm not in the shop all that much – just a few hours each day. I had some stomach trouble a few years back and I have to take things more quietly these days. Doctor's orders.' He grimaced. 'Comes a bit hard when you're used to slogging away, but, well, what can you do? When a doctor tells you to take it easy, you do.'

'But you're still the manager?' Karsten pressed, unable to prevent his gaze wandering over the expensive leather-upholstered sofa and chairs they were sitting on.

Lessner nodded emphatically. 'Harts is a joint-stock company,' he said, 'but I have a controlling interest. The other shareholders – directors, I should say – are all elderly and don't involve themselves in the running of the business. Besides, I know clothing in and out, they don't. We've branches all over, by the way – Bergen, Trondheim, Kristiansand, Stavanger, Narvik, even right up north in Tromsø. Our Tromsø branch is bigger than the main shop in Oslo, in fact.'

'And they're all doing well?' Karsten couldn't help asking as he took another sip of his drink.

'Well . . .' Lessner hesitated. He took a sip of his own whisky, glanced from Karsten to Haraldsen and back again to Karsten, then continued: 'Times are hard. We're up against some keen competition these days, and we've been discussing making a few changes.'

'Changes? What sort of changes?'

Lessner shifted uneasily in his chair. It was obviously not a subject he wished to discuss. 'Oh, giving the shops a facelift as you might say. Brightening them up a bit. We thought we'd aim more at the younger generation; that's where the money is.'

'Would these changes have affected Brandt?'

31

Lessner seemed to have been expecting the question.

'Yes, I may safely say that they would. In fact, we've been wondering whether we shall need him in the new set-up. Whether we ought to keep him on.'

'He's fifty-five. He wouldn't find it easy to get a new job, would he?'

Lessner gave a cynical laugh. 'Maybe not, but these days we taxpayers pay so much to support people who're out of work that that'd be no problem. Some of them are pulling in as much out of a job as other people do in one.'

'There are a lot of people who'd rather have a full-time job than receive what they consider to be charity,' Haraldsen suddenly put in. 'It's just that they can't find work.'

'Exactly,' said Karsten, developing the theme. 'So if Brandt knew that he was in danger of losing his job . . .'

'I didn't say that,' Lessner interrupted. 'All I said was that the directors had been discussing making certain changes. But Brandt doesn't know anything about it. Nobody in the shop does, as far as I know.'

'These things have an unfortunate habit of getting out, Mr Lessner,' said Karsten, 'and if Brandt had got wind of it he might have been depressed . . .'

'If you're insinuating that Brandt's done away with himself, Constable, you're barking up the wrong tree,' Lessner said heatedly. 'The wrong tree entirely. He's not the type. He's the born underdog, the type that takes everything lying down. He's earned quite a bit over the years and he's careful with it, too, so it wouldn't surprise me if he had a tidy sum put away for just such an eventuality. No, Brandt'll be all right. He's not married, either, don't forget, so he's only himself to think about. It would have been different if he'd had a wife and children to support. The others have, the other assistants, I mean. Besides, we directors aren't exactly heartless monsters, you know. We've thought about everybody's commitments, their dependants and that, regardless of age and length of service.'

'That's the second time you've brought up the subject of age. First you said Brandt was the oldest member of the staff, now you say that you haven't gone by age and seniority, you've taken account of family obligations. I have the impression that Brandt's only real fault is that he's fifty-five. Am I right? What I'm getting at is that that's the main reason he'll be the first to go if you reorganize the business. You said yourself you couldn't think of a single thing to his discredit.'

Lessner pondered this before replying. 'The whole idea of restyling the shops is to attract younger customers, and to serve them you need people of their own generation, more or less. I know fifty-five isn't old, but Brandt's an old fifty-five, if you see what I mean. He'd never be able to speak the youngsters' language, meet them on the same level. And you have to if you're going to sell to them, you know that as well as I do. Another thing: he's no imagination. He'd never be able to contribute to the changeover with any new ideas, he's far too set in his ways. Too conservative by half. And there's something else: he's fanatically teetotal and he doesn't smoke, either. He's a rabid anti-smoker, in fact. He's entitled to be, of course, but you can't go ramming things like that down people's throats these days, especially not young people's. No, it's a pity, but he's just a non-starter.' At that moment the door opened and a short and exceedingly stout woman waddled into the lounge and came to a sudden halt in the middle of the floor.

The two policemen leapt to their feet, while Lessner remained seated. He made the introductions and then told his wife to sit down. She did so, muttering 'police?' in a puzzled voice.

'Brandt's disappeared,' Lessner explained briefly.

'Brandt? The one who works for you?'

Lessner nodded. 'Who else? He's the only Brandt we know.'

'But that's awful. Disappeared in what way?' The woman placed a pudgy, heavily ringed hand on her bosom and rolled her small eyes, which were embedded in folds of skin.

Without being asked, Lessner poured his wife a tumbler of whisky and replenished his own and Karsten's glasses.

Now there's a man after my own heart, thought Karsten. None the less, he deemed it politic to ask for a little water this time to dilute his drink. After all, I am on duty, he reminded himself, casting a sidelong glance at Haraldsen who, however, seemed to be wrapped in thought.

33

Feeling a sudden urge to go to the bathroom, Karsten got to his feet. Lessner made no attempt to show him the way, merely giving him directions: 'Up the stairs, second on the left.'

Every man for himself in this house, obviously, Karsten smiled to himself. When he got back it was to hear Mrs Lessner's rather petulant voice: 'If the police are mixed up in this they must think poor Brandt's dead. But why come to us? I mean to say, we didn't *know* him. Not socially, I mean.'

Before coming in she had taken the time to put on a few clothes, but either she was still a bit befuddled after the party and had had too little sleep or she had been in a great hurry to find out who her husband's visitors were, as it was a strange ragbag she was wearing – a green blouse, a fawn tweed skirt laced with broad blue stripes, black, high-heeled shoes with ankle-straps, and around her neck a glittering necklace of what Karsten assumed were imitation diamonds. Maybe she's slept in it, was his first thought.

'It's the obvious place to come to, Baby,' Lessner replied. 'As Brandt's employer, naturally I know most about him.'

'Baby' Lessner sniggered, and Karsten looked away. A moment later his gaze returned to Lessner: 'Can you give me a list of your employees – names, addresses, how long they've been with you?' He drained his glass and set it firmly down on the table.

Haraldsen rose and walked across to study a painting on the wall.

'Weidemann,' came from the mountain of flesh that was Mrs Lessner.

'Yes, so I see,' Haraldsen said. 'My parents have two of his. Bought them before he made his name.' He gave the woman a disarming smile.

'I have all my files at the office,' said Lessner, 'but I'll go and make you a list.' He rose rather unsteadily to his feet and made for the door.

'We only have name artists on our walls,' said Mrs Lessner, making no attempt to disguise her childish satisfaction with the fact. 'It's an investment,' she added, pouring herself another generous tot of whisky.

Her husband paused with his hand on the door jamb: 'I own

a little land, too,' he said. 'Woods.' And then, as though he felt he owed the two policemen a further explanation of his manifest affluence, he added: 'And a sawmill.' He frowned at his wife and left, leaving the door open. Five minutes later he was back with a handwritten list, which he handed to Karsten. 'I don't think any of them know anything about Brandt's private life,' he said, shrugging his shoulders. 'As I told you, he kept his affairs very much to himself. Introverted as they come.'

Karsten and Haraldsen took their leave and went out to their car. Once inside, Karsten couldn't help commenting: 'I'm beginning to feel sorry for this chap Brandt. Imagine working for a type like that. And as for that woman . . . '

'Yes,' was all Haraldsen had to offer in reply. He concentrated on his driving and appeared to be lost in thought. After a few minutes' silence he ventured: 'I've read *In Retrospect*.' He glanced shyly at Karsten, who at first failed to grasp what he'd said.

'You've what?' he exclaimed, as it dawned on him. 'But you're so young! I'd no idea you were interested in poetry.'

'I'm not all that young, I'm twenty-eight. I look younger, though, I know. And as for poetry –' He broke off and smiled. 'I've even had a go at writing it myself. Wasn't very successful, however. Why've you only published the one collection, by the way? Why didn't you carry on?'

'Because . . .' Karsten fell silent and stared out of the window. Why *had* he stopped? he wondered. *In Retrospect* was something he'd written when he'd first found himself falling in love with Wendy, long before they got married. Within certain circles the anthology had attracted quite a lot of attention. The reviews had been so favourable that they'd almost frightened him when he realized what was expected of him in future. That made him extra-critical of his own efforts. But then the problems had started, one after the other, and he'd found it impossible to get anything down on paper. He'd had his hands full just getting through the daily business of living. Poetry had been thrust into the background. 'Probably because I'd lost the knack,' he finally confessed.

'That's a shame,' said Haraldsen, genuinely sympathetic.

'With your talent . . .' His voice trailed away and he again concentrated on his driving.

Karsten closed his eyes and thought sadly of how long ago it had been since he had proudly stood with the first copy of his book in his hands. When Wendy had moved out, taking all her possessions with her, she'd left her copy behind, despite the fact that he'd inscribed on the flyleaf: 'To my own beloved Wendy.'

7

The Ulleval Hospital heist had taken place on Thursday, the twenty-sixth of February, and for those assigned to the case there had been little sleep since. Rudolf yawned. This Sunday was to have been his day off as well as Karsten's; instead, here he was on his way to see a man called Johansen. To be truthful, he couldn't understand it himself. Magda claimed that he was turning into a workaholic, and that if he didn't soon let up he'd end up on the sick list. Maybe she was right. A good policeman should never allow his personal feelings to intrude upon his work, but the fact was that he felt a sneaking sympathy for old Mrs Brandt, sharp-tongued though she was. It was that that had impelled him to give up his weekend – that and his hatred for the drugs racket.

Johansen's flat took up half the top floor of an old turn-of-the-century block. It was all high ceilings and tall, narrow sash windows.

'Beats me what can have become of him,' Johansen said when Rudolf had introduced himself and been settled in a somewhat threadbare armchair. 'If he'd been planning to go away he'd have told me when we played chess together last Wednesday, after he'd been to see his mother. But he never said a word. He was just the same as he always was. In fact, he said that if I cared to come into the shop on Monday, tomorrow, he could let me have a good winter overcoat pretty cheap. They were going to sell off old stock to make room for spring fashions, apparently. Thirty per cent off, he said; that's quite a lot. Only I had to be quick off the mark. He was thinking of getting himself one – and he has staff discount on

37

top of the thirty. Said he'd bought a coat only a couple of years back, but prices are rising so fast he thought it would be a good investment to buy another now. We had a cup of tea and a few sandwiches, and then we packed up. He left round about ten, I'd say.'

'He's never said anything about having a girlfriend – a woman he might be staying with now?'

Johansen shook his head emphatically. 'He did have a girlfriend some years ago, he told me once, but it never came to anything, I don't know why. Since then he's been pretty much of a loner. As far as I know, all he does is to visit his ma every Monday, Wednesday and Saturday and play chess with me. That's on Wednesdays and Saturdays, too. I'm a bachelor myself, you know. Only got one relative – a nephew, goes to university in Trondheim. He'll be finished this summer. Moving into Brandt's flat.'

Rudolf looked at him sharply. 'Oh? How long's Brandt been living here?'

'Five years. Bit more, actually.'

'What about your chess games then?'

Johansen shrugged; he looked a bit embarrassed. 'I hope we can stay friends, of course, and if he doesn't move too far away we can go on meeting just as we do now.' After a slight pause he went on: 'But with everything getting to be so expensive, I have to think about myself a bit too.'

'Sorry,' said Rudolf, 'I'm not quite with you.'

'I own the building,' Johansen explained, brushing some specks of dandruff off the shiny shoulder of his suit, 'and my nephew's promised to help me do it up. All of it. He'll soon be a qualified engineer and earning good money, once he finds himself a job. On top of that he's offered to pay more than Brandt pays – or can, for that matter. And he's planning to buy a car, and that'll mean that I shall be able to get about more, weekend driving, that sort of thing. It'll bring more colour into my life, you might say, having him here. Like I said, you've got to think of yourself a bit these days. And then there's the other side of it – blood's thicker than water, you know, and Thomas is one of my own. The only one I have left. He's the only son of my only sister, and she died five years back; been a widow for

38

years, she had.'

'Do you think Brandt has a good bit put by?'

'I doubt it. He was always on about how dear everything's getting. No, I think he can just about manage and that's all. If he'd had a bit of money behind him he wouldn't have been so worried about having to move. Every time I bring the matter up, he asks me to hang on for a bit. He's always on the lookout in the papers, but he hasn't found anything suitable yet that he can afford.'

Small and stocky, clad in a pair of worn slippers and a suit that had seen better days, Johansen was in his late sixties and was beginning to show his age. His face was lined and sagging, and was dominated by a Roman nose; grey hairs sprouted from his ears and nostrils, and he wore ill-fitting dentures. He may own the place, Rudolf thought to himself, but he's let himself go along with the building. Mean as muck, too, obviously. The man's watery blue eyes seemed to light up only when he was talking about money. Instinctively, Rudolf disliked him.

'I should like to see Brandt's flat, if I may.'

Johansen padded out to the kitchen, to return almost immediately with two keys hanging on a loop of greasy-looking string. To the string was attached an improvised cardboard tag with 'Brandt' printed on it with a ballpoint pen.

'He lives below, on the second floor,' Johansen volunteered.

They descended a flight of stairs, their treads worn by constant use. Johansen stopped outside the flat below, inserted an old-fashioned key into an equally old-fashioned lock, and turned it. Then he slipped the other key, a Yale, into another lock and opened the door.

'Brandt's so afraid of burglars,' he said with a condescending smile. 'Anyone'd think he had a fortune stashed away in here.'

'Ever had a break-in?' asked Rudolf, more for the sake of something to say than out of professional interest.

'No, touch wood,' the landlord replied.

They found themselves in a poky little hall with dark-brown wallpaper, a small mirror to the right of the door, and a hall stand to the left on which hung a raincoat and a trilby hat; a pair of slippers stood neatly side by side on the floor. Johansen saw Rudolf looking at them.

'First thing he does when he gets home,' he said. 'Changes into slippers.'

The living-room was papered in the same dark-brown. Two windows provided a view of a cheerless back yard. Opening off the hall to the left was a small kitchen. From the living-room a door led to the bedroom, where space had been found, just, for a bed, a chest-of-drawers, and a low table beside which was an armchair. The single window looked out on to the street. There was no bathroom. Johansen explained that the toilet was in the passage outside. The flat was so incredibly tidy as to appear virtually unlived-in. It's more like a third-rate hotel room than somebody's home, Rudolf mused.

'Brandt's a very particular sort of chap,' Johansen explained, as if reading Rudolf's thoughts. 'Never leaves anything lying about when he goes out. Likes it to look nice when he gets home, he says.'

A few cheap prints broke the dull expanse of wallpaper. On the television set stood a photograph of Mrs Brandt which Rudolf surmised must have been taken some ten or fifteen years ago. She was wearing a bold-patterned summer dress and smiling down at a bunch of flowers held to her breast. In the background could be seen three garden chairs grouped around a table laid for a meal. As far as Rudolf could see it was the only photograph on display in the flat.

'As I told Miss Borg when she phoned yesterday,' said Johansen, 'Brandt's case is here. So if he's gone away he can't have gone far – or for long.'

'We'll just have to hope that he shows up for work tomorrow, then,' said Rudolf.

'If he does, he's pretty well bound to come here first,' Johansen said, 'and I'll hear him. Sounds carry in an old building like this, you know. I'll nip down and tell him to give you a ring. No, on second thoughts I'll just leave a note. That'll do.'

'Ye-s, do,' said Rudolf, his mind on other things. 'This furniture, is it yours or his?'

'Both. I only let furnished. Wouldn't pay otherwise,' Johansen answered. 'But Brandt had some things he wanted to bring with him when he moved in, so apart from that corner

40

cabinet there and the armchair in the bedroom, all the furniture's his. But as I told him right at the start, if that's what he wanted to do, fair enough. Whether he uses my furniture or leaves it all standing in the cellar's up to him. Either way, the rent's the same. I only let fully furnished, as I told you.'

Out in the street again, Rudolf sniffed the wintery air appreciatively. It was very cold and there were not many people on the streets. As he drove along Parkveien on his way back to Victoria Terrasse, he glanced through the railings at the Palace Park, where patches of withered brown grass were beginning to appear in the carapace of frozen snow. An old lady was busy feeding the ducks crowded into the small expanse of open water where the park-keepers had broken the ice. She seemed to be carrying on an animated conversation with them as Rudolf could clearly see her lips moving. Or maybe she was simply talking to herself. Either way, Rudolf envied her her peaceful task.

On his desk there was a note to say that there was no Georg Brandt in the files, that the photograph of him had been circulated through the usual channels and a description sent out, and that Mrs Brandt wished to talk to him. With two stubby fingers he laboriously typed out his report on his morning's work on the ageing typewriter that he'd 'inherited' many years ago. Complicated reports he always wrote by hand first; it was only the simpler ones he felt confident enough to type straight off. Carefully he placed the copy in a file marked 'Brandt, Georg' and then made his way to Chief Inspector Albrektsen's office, which proved to be empty. So ought mine to be on a Sunday, he thought wrily. He laid the report on his superior's desk, and just in case Albrektsen decided to drop in, scribbled a note to say that he was going to look in on Mrs Brandt again and call it a day.

The old lady had nothing new to tell him. If anything, it was to hear a few cheering words from him she'd asked him to call. But, of course, he had none.

What was left of his Sunday off he spent at home with his wife. But he found it hard to settle down to domesticity. His mind kept returning to the two cases on which he was working. Might just as well have stayed at the office, he mused glumly.

41

8

At exactly seven-thirty next morning Rudolf was dragged from his sleep by the ringing of the bedside phone. Magda sat up with a jerk and grabbed the receiver almost without realizing what she was doing.

'It's for you,' she said, handing it to her husband. She yawned widely, scratched herself languorously beneath her full breasts, cast a disbelieving eye at the alarm clock, which she now saw they had forgotten to set, yawned again, less widely this time, and padded out to the bathroom and thence to the kitchen. She knew it would pay her to get started on making breakfast right away. Years of experience had taught her that Rudolf would be wanting to be out of the house immediately. The voice on the other end of the line had sounded rather animated, to say the least. She had just put the kettle on for coffee and was engaged in cutting the bread when her husband came tearing into the kitchen.

'Never mind the bread,' he said without as much as a 'hello, dear' or 'good morning'. 'A dentist's just found a dead man in his chair. I've got to run.'

'Not before you've had a cup of coffee and a bite to eat, you haven't,' said his wife firmly. 'Even you can't resurrect him, and if you think you can live and work on air, you're mistaken. That's just asking for trouble.'

'Love and air, isn't that what they say?' Rudolf replied absently.

'Love? That'll be the day. Or night. I didn't know you knew

the word. When do you ever have time for trifles like that?'

Without answering, her husband hurried off to the bath-room, but the shaft had gone home. He had a quick shower, and ten minutes later he was back, shaved, dressed and ready to go. But Magda refused to let him leave before he'd gulped down two cups of coffee and eaten a slice of toast.

'Why do you have to go to such extremes?' she asked, half-joking, half-serious. 'One moment you're eating fit to burst, the next you're practically starving yourself! There's something called the happy medium, you know.'

'If you ever came across someone who's found it, let me know, will you?'

'Did you say a dentist had found a dead man in his chair, or did I misunderstand you?'

'No, that's right. In his chair, in his surgery. I'm going straight there. The others are on their way now.' He gave his wife a quick peck on the cheek, patted her shoulder in an embarrassed sort of way, and hurried out.

The flat was already crawling with policemen when Rudolf got there. He knew them all: Allan Arvik, tall and gangling, with a prominent Adam's apple that bobbed up and down like a cork on a rough sea; Kristoffer Lee, also thin, but not as scrawny as Arvik, who with his short, fair hair and slightly bulging eyes had the look of a startled rabbit; and Leif Robotten, tubby, avuncular, invariably good-humoured and never flustered. Rudolf ticked them off on a mental roll. They were all there, all the team – all except his brother Karsten. No, he thought, he wouldn't be. Sleeping it off. Either that, or he's fallen for a hair of the dog after all. Rudolf cursed inwardly. Still, he reflected, it was better that Karsten should stay home till all signs of his hangover had disappeared, rather than that he should report for duty bleary-eyed and oozing stale booze from every pore, dragging his feet and just going through the motions of doing his duty. Rudolf forced his mind back to the job in hand. His practised eye registered the presence also of the forensic experts, the fingerprint men, the cameraman and the police surgeon.

He saw that the surgeon was Moe, grumpy as always at being dragged out of bed at such an early hour. Early for him, anyway. Still, fair's fair, Rudolf told himself. Moe worked long hours, often far into the night, six days a week. Articles and books poured from his pen and he had built up quite a reputation as a public figure.

'What happened, exactly?' Rudolf asked Allan Arvik.

'Brenner, the dentist, the chap whose place it is, came in at a quarter to seven and found a dead man in his chair. Phoned us immediately, naturally.'

'Who's the man?'

'Brenner doesn't know. He's been away for a week, up at Voss, skiing. Came back yesterday. There's nothing on the chap to identify him, either.'

'How was he killed?'

'I don't know. He wasn't shot or strangled, that much I do know. I tried to tap Moe, but he's his usual cheery self. Might as well talk to a brick wall. We shall just have to wait till after the PM – as usual.'

'How's Brenner taken it?'

'It's knocked him flat. He's in there, in the living-room, having a lie-down.' Arvik gestured towards a closed door at the end of the passage. 'It's an old flat, as you can see. Been converted into a surgery and waiting-room and a sort of living-room. There must have been two big lounges before. There's another room, general-purpose sort of thing, a bedroom, a kitchen and a bathroom. Bit rambling, but that's the way they built them in those days, wasn't it? Brenner doesn't live here, lives out at Lysaker. The only thing he can see that's missing is a towel.'

'A towel?' Rudolf repeated in bewilderment. 'That's a funny thing for anyone to take.'

'Well, that's all, he says. There's no sign of the door having been forced, so how the chap got in's a mystery. Hadn't a key on him. That's strange in itself, wouldn't you say?'

Rudolf nodded. 'How long's he been dead, any idea?'

'Probably since Friday. Could be Saturday. That's all I've been able to get out of Moe.'

'No signs of violence?'

'Not as far as I know. He could have died a natural death, of course, but you'd hardly think so under the circumstances.'

44

Rudolf went in to where Dr Moe was busy with his examination. The doctor glanced up and before Rudolf could say anything told him to save his questions for later. Rudolf gave no sign of having heard; instead, he peered intently at the body.

'It's murder, Doctor,' he said at length. 'At least, that's my opinion, and until someone convinces me that I'm wrong I shall stick to it. I know who he is, you see. Chap called Georg Brandt.'

The buzz of conversation suddenly died away.

'You psychic or something?' asked Allan Arvik, appearing at his elbow.

'The reason I know who he is is that his mother reported him missing on Saturday. She hinted at drugs, so keep your eyes skinned, Doctor.'

Instead of taking offence, Dr Moe joined with the others in asking for further details. Rudolf explained that Brandt had last been seen alive on Thursday evening when Harts had closed late at seven. 'He was supposed to visit his old mum on Saturday,' Rudolf continued, 'but he didn't show up and she started to get worried. She's in a home, an old people's home – "Rosemullion" it's called. Bright as a new pin, she is, but a bit shaky on her legs. Anyway, the matron got in touch with me and said that Brandt's mother "felt" that something had happened to him. So I went and had a word with her. Well, she was right, wasn't she, poor soul?' he concluded, surveying the group gathered about him.

'What was it exactly she said about drugs?' the doctor wanted to know.

Rudolf told him, recalling his conversation with Mrs Brandt as best he could word for word.

'But if he'd been into drugs, taking them or trafficking in them, he wouldn't have told his doting mother, surely?' Dr Moe objected, sceptical as always.

'Who knows?' Rudolf replied reflectively. 'Perhaps he felt a need to confide in someone, and who's more likely to keep a secret than a loving mother? Especially when she's no other living relative, just her darling son.'

9

When Karsten got back to his flat on Sunday afternoon it was to find it empty. On the back of the note he had left, Ada had scribbled: 'Got tired of waiting. Luv, Ada.'

She couldn't have waited very long, mused Karsten sourly. At any rate she hadn't taken the time to clear up before she left. Reluctantly he set about the task of clearing away the débris, though all he really wanted to do was to crawl into bed and go to sleep. And never wake up, he thought grimly; Haraldsen's words still rankled.

Of course it was a pity he'd never written any more – he knew that better than anyone. Probably it was simply because he'd dried up and had no more to say. Well, if that were the case he just had to accept it. But there was no denying that it hurt. And Wendy hadn't even bothered to take her copy of his poems with her . . .

Why had Haraldsen had to bring up that blasted book now, so long afterwards?

The least Ada could have done was to tidy round a bit before she went, he told himself bitterly. If he'd ever toyed with the idea of marrying her, he dismissed it from his mind now. Sexual equality was all well and good, but a spot of give and take still didn't do any harm.

All the time he was clearing up and airing the flat his thoughts kept returning to his published collection of poetry. As if he wasn't down enough already! Even if Haraldsen *had* read them and professed to like them, he needn't have brought it up, need he? Damn the man! Karsten thought savagely. Didn't he realize what unhappy memories he was bringing to life?

Overflowing ashtrays and empty glasses and bottles crowded every table and in some places chairs. He even found a couple of glasses in the bathroom. Instant through-put, he thought with a wry smile. Someone appeared to have been sick in the washbasin and to have tried half-heartedly to remove the traces. Karsten overcame his repugnance and completed the job.

He poured any dregs of whisky he came across in the bottles into a jug; he wasn't mean, but it seemed a pity to waste it, considering what it cost. Some of it he poured into a clean tumbler. He added soda water and tossed it back where he stood, beside the kitchen sink. 'Ah, that's better,' he sighed gratefully. Feeling restored, he lit a cigarette and poured himself another drink, which he took into the living-room. It looked a bit more presentable now, but it still needed a good going-over with a vacuum cleaner and a damp cloth.

He crossed to the bookcase and took out a slim volume. *In Retrospect. An Anthology of Poems by Karsten Nilsen*. Idly, he turned the pages: every single poem had to do with Wendy; if it wasn't about her it was inspired by her.

'Hell!' he exclaimed, loud enough for him to realize how quiet the flat was. How empty. He felt like crying.

Instead he went back into the kitchen and drank up the rest of the whisky in the jug. Then he weaved his way to the bedroom, removed his shirt and trousers, and sank gratefully down on to the bed. Seconds later he was sound asleep, although it was only a quarter past seven.

When he woke it was half past eleven. His mouth felt parched and furry again. Shakily he rolled off the bed, rose unsteadily to his feet, and reached up to a suitcase perched on top of the wardrobe. From it he extracted a half-bottle of beer. Unknown to his friends, he always had a few bottles put by 'for emergencies'.

Suddenly he found that he was hungry. No wonder, he told himself, I haven't had a thing to eat all day. Only drink, his

47

conscience added, but he suppressed the thought. Quickly he fried a couple of eggs and some bacon. Washed down by the beer, warm though it was, the food restored him. He lit a cigarette, but for some strange reason failed to enjoy it. Stubbing it out he made his way to the bathroom, cleaned his teeth and tumbled into bed – in his pyjamas this time, and between the sheets. Once again sleep claimed him as soon as his head touched the pillow.

When he was awakened by the alarm clock on Monday morning he felt better than he had for a long time. He was almost *glad* to be awake! It was a pleasant feeling – and a novel one. A hot bath further enhanced his new-found zest for life, and for the first time for weeks he made himself a proper breakfast.

He realized he must still have quite a lot of alcohol in his veins, and decided once again not to take his car. There'd been a lot of similar decisions lately, he reflected; too many. But this morning it annoyed him that he couldn't just climb into his own car and drive to the office, but had to wait in the cold for a tram instead.

Today, he vowed to himself, was going to be non-alcoholic all the way.

10

From Brenner's surgery Rudolf drove back to his own office.
He found his brother's report lying on his desk. It added a few
more pieces to the jigsaw; not many, but some. A picture of
Georg Brandt was now beginning to emerge. In the margin
Karsten had lightly pencilled: 'Don't they make outsize tights?'
Never knew you could get garters these days. Pity they were on
Mrs L!'

He was still perusing the report when Chief Inspector
Albrektsen entered. Fairly tall, Albrektsen was in his mid-
fifties. He had grizzled hair, cool grey eyes, an aquiline nose
and a strong mouth. Come rain, come shine, he ran a couple of
miles every morning before breakfast. But although he was a
health-food enthusiast and neither smoked nor drank, he never
made any attempt to thrust his views on others. Live and let
live was his motto. He and Rudolf got on well together.

This morning he was looking his age. While the rest of the
Murder Squad had been busy at the dentist's, he had been at
Ulleval Hospital. A girl had been rushed in, clearly suffering
from the effects of both alcohol and drugs. Her condition was
critical, and Albrektsen had been afraid to leave her bedside in
case she should regain consciousness in his absence. True,
there was a constable on duty there day and night, tape
recorder at the ready, but Albrektsen had more faith in
Albrektsen than in such impersonal aids as tape recorders.

Rudolf told him the latest developments in the Brandt case,

49

and when he finished the Inspector agreed that there might be a link-up with the drugs theft from Ulleval. It was unlikely, but the possibility couldn't be ruled out.

'It's worth following up, anyway, Rudolf,' he said encouragingly.

Karsten came into Rudolf's office while the two were still talking. To his brother's surprise and relief he looked not only fresh and rested but also full of beans.

'I've just heard that Johansen's on his way down to the morgue to identify the body,' he said. 'But there's no doubt it's Brandt, is there?'

'No, not really,' Rudolf replied. 'His mother was already convinced he was dead when I saw her Saturday, strangely enough. I'm not looking forward to having to tell her she was right, though.' He looked at Albrektsen. 'Moe seemed to think Brenner was far too much in shock to make a statement at his surgery, so he sent him home to Lysaker to rest. That's all right, only I can't shake off the feeling that he's just putting it on. I've asked Records to check him out; *and* his wife. Gustav Lessner and *his* wife, too. He's the chap who runs Harts; practically owns it, in fact. Plus Johansen and his nephew. And all the staff at Harts, of course.'

'What about the matron at "Rosemullion"?' Karsten enquired.

'No, not her. She's OK, I'm sure. We'll stick to nearer home to start with. But you might check whether any of the other people who live in those flats heard or saw anything out of the ordinary.'

Chief Inspector Albrektsen made for the door. 'Well,' he said, 'you seem to have it all under control. I'll go and report to the Old Man.' The Old Man was the Deputy Commissioner, Tor Tygesen.

'I like working with Haraldsen,' Karsten said when the two brothers were alone. 'We get on quite well together. So if you could spare him . . .'

Rudolf looked at him quizzically, expecting to see an ironic smile on his face. Ever since his brother's promotion Karsten had taken to pulling his leg gently when they were alone, but this time it was evident that he was in earnest.

50

'He's a good scout,' Karsten added, unconscious of the pun.

'You can manage without someone to hold your hand, can't you?' asked Rudolf. Then, relenting: 'Still, if he's free it's OK by me.' But he couldn't help wondering what had caused Karsten's sudden change of heart. Why, only the other day he'd protested violently when Haraldsen had been assigned to accompany him to Lessner's.

His musings were interrupted by the ring of the phone. Johansen had identified the body as Brandt's. And now he'd been taken ill, whatever that might mean. It had been a blow, losing his chess partner and best friend.

'Best friend my foot!' snorted Rudolf. 'If that's friendship, give me enmity any day.'

Karsten went to get Haraldsen, and together they went off to interview the other tenants where Brenner had his surgery. Rudolf was informed that Johansen had been given a couple of tablets to calm his nerves and driven home in someone's private car 'because of the neighbours'. WPC Gunhild Mortensen had gone up with him and seen him into bed. Did she tuck him in, I wonder? Rudolf wondered idly. The very sight of Gunhild was calculated to put new life into any man, he thought. She had long, ash-blonde hair, merry blue eyes, a full, smiling mouth, and the figure of a Greek goddess. 'A real smasher' was the verdict of her colleagues. And she was a trained nurse to boot. She'd found nursing too unexciting; she wanted something with more spice and variety to it. At least, that was the reason she'd given when she'd applied to join the police, but it couldn't have done any harm that her father was a retired police officer and that an uncle on her mother's side had once been Oslo's chief of police.

The thought of Gunhild set Rudolf thinking about his wife, Magda, and her sarcastic remark early that morning. What was it she'd said? 'Love? . . . When do you ever have time for trifles like that?'

Sadly, he had to admit that her sally had be justified. He hadn't exactly been an ardent young lover lately. Still, he wasn't young, was he? The trouble was, he thought ruefully, he wasn't ardent, either. Come to think of it, he wasn't even a lover – well, not since . . . when was it? Christ, he thought, as realization hit him, it must be weeks! He consoled himself with the thought that it took two to make a bargain – until he suddenly recalled an article he had read some time back in one of the women's magazines that always seemed to be cluttering up the flat. What was it it had said? 'A mountain of flesh is not a pretty sight. No woman is attracted by a man who looks like a walking advertisement for a butcher's shop, all hams, rump steak and belly of pork. Lean meat's the thing; no one wants a bladder of lard.'

A vision of Johanna Borg at 'Rosemullion' floated unbidden into his mind. He shuddered inwardly at the memory of the pitying smile she'd given him as he'd puffed and blown his way up those damned stairs. There was no doubt about it, he told himself, not for the first time: he had to set about getting his weight down. Still, it wouldn't do Magda any harm to lose a bit, either, he thought. With a sigh he hauled himself to his feet and went out to his car. It was no good trying to put it off any longer: he had to tell Mrs Brandt that her son was dead. It was a task he dreaded.

He need not have worried, however. The old lady took it with stoical calm.

'I knew it,' she said. 'I've known it all along. I'll tell you something, young man . . .'

Despite himself, Rudolf stole a glance behind him. They were alone. It was him she meant. 'Young man!' And only a short while ago he'd been thinking . . .

'I've lost a lot of people who were close to me in my time,' she continued, 'a lot of people I loved. Really loved. So I know from experience that the reaction sets in later. Tonight I shall wake and realize that I'm all alone in this world. That I've no one left. And *then* the tears will come. The next few days will be awful. It's not easy, you know, to reconcile yourself to the loss of someone who was as close to you as Georg was to me. He was my only child. I never had another, and when my husband died fifteen years ago we sort of lived for each other, Georg and I. And through each other. I can't help asking myself why I'm allowed to go on living when I'm eighty-six, whereas Georg – he wasn't even fifty-five . . . '

'You said something about drugs last time I was here,'

Rudolf prompted gently.

The old lady looked at him blankly for a moment: 'Yes, so I did, so I did.'

'It wasn't just for something to say, was it, Mrs Brandt?' Rudolf urged, treading carefully.

'It's all you read about these days.'

'You meant something by it, though, didn't you?'

'Poor Georg. He was so kind. Wanted me to go and live with him. Thought it would be better than being shut up here. But I like it here.' Mrs Brandt clasped her hands tightly together in her lap and looked at Rudolf defiantly.

'Did your son ever mention a dentist called Brenner?' Rudolf asked.

'Brenner? Never,' the old lady replied firmly.

'Do you happen to know who his dentist was, his regular dentist?'

'I know everything about my son, Sergeant, everything. Georg used to go to a Sverre Ranheim. Only Ranheim packed up and went to Spain, so Georg didn't have a dentist. He never said anything to me about having toothache when he was here last Wednesday, but of course it could have developed since. Still – no, I don't know why he should have gone to Brenner.'

Knowing as he did what a retiring sort of person Brandt had been, not to put too fine a point on it, what a nonentity he had been, Rudolf thought it would seem rather silly to ask if he had had any enemies. But it had to be done. After all, the man had most probably been murdered. He reminded Mrs Brandt of the fact before putting the question. Even so, she appeared to be taken aback.

'Georg? Enemies? No, did you ever hear such a thing!'

'It was only a question, Mrs Brandt,' Rudolf hastened to assure her. 'Routine,' he added soothingly, remembering what Johanna Borg had said about Brandt's having been a real mother's darling. 'I haven't heard a word said against him. But someone must have thought that they had no choice but to kill him.'

The old lady sat for a while lost in thought. Then she declared decisively: 'My Georg was the best son anyone could wish for, Sergeant. He must have been killed by mistake. *I* can't think of any other explanation, anyway.'

Rudolf rose to his feet. 'Well, Mrs Brandt, be that as it may, at least I can promise you that we shall do all we can to find whoever did it –'

'Young man,' Mrs Brandt interrupted him, wagging her finger at him to give added emphasis to her words, 'all that matters to me is that I've lost Georg. It's not important to me whether you find who killed him or you don't. Even if we still had the death penalty, hanging his murderer wouldn't bring my son back, would it now? So you're off,' she continued, changing her tone. 'I know you mean it well, and I'm grateful, I wouldn't like you to think I'm not. But now . . . now it'll be nice to be alone. Perhaps I shan't have to wait until tonight before I can cry. Perhaps the tears will come now, and if they do, I wouldn't want you to be here.'

Rudolf allowed his gaze to wander over the cluttered room. His eyes finally came to rest on the proud little old lady in the wheelchair before him. He thanked her for taking the news so bravely, then suddenly, to his own amazement, bent down and patted her comfortingly on the shoulder. He turned in the doorway, but didn't stop. Instead, he gently closed the door behind him and strode resolutely away down the passage. He'd seen that her eyes were already filling with tears.

In the car Rudolf swore to himself that Georg Brandt's death was going to have priority as far as he was concerned, and began to wonder whether anything of interest had been found in the dead man's flat. He doubted it; he himself had seen nothing, but perhaps the team of experts who'd gone over it afterwards had come up with something?

He drove to Brenner's surgery, where he found Constable Vetlesen, all alone and clearly none too happy at the fact. Vetlesen was not only a very young man, he was also just out of police college, and the combination of an old-fashioned flat that was both a dentist's surgery and the scene of a murder was evidently causing his imagination to run riot.

Who'd killed the poor chap, and why? And how had they killed him? Vetlesen could hardly wait for the pathologist's report. He had already convinced himself that it was murder; no one would let himself into a dentist's without a key, to die!

Every room had been thoroughly gone over by specialists, as he invariably put it in his enthusiastic letters home to his parents in the country, but as far as he knew nothing had been found to cast light on the case. He was expecting another team of experts to have a go. In the meantime he was having a good look round himself, more to pass the time than in the hope of finding something of interest.

All this and more he had poured out to Rudolf, whose thoughts continued to centre on the young policeman all the way out to Lysaker, where the Brenners lived. The house, when he finally managed to find it, turned out to be in a secluded cul-de-sac, well off the main road. Old and solidly built, it was badly in need of a coat of paint. It didn't look particularly opulent from the road, and the interior, when he entered the house a few minutes later, proved to be in keeping with the façade.

Mrs Brenner opened the door to his ring. On hearing who he was she immediately assured him that her husband was still far from recovered from the shock. She ushered Rudolf into a large, L-shaped lounge with an open fireplace in which a cheerful log fire was burning. Rudolf's eye took in two three-piece suites, parquet flooring, and a scattering of rugs and carpets. The walls were hung with an array of what were to him incomprehensible pictures. It's not exactly a hovel, either, he said to himself.

The dentist was reclining on one of the settees under a tartan travelling rug. Two coffee cups stood on the table by his side. Mrs Brenner asked Rudolf if he'd like a cup of coffee, but the question was framed in such a manner that it was evident that she was hoping he'd say no. Out of sheer bloody-mindedness Rudolf couldn't resist thanking her politely and saying yes, he'd love one, it was such a rotten day.

The Brenners made a handsome couple. Forty, he judged, give or take a year or two. He was dark, with curly hair, cut short, and the longest set of eyelashes Rudolf could remember ever having seen on a man. She was a honey blonde, though how much was natural and how much the work of a good hairdresser Rudolf was unable to guess. She had slender, restless hands; Rudolf soon found himself wishing she'd keep them still.

'It's been an awful shock for Peter, and for me,' she said, dropping four lumps of sugar into her coffee and stirring it as she spoke. Idly, Rudolf found himself wondering how she managed to indulge so in sugar and still keep her figure. 'That's why – because of the shock, I mean . . . ' Her voice trailed away and she looked helplessly at her husband. 'You see, Peter lied earlier when he said we got home last night. Actually we came home on Thursday evening. We – we'd had a row. It wasn't exactly the first one,' she added bitterly.

Ignoring his wife's remark, Peter Brenner took up the story. 'I was in the surgery Friday. Well, not the surgery exactly, the flat. I went straight to the bedroom. Tumbled into bed and dropped off right away. I haven't been getting much sleep lately and I was pretty tired before we went away. Rowing didn't help, either, nor the fact that the hotel was full of kids. It wasn't much of a holiday for either of us. You can imagine! That's why I flaked out the way I did. It couldn't have been more than half past ten.'

'He hasn't actually put it into words, but what he's trying to say, Sergeant,' Mrs Brenner put in petulantly, 'is that it was all my fault. The quarrel, I mean. It always is, according to him.'

'Cut it out, Elsa,' Brenner said wearily. 'The Sergeant hasn't come all the way out here to hear about our family tiffs.'

'There's no sign of your place having been broken into,' said Rudolf, eager to change the subject. 'The door's not been forced or anything like that. So how did Brandt get in? Who has a key, apart from you and your wife?'

'*I* haven't a key,' Elsa Brenner protested vehemently, two spots of colour appearing in her cheeks. It was obvious that she was having difficulty in containing her anger. 'You see, my husband's fond of taking his fancy girlfriends there, and you can imagine how awkward it'd be for him if I were to turn up unannounced.'

'Please,' groaned the dentist, closing his eyes.

'My husband's very fond of young girls, Sergeant,' the woman continued unperturbed. 'That's why he . . . er, keeps two establishments.'

Brenner gazed malevolently at his wife. 'That's enough.

More than enough. In the first place it's all a downright lie, and in the second place I'm quite sure that Sergeant Nilsen isn't interested in all these sordid disagreements.' He paused for a moment before adding with another malicious glance at his wife: 'Or would you like me to tell him about a few of *your* little escapades? Eh? Let's drop the subject. We can have it out later.'

Rudolf was feeling increasingly uncomfortable. 'You didn't answer my question, sir,' he said, trying to get the interview back on the rails. 'Who else has a key to your surgery, to the flat?'

'Only us,' the dentist replied, looking quickly at his wife. 'When my wife says she hasn't a key, what she really means is that last time we had a row she got so het up she threw hers back at me. Whether anybody's had a copy made I don't know, of course.'

'What about you, Mrs Brenner?' Rudolf pursued. 'What did you do when you got back Thursday?' He noticed that she had done nothing to refute her husband's tale about the key.

'Nothing!' said Peter Brenner, not giving his wife a chance to reply. 'She just shut herself up in her room and sulked.'

Rudolf acted as though he hadn't heard the dentist's outburst. Instead, he looked enquiringly at Mrs Brenner, who evaded his glance and mumbled indistinctly something about not having felt very well and staying in bed. There was no one who could corroborate her story, apart from her husband.

'But one can't attach much importance to what *he* has to say,' she added viciously.

'When did you leave your surgery on Friday, Mr Brenner?' Rudolf enquired.

'Round about two, I should think. I didn't look at the time. Everybody thought we were in the mountains, you know, and I couldn't very well phone any of our friends and explain why we'd packed up early. So I just wandered around the town for a while and then went home.'

'And all that's missing's a towel, I gather.'

The dentist waved his hand deprecatingly. 'It was silly of me to mention it, really, but that's the kind of thing one does in shock. Forget it, Sergeant, I've more than enough towels. It can't possibly mean anything. I always keep a fair sum of money in the flat. There's a safe, but I don't very often use it, actually. It's what they always go for first, isn't it? So I hide my money away in the strangest places – among towels piled in a drawer, in an old envelope, behind a picture, you know the kind of thing. But it's all there. Your men found it all, of course, when they went through the flat. So are the other things of value that I have there – a few gold trinkets. So that bit about the towel . . .' He shook his head.

'Have you been home all this weekend?' Rudolf asked, allowing his gaze to travel round the room.

'Home?' repeated Brenner, making no attempt to hide the bitterness of his feelings. 'If by home you mean this place, yes.'

Rudolf had had enough of the couple's perpetual squabbling. He determined to have them in for proper questioning at Victoria Terrasse. That'll settle their hash, he thought with satisfaction. He informed them of his decision. 'I'll let you know when I'd like you to come in,' he said.

'But we can't tell you any more there than we have here,' wailed Elsa Brenner.

Her husband was more co-operative. He assented without a murmur when Rudolf asked if he'd mind if the police had a look round the house. Rudolf phoned Allan Arvik, who promised he'd get on to it right away.

It was remarkable that two seemingly well-bred people should make such awful accusations about one another in the presence of a stranger, and a policeman at that, Rudolf reflected. In fact, not only was it remarkable, it was very suspicious, almost as though they were doing it on purpose, putting on an act purely for his benefit.

He decided to see what the people at the hotel in Voss had to say about the couple. Wouldn't do any harm to check the register, too, for the days they claimed to have stayed there.

There's more to those two than meets the eye, he told himself as he drove away. They're hiding something, I'm damned sure they are, though whether it has anything to do with this case I don't know.

11

Karsten resolved to start with the flat directly above the dentist's. The brightly polished brass plate under the old-fashioned bellpush said: K.L.O. Evensen.

The sound of the bell had barely died away before the door was opened by an old man. Almost as though he's been expecting us, Karsten thought. The man hardly glanced at their identity cards.

'My name is Konrad Ludvik Olav Evensen,' he declared. 'I'm retired. If you'd like to know how old I am, I'm exactly eighty-one years and two months. I'm a widower. No children, I'm pleased to say. I've worked practically all my life as a printer – at *Aftenposten*. Lived in this place since the year dot. Well, not really, of course, but it seems that way. Moved in just after the war. I don't go out very much. Don't listed to the radio either; hardly ever, anyway. And I don't have a television. Don't need it.' He leered at the two policemen. 'I get all the entertainment I need from the flat below. Well, there you are,' he concluded triumphantly. 'Me in a nutshell. Saved you some time, didn't it? Right, now let's have your questions.'

Throughout the old man's monologue Karsten had stood silent, hardly daring to look at Haraldsen by his side.

'But won't you come in and sit down?' Evensen said before either of the two policemen could say a word. He showed them into his living-room. 'Not that chair, there's a spring gone.

Don't take the corner of the sofa, either, that's my place, but otherwise you can sit where you like.'

Haraldsen lowered himself cautiously on to a stool. Karsten hesitated for a moment, then gingerly seated himself on a rickety-looking dining-room chair.

'I know why you've come, so you don't need to go warning me about what I say being taken down and used in evidence and all that sort of thing,' the old man said. 'I don't suppose you suspect me of killing that poor chap, anyway, do you?' He looked at them quizzically.

'At the moment we don't suspect anyone,' Karsten reassured him. 'Tell me, how do you –'

That was as far as he got. 'Let's get back to that later,' Evensen interjected. 'Come on, fire away. Let's have your questions.' He laughed. 'I can save you one question, anyway. I was home all the time, Friday, Saturday and Sunday.'

Evensen was tall and thin, with a slight stoop, and had a face so lined that it reminded Haraldsen of the hachures on a map; to Karsten it conjured up visions of a giant marshalling yard he'd once seen from the air in Germany. The old man's bald pate was encircled by a chaplet of grey-and-white hair. The picture was completed by small, twinkling blue eyes, a craggy nose, high, gaunt cheekbones, and a mouth that would have been quite pleasant had it not been spoiled by a few stray specks of spittle. He was wearing grey worsted trousers that had evidently seen better days (part of a suit, was Karsten's immediate summing up), a trendy high-necked pullover, and a smoking jacket that looked as old as its owner.

'All last week, apart from Friday, that is,' the old man rambled on, 'it was quiet down below. I was bored to tears. But Friday something strange happened. It began about half past six. I'd been awake since five. Wide awake. I'd had three cups of coffee, so you can imagine. I can remember thinking that it was funny that someone should be rummaging about in Brenner's flat. Sounded as if they were looking for something. I knew Brenner was away, you see – he told me so himself before he went. We met on the stairs. So I kept my ears open. Nothing wrong with my hearing, I can tell you. Nothing wrong with my eyesight, either. I wear glasses for reading, that's all. Anyway,

I felt I ought to listen in case it was burglars. It went on for quite a while, then it went quiet. I realized that whoever it was was probably getting ready to leave. Then I heard the doorbell ring. Brenner's. Well, I assumed it was Brenner's. You can hear them all when it's quiet like that, early in the morning. I nipped across and opened the door and looked over the banister. I could only see the back of the man at the door. It *was* a man. He was talking. I heard a woman's voice ask if he had an appointment. Husky it was, she was sort of whispering. I couldn't hear what he answered, he was mumbling so. He must have had toothache and been pretty desperate, don't you think, otherwise he wouldn't have come so early. He can't have had an appointment, not with Brenner being away, can he? But I distinctly heard the woman say that her son hadn't come yet, but that the chap could come in and wait. He went in then and they closed the door. Well, by that time I was really curious. I knew Brenner's parents had been dead for donkey's years, you see. Then there was some more banging about, and after that it was completely quiet again. I didn't quite know *what* to do. I pulled a pair of trousers on over my pyjamas and slipped on a shirt and jacket. Thought I ought to go down and have a look. I thought I'd ring the bell and see for myself who it was who'd opened the door. If it had been burglars I could always play the innocent and pretend I'd run out of tea or sugar or something. I wasn't scared because I knew no one'd be scared of me.' He chuckled. 'Being old has its advantages at times.' He grew serious again. 'I'd just got down to the bottom of the stairs when the door opened. Brenner's. And who do you think came out? You'd never guess! A woman, all in black. And when I say "all", I mean all. She had a darned great veil over her face and dangling down her back, right down to her feet. It's true. I didn't realize it at first – it was only when she hurried past and ran down the stairs. It trailed after her. She may have been getting on, but she belted down those stairs like nobody's business. No waiting for the lift. You'd never seen such a sight! Gave me quite a turn, I can tell you. Anyway, after a bit I got myself sorted out and rang the bell. Nobody opened the door, so I decided the chap must have gone before the widow, though I remember thinking it strange that I hadn't heard him. I

61

thought he must have crept out, otherwise I would have. As I told you, my hearing's first-class. He'd have had to have been pretty quick, too, because I hadn't wasted much time getting dressed and going out. Anyway, no one opened the door, so I assumed that he *had* gone and I came back up and phoned Brenner. Phoned him at home, I mean. No one took the phone. Then I tried down below, but there was no answer there, either. Not that I'd expected one. After all, why would Brenner have told me he was going away if he wasn't?' Evensen looked questioningly at the two policemen.

'Why didn't you call us?' asked Haraldsen. 'The police, I mean.'

The old man shook his head. 'I've never had anything to do with the police in all my sinful life,' he said. 'Never been in trouble with them, never even been inside a police station. Besides, I was afraid of making a fool of myself. What could I have said, anyway?'

'No, I must admit it would have been a bit difficult,' Haraldsen admitted. 'Well, what *did* you do?' They were both beginning to take a liking to the old chap, garrulous though he was.

'I tried to find a simple explanation. A natural one. Only I couldn't get that widow out of my mind. Nor the fact that she'd said that about her son. That worried me. I mean to say, I *knew* Brenner's parents were dead. Well, obviously Brenner could have lied to me, but why should he? It doesn't matter to me whether they're alive or dead. You know, I can't remember when I last saw a woman dressed up like that. They don't these days, do they? Don't even wear a black patch or an armband, not to mention full widow's weeds. And then it struck me: it must have been one of Brenner's fancy girlfriends – he has a few, I can tell you – who didn't want anyone to see her. One who didn't know he was on holiday.'

'One who had a key, then,' said Karsten.

'Obviously.' Evensen looked at him for a moment without speaking. 'There's a whole bunch of them. Girls, I mean, not keys.' He chuckled at his own joke. 'I started to think about Brenner and his harem. That's how I've always thought of it privately, as his harem. Still, his wife's in on it, too. The parties they've had! You wouldn't believe it! And at exactly twenty-five minutes past ten I heard someone moving about in the flat again. I was just making up my mind to go down and have a look when I realized it was Brenner.'

'How could you know that?' asked Haraldsen, genuinely curious.

'Easy. I heard him cough. Nobody coughs the way he does. Several times it's woken me up when I've been having a nap after dinner.'

'How'd you know the exact time?' Karsten enquired.

'I'd just put my watch right by that old grandfather clock there. Inherited it from a cousin; he'd inherited it from his grandmother. Well, she was my grandmother, too,' Evensen added, as though he were afraid they might think he'd come by it unlawfully. 'Lovely, isn't it?'

'Yes,' Karsten agreed, 'but it's wrong.'

'It wasn't last Friday,' said the old man firmly. 'I hadn't long put it right by the wireless. I do sometimes, when I can be bothered. I haven't today because I knew I wouldn't be going anywhere.'

'Were you going somewhere Friday, then?' asked Haraldsen.

Evensen wiped his mouth with the back of his hand, making Karsten wince inwardly. 'No, but the weekend was coming up. That's why I always make sure it's right to the second on Fridays. Gives me a bit of company. Rest of the week it doesn't matter so much, there're always plenty of comings and goings in the other flats then.'

Funny old codger, thought Karsten to himself. Aloud he said: 'Did you say anything to Brenner about what you'd seen?'

'Good Lord, no! If I had done he'd have realized that I was keeping tabs on him, all his fun and games, hanky panky . . .' The old man looked genuinely appalled at the idea.

'Know when Brenner left?'

'Two o'clock, on the dot. Both the clock and my watch were keeping perfect time then.' Evensen looked at the two policemen as though defying them to question the accuracy of his timepieces. 'But now I suppose you want me to go back with you to Victoria Terrasse and make a formal statement, eh? I know the ropes, you see. Read a lot of detective stories.

63

Always have.'

Karsten gave him a friendly smile: 'Well, if you wouldn't mind . . .'

Haraldsen threw him a puzzled glance, until it dawned on him that Karsten was being nice and didn't want to hurt the old man's feelings. And it was true, he'd been very observant and helped them a lot.

'Of course, it's no trouble,' said Evensen with old-fashioned courtesy. 'On the contrary, it'll make a change. Nice little outing.'

'First I'd just like to see how well sounds carry in these flats,' Karsten said.

'Go ahead,' said the old man gallantly. 'I'll stay here, stand by my post. I'll get my coat on while you're gone.'

12

The two policemen went below to look in on Vetlesen, who was glad to have his solitary vigil interrupted once again. He told them that Rudolf had been in and then gone on to Brenner's house at Lysaker. The new team of experts hadn't yet arrived. Karsten recounted what Evensen had said about Brenner's activities and how easily sounds carried, and enlisted Haraldsen's aid to find out for himself.

'Cough, jump, open a drawer or two, move a bit of furniture. Flush the toilet, talk to yourself – normally, then raise your voice – whistle – "Colonel Bogey", anything. Start in the surgery and work your way from room to room. We'll go back up to Evensen's and see how well we can hear you. OK?'

Vetlesen nodded unhappily. 'I shall feel a right Charlie, doing all that,' he mumbled.

'You'll be all right,' Karsten told him. 'Never heard of a one-man show?'

'I don't know whether it's worth mentioning,' said Vetlesen diffidently, 'only – well, there's something strikes me as strange.'

'And that is?'

Vetlesen looked uncomfortable, as though he regretted having opened his mouth.

'What is it that strikes you as strange?' Karsten prompted.

'It's just that, well –' The young policeman's voice came to a stop. 'It's just that –' he began again, 'that – well, if this

Brenner's such a ladies' man, like the old chap upstairs says he is, why's he got a whacking great clock over his bed and a calendar as well? It's as if he's keen to remind people that time's up and they should go. I mean to say, wouldn't you have thought he'd rather have had a nice picture? Nymphs and fauns, satyrs, you know, something a bit – well, a bit more to the point? Evocative, that's the word I want, evocative,' he concluded triumphantly, swallowing hard and giving Karsten and Haraldsen a sheepish smile.

The three of them went into the bedroom. On the floor was a fitted carpet, deep and white. The centrepiece was a big brass bedstead. Room for three, thought Karsten, suppressing a smile. On each side of the bed stood a white table, each with a gleaming brass lamp, topped by a white silk shade, and a heavy crystal ashtray. The window was draped with heavy velvet curtains in a delicate shade of pink. On the walls were erotic Japanese prints in wide gilt frames. From the ceiling hung a crystal chandelier. There were three double lamps. 'There's an awful lot of light for such a relatively small room, don't you think?' Karsten couldn't help remarking. 'And it's supposed to be a love nest at that. Where's the cosiness?' In each corner, on the opposite site to the bed, stood a white dressing-table with a large mirror. A white wardrobe and a white chest-of-drawers with brass handles completed the furniture.

'I've been experimenting,' Vetlesen suddenly volunteered. 'The mirrors on the dressing-tables are tilted so that if you lie on the bed you can see yourself in both at the same time. And if you stand in the doorway, in that mirror there' – he indicated the mirror above the bed between the clock and the calendar – 'you can see everything, the bed itself and the bed and the calendar and the clock and everything reflected in the other mirrors.'

Haraldsen laughed. 'All done by mirrors, eh?'

'I've never been in a brothel,' Vetlesen ventured, his cheeks reddening. 'But if I were to imagine what one looks like, a high-class one, if there is such a thing, and I suppose there is, I should think it'd look something like this, wouldn't you?' He looked appealingly at his two companions. 'Just look at how stylish it all is, all pink and white. Not very cosy, though, I agree with you, Karsten; functional, more, I'd say. Only one thing spoils it: that blessed calendar. Sticks out like a sore thumb, doesn't it? And the clock. If the calendar had been pictorial – a Pirelli, for instance, only they don't make them any more, do they? – I'd have understood it better. But that thing – it's just a wad of numbers that you have to tear off every day. And look at the size of it! And the clock. Ugly as sin. Well, *that's* in keeping! No, it beats me,' he concluded, shaking his head.

The bathroom and toilet were separate. But whereas the former was a vision in mauve and pink, with wall-to-wall carpeting and a matching shower curtain, a pile of fleecy hug-yourself-dry towels and a medicine cabinet with a mirror door, the toilet was spartan in the extreme, a tiny cubicle with institution-green walls, a stained washbasin, a speckled mirror, a worn-down piece of soap, and a pack of paper towels.

'Serves its purpose,' Karsten commented, 'but that's about all. Probably used by his patients too. Perhaps that's why it's not as plush as the bedroom and the bathroom. Still, you'd think he'd brighten it up a bit, wouldn't you?'

The living-room-cum-lounge seemed to have been furnished more with an eye to partying than to everyday living. Here too there was a fitted carpet, a warm grey in colour, and grouped around a rectangular table with a smoked-glass top and brass frame were a four-seater sofa and several deep armchairs, all upholstered in a velvety grey fabric. Karsten tried one of the chairs and felt engulfed. In contrast to the bedroom, there were very few lamps. Even when they switched them all on, despite the light from the window the room remained half in darkness. But the shadow wasn't too deep to prevent Karsten spotting the cocktail cabinet.

The waiting-room was a cut above most such places, but compared with the other rooms it appeared uncommonly antiseptic and sterile. Four tubular-steel chairs stood against the wall and there was a low table on which lay a few magazines. Apart from the chair in which the body had been found the surgery contained an impressive array of instruments and other dental accessories.

'Looks like every other dentist's surgery,' said Haraldsen. 'A proper chamber of horrors.'

Constable Vetlesen was eager to know how Brandt had died.

'We haven't had the result of the autopsy yet,' said Karsten. 'Moe's promised to let us have it as soon as he possibly can, but he needs time. He's a crabby old stick, but there're no flies on him. He's not likely to miss anything. Still, never mind Moe, let's get something done here. We'll go up now. Give us a minute or two to settle in – you'll probably hear it when we ring the bell – and then go into your song-and-dance routine.'

Vetlesen nodded, plainly ill at ease, and swallowed painfully. Karsten looked at him.

'You eaten?'

The young constable swallowed again. 'No, not really. It was a long time ago.' The truth was that he didn't feel very much like food; the atmosphere in the flat was not conducive to hearty eating.

Karsten seemed not to notice. 'Nip down and get yourself something, then,' he said breezily. 'We don't want you fainting on parade. Only make it snappy, won't you?'

Glad of a chance to get away, Vetlesen hurried out. The other two policemen continued their inspection.

'He's not very happy being in here all on his own,' Haraldsen remarked. 'Still, who's to blame him? It's enough to give anyone the creeps.'

Together they went into the kitchen, which was small, bright and well equipped.

'All mod cons,' said Karsten, casting an appreciative glance at the ultra-modern stove, the electric bread slicer, fridge, dishwasher, even a waffle iron. 'And then some,' he added. 'Doesn't look as if it's been used very much, though, does it?'

Haraldsen slid back the door of the cupboard above the sink. 'He doesn't confine himself to twosomes, obviously,' he said. 'Just look at this little lot.' He counted quickly. 'Twelve. Who's he hobnob with, the Apostles?'

Karsten laughed. 'Hardly, not if he serves things like this, anyway.' He had opened a large store cupboard, and he indicated rows of bottles, many still in their gift cartons, and unopened packs of cigarettes. 'No fear of running short, is there,' he said, 'not with a stock like this.' He sounded a trifle wistful. 'We should have been dentists, you know, not policemen. Pulling 'em out instead of pulling 'em in!'

In a drawer he found a complete set of silver cutlery.

'I thought he didn't live here,' said Haraldsen. 'Looks as if he has some pretty big dinner parties though, doesn't it? But who with? Doesn't seem to tie in with what Evensen said. Girlfriends and all that. Even if he has a whole string surely he doesn't have them all to dinner at the same time? Lord of all I survey sort of thing.'

Karsten hesitated. He thought of all the parties he'd had since his wife had left him. They hadn't been twosomes, either; people milling about all over the place. But everything was always so casual: there was never any question of a sit-down meal. People mostly just drank, but if anyone was hungry they simply went into the kitchen and cut themselves a sandwich or two. Otherwise it was only peanuts and crisps and that kind of thing.

'No, I don't understand it, either,' he said finally. 'After all, they only live at Lysaker. If it'd been in another town, or further out even, but Lysaker, why, it's as good as part of Oslo. You can't very well invite people for dinner when you live forty, fifty kilometres away and expect them to take a taxi home afterwards. Cost a fortune. And it's no fun if half the guests aren't drinking because they have to drive. But Lysaker . . .'

'There's something called a train,' Haraldsen replied drily.

'Not at three o'clock in the morning there isn't,' said Karsten.

'But does it make sense to you that the place should be used as both a home and a love nest *and* as a dentist's surgery?' Haraldsen persisted.

'No,' Karsten replied, 'no, it doesn't. Think if Brenner was going to have one of his lady friends in and he told his wife he was working late or going to a meeting or something. If she got a bit suspicious and turned up here there'd be hell to pay. You'd think so, anyway.'

'It's a strange place altogether if you ask me,' said Haraldsen thoughtfully. 'I'd go round the bend living here. The bedroom's like a brothel – the whole place is, come to that. I'm sure it's all very tastefully done and it must have cost a mint of money, but there's something cheap about it even so. Tawdry, isn't that the word? What sort of people are they, these Brenners, I wonder? And where do they get all their money from? I know dentists earn well, and they can probably stash a lot away without the taxman getting his grubby paws on it, but this –' he indicated the opulence about him. 'This, and a house at Lysaker, and who knows what else besides. I'm beginning to wonder where the Lessners get all *their* money from, too. Might not do any harm to tip the Inland Revenue off, get them to go through the books. What do you think? Be easier with them than with the Brenners. Though land . . . woods . . . a sawmill . . . no, they've dozens of loopholes too. Not like us.' He smiled wrily.

'I'd rather be a pauper than be stuck with someone like Lessner's wife,' said Karsten feelingly. 'She looked like a bloody great slug.' He grimaced at the thought of having to go to bed with her every night and waking up to find her still beside him in the morning. 'I wouldn't touch her with a bargepole. Not even if I looked like Lessner,' he added as an afterthought.

Vetlesen came back clutching a package of sandwiches and a carton of milk, and Karsten and Haraldsen went back up to Evensen's flat. He welcomed them eagerly, chuckling to himself. 'Never thought I'd be a witness for the Crown,' he crowed, and went on to say how much he was looking forward to recounting all the goings-on in the flat below. 'Serve him right,' he said vehemently, 'supercilious devil. But your friend's taking his time, isn't he?'

The words were no sooner out of his mouth than the unmistakable strains of 'Colonel Bogey' came floating up through the floor. Shortly afterwards they heard Vetlesen cough, and they could clearly hear him talking, although it was impossible to make out what he was saying. They heard the scrape of a chair, a drawer being pulled out, and the flushing of the toilet. Karsten half-expected to hear the creak of bed-springs, too, but there he was to be disappointed; Vetlesen's imagination, or his nerve, or possibly both, must have failed him. There was no doubt that Evensen was right. Give and take a little, he would have no difficulty in keeping track of what

70

went on in the flat below, especially as it was always so quiet in his own home. No wonder he doesn't need a television, thought Karsten. He must be able to hear everything as well as Brenner can himself.

'You're quite at liberty to search my flat, you know,' said Evensen, throwing out a hand in a generous gesture. 'Don't pinch my valuables, though, will you?' he laughed.

Nothing wrong with his sense of humour, that's for sure, thought Karsten. Still, perhaps the old chap needed it; it couldn't be much fun living all alone in a dingy flat like that. A lifetime of work and this is all he has to show for it. But Evensen seemed contented enough.

'Who owns this building?' asked Haraldsen abruptly.

'Alf Kristoffersen,' Evensen replied. 'Alfred the Great. "AK" to his friends. You must have heard of him.'

'It's impossible not to,' said Karsten. 'He'll soon own half the town.'

'Well, yes, perhaps, but he's still quite a way to go before he catches up with Svendsby.'

'Maybe, but he's not doing badly, is he?'

'He drops in occasionally,' Evensen informed them. 'He's good at that. Goes around and chats with the old people in his flats.'

'So it's true, then,' said Haraldsen. 'I heard him say he did, saw him once on television.'

Evensen nodded his assent. 'But don't you think we ought to be going?' he said. (He's like a dog that knows it's going to be taken for a walk, was the thought that leapt into Karsten's mind.) 'We'll take the lift. I have to be careful on the stairs, Mrs Olesen scrubs and polishes them so much, they're like a skating-rink, but once I'm in the street it's no problem unless there's a lot of ice about.' He reached for his walking-stick. 'Better take a book, too, I suppose,' he added. 'Be hanging around half the day, I expect, while my statement's being typed.' A sudden thought occurred to him: 'Hope you'll get someone to run me home again afterwards.'

Karsten assured him that they would.

Evensen crossed to the bookshelf and took out a tattered-looking volume. Karsten glanced at the title: *The Corpse with the Creaking Voice*. Neither he nor Haraldsen had ever heard of it; nor had they heard of the author.'

'It's jolly good,' Evensen declared. 'I've read it lots of times. Perhaps even you two could learn something from it.'

'Yes, perhaps we could,' Karsten agreed good-humouredly. 'They don't teach us anything at police college, you know.'

13

Two constables were detailed to make routine enquiries in the street where Brandt had lived and two more were sent to do the same in the street where Brenner had his surgery. Rudolf and Arvik made their way to Harts.

Rudolf was annoyed with himself. Experienced policeman though he was, he couldn't seem to get old Mrs Brandt out of his mind. It affected his driving and, completely out of character, he found himself cursing the traffic, other people's 'bad' driving, and the lack of parking space.

Arvik tut-tutted occasionally and shook his head in commiseration. Rudolf felt sorry for his companion; after all, none of it was his fault. On the other hand in some perverse way it irritated him that Arvik was so willing to agree with him. Rudolf knew perfectly well that he was out of sorts and acting unreasonably, and he would have preferred Arvik to have rebuked him every now and again instead of just going along with him. Poor chap, he thought, as the unjustness of his attitude struck him, he just can't win. It didn't improve matters that he was beginning to get decidedly peckish.

Still feeling vaguely depressed and at odds with the world Rudolf followed Arvik into the shop. To the surprise of them both, despite the fact that it was a Monday the place was full of people, and the assistants looked as though they were being run off their feet. It was only when he saw a large notice proclaiming '30% off all winter overcoats' that Rudolf understood why and remembered what Johansen had said. He glanced around: yes, it was mostly heavy overcoats that were being sold.

Surprisingly large inside, the shop was rectangular in shape. Five narrow cubicles where customers could try things on lined one wall. The other was taken up by a heavy counter, at one end of which stood a cash register. Its frequent plinging came to the policemen on a carrier wave of subdued conversation.

Rudolf waited until one of the assistants was free. It happened to be Iversen, who beamed at them and enquired what he could do for them. They identified themselves and Rudolf asked if there was a back room where they could talk undisturbed. It was clear that Iversen was not at all happy at the idea, but, having no option, he reluctantly led them through a curtained doorway half-hidden by a rack of reduced coats. It was a cramped little cubbyhole, obviously the place where the staff were accustomed to have their lunch and snatch a cup of tea or coffee. A large kettle stood on the hotplate and there was a table crowded with cups and saucers, some clean, others dirty. There were only three chairs. Iversen motioned Rudolf and Arvik into two of them and himself took the third.

'It's about Brandt,' said Rudolf, as soon as they were all seated.

Before he could go on Iversen broke in anxiously: 'He's all right, isn't he? Nothing wrong, is there?'

'He's dead,' Rudolf informed him bluntly, his eyes on the man's face. 'That's why we're here. Mind if we record this little interview? It's quicker than taking it all down.'

Iversen moistened his pale lips with the tip of his tongue. 'But . . . I can't help you, Sergeant,' he stammered.

'How about letting me decide that?' Rudolf replied. '*Is* it OK my using a tape recorder? You're quite at liberty to say no. Constable Arvik here'll take notes instead.'

'No, use the recorder, it's quite all right by me. It's just that I don't see what I can tell you about Brandt – not that would be any use, I mean.' He paused for a moment, then blurted out: 'Was he attacked – beaten up or something like that?' His eyes roved over the tiny room and came to rest on the curtain hanging in the doorway, as though he half-expected Brandt's killer to step out from behind it.

Rudolf elected not to hear. 'What did you think of Brandt? What was he like?'

'Oh, he was a nice chap,' said Iversen without hesitation. 'Quiet, kept himself pretty much to himself. Good salesman, good at his job. Yes, he was a nice chap altogether.'

'Were you particularly friends with him? You or anyone else?'

The tip of Iversen's pink tongue came into view again, only to disappear immediately. 'No, I can't say that I . . . that any of us, in fact . . . he was a retiring sort of fellow, as I said. Withdrawn. He never discussed his private life with the rest of us. Still, why should he have? That was up to him. But then, of course, by the same token, when he didn't share his with us, we didn't share ours with him. It worked both ways. Stands to sense.'

'Did you know that there were plans to revamp the shop – to do it up and concentrate on other lines? And that as a result Brandt might have lost his job?'

Iversen now made no attempt to hide his agitation. 'We'd heard rumours, of course. There'd been hints, there always are, aren't there?' He looked at them appealingly.

'Where'd they come from, these rumours or hints or whatever you'd like to call them?'

'That I don't know. All I know is that we talked about it among ourselves.'

'Think Brandt knew about it? Or that he was in ignorance because he wasn't in the swim, so to speak?'

'Oh, I'm sure he knew. He could hardly have helped it. Nobody made any secret of it.'

'How'd he react?'

'Took it calmly enough as far as I could see. The only thing I noticed was that he became even more withdrawn.'

'What did you think when he failed to show up for work on Friday?' Rudolf asked.

'I thought it a bit strange. So did the others. He was hardly ever away ill, and the few times he was he always took pains to let us know. Even when he'd no phone of his own. He got one about four years ago, I suppose it would be, shortly after he moved to where he lives now – lived. He didn't even have one in the house before, as far as I know; must have gone out. So naturally we thought it was funny.'

'Who's your dentist?'

Iversen stared at Rudolf in perplexity. 'My dentist? What on earth's my dentist got to do with Brandt?'

'Answer the question, there's a good chap,' Rudolf urged him.

Small beads of perspiration had broken out on Iversen's forehead. 'I go to one called Brenner, Peter Brenner. Have done for a long time, many years.'

'Did you recommend Brenner to Brandt?'

'I? I've never recommended Brenner to anyone as far as I know. Not that there's anything wrong with him, it's just that I haven't. But where's Brenner come into it all?'

'Are you absolutely sure you didn't advise Brandt to go to Brenner?' Rudolf persisted.

'Why ever should I? He never said anything to me about needing a dentist. I can't see why . . .' Rudolf gazed at him expectantly. 'No,' Iversen went on, 'Brandt never said a word to me about there being anything wrong with his teeth. Was there?'

Again Rudolf chose to ignore the question. Instead he asked Iversen to relate exactly what he had done from the time the shop closed at seven on Thursday and through to when it had opened that day. Afterwards he interviewed the rest of the staff, one by one, but none of them had anything of value to add to what Iversen had already told him.

When the two policemen got out into the street again Rudolf stood for a time peering into the shop through the window. This time the staff seemed to be busier conversing among themselves than attending to their many customers. 'That's caused a flutter in the dovecotes, hasn't it?' he said, smiling at Arvik.

Arvik nodded. 'Iversen – Brandt – Brenner, it *must* have been Iversen who recommended Brenner. I can't see why he should be so intent on denying it, though.'

'Neither can I,' Rudolf agreed absently. He was thinking that Dr Moe had promised to drop everything else and concentrate on the Brandt post mortem. He'd actually promised to have his report ready by six. 'Now we've got to check their alibis,' he said. 'But something tells me that all of them, Iversen included, are sure their families and friends will back them up – wives, kids, relations, the lot.'

'Doesn't have to mean they're all telling the truth, though, does it?'

'No, that's the devil of it,' Rudolf agreed with feeling.

Together the two men hurried to where they'd parked their car.

14

Karsten left Evensen to Constable Arvik and he himself returned with Haraldsen to the building where Brenner had his surgery. They had to find out if any of the other tenants had noticed anything out of the ordinary on Friday, Saturday or Sunday.

They tramped from office to office, from flat to flat, but drew a blank everywhere. At last they found themselves before the door of the caretaker's flat. Karsten rang the bell and when they had explained why they had come they were admitted by a tall, gaunt woman who introduced herself as Mrs Inga Olesen. The flat appeared to consist of three small rooms and a poky little kitchen. In the living-room, which looked out on to the same dismal back yard as Evensen's did, the stained wallpaper was full of wrinkles; at one place a tear had been clumsily patched with Scotch tape. The walls looked as if they belonged to a crazy house in an amusement park. They were probably plumb enough, Karsten realized; it was simply that the pictures on them hung at all angles. The furniture wouldn't have been out of place in a junk shop, and the linoleum was holed and threadbare. The caretaker himself, Rolf Olesen, was about the same age as his wife and was seated in a chair reading a magazine. He didn't get up. Some caretaker, was Karsten's first thought. The words of a 1960s Rosemary Clooney hit, 'This Old House', came unbidden into his mind. Must have been written about this place, he smiled to himself.

'So Brenner found a dead man in his chair, did he?' Rolf Olesen said when the two policemen had reluctantly seated themselves on a greasy-looking sofa. 'Pity it wasn't him! Pleased a lot of people, that would.'

'Rolf!' his wife rebuked him sharply.

'Rolf!' he mocked. 'Bah! 's right, you know it is.'

Karsten noticed that the man's eyes were bloodshot, and his whole appearance bespoke addiction to cheap liquor.

'Care to amplify that remark, Mr Olesen?' he said. Haraldsen had a tape recorder ready in his pocket, but Karsten was afraid to use it in case the sight of it caused the caretaker to dry up.

'Rolf . . . ' said Inga Olesen in a warning tone.

'For God's sake stop Rolfing me, Inga!' Olesen said irritably. 'Why shouldn't I tell 'em? Bound to find out sooner or later, anyway. And who's got a better reason for tellin' 'em than I 'ave, eh? Tell me that.'

'But Rolf!' his wife protested, desperation showing in her face.

'To hell with it!' exclaimed Olesen. 'Sick and tired of shutting up, I am. Sick and tired! Tell 'em all about bloody Brenner and our Greta, I will. 'Ow he made us so ashamed we felt like doin' away with ourselves.'

'Greta?' Karsten prompted.

'Our daughter,' explained Mrs Olesen, tight-lipped. Turning back to her husband she said: 'Don't forget how good she is to us.'

'Don't do no more than pay for board and lodging, does she?' Olesen retorted. 'And even then it's you as goes buyin' toothpaste and soap and all them fancy creams she uses.'

'Please, Rolf,' his wife implored. 'Please.' She looked at Karsten and said in a tired voice: 'My husband's had an accident. Been off work the last ten years. He can hardly walk.'

'Fell off a ladder. Weren't my fault, though,' Olesen put in. 'And the landlord, Alfred the Bloody Great, you know 'im, 'e wanted to throw us out. No use for a bloke as spent 'arf 'is life sittin' down and in bed. Only Inga 'ere showed 'im she could work as good as a man, better'n some, so 'e let us stay on. And if ever I meet the bastard, 'e asks me 'ow things are with me

79

wife, with the caretaker! We'd've moved long ago, only all we've got's my pension, national 'ealth, y'know, disability, and the bit Inga can earn charrin'. She don't just do the offices and shops, 'elps out in some of the flats, too. If it 'adn't been for 'er we'd've starved years ago. But she's got sciatica somethin' cruel, so 'tain't easy for 'er, I can tell you.'

'We've managed all right so far,' said his wife encouragingly, 'and if I'm not complaining . . .' She forced a smile, twisting her finger round and round in a fold of her apron. One pocket had gone at the seam, Karsten noticed.

Rolf Olesen was small and running to fat. His trousers were stained and shabby and his pullover had gone at the elbows. He hadn't shaved, and Haraldsen, who was seated nearest, couldn't help wondering when he'd last had a bath. The sight of the unkempt, evil-smelling, irascible man slumped in the chair depressed him. Still, he thought, ten years . . . He looked about him. Old-fashioned crocheted curtains. His grandmother had had some like that, he remembered. Had Inga Olesen crocheted them herself? he wondered. And what about all the cushions? Had she embroidered them as well? If she had, it must have been a long time ago, he thought.

His musings were interrupted by another outburst from Olesen. 'Brenner . . . Right bastard 'e is, real nasty type. Our Greta! Dumb! Dumb as they come. Likes of 'er oughtn't to be allowed out without a lead. She's twenty now, but she weren't no more than seventeen when Brenner told 'er he knew of a firm in Stockholm as was on the lookout for photo models. Said 'e'd take some pictures of 'er and send them in. Thought she had a good chance with 'er figure and all. Pair o' knockers on 'er like cannonballs, she 'ad. You know 'ow they are at that age.'

Inga Olesen opened her mouth as if to protest, but her husband carried blithely on, careless of her susceptibilities.

'Only thing was, she 'ad to undress. 'Course she would,' he said, his voice heavy with scorn. 'Told 'er they made bikinis and that kind of thing, and they needed to see what she was like in the nood, to see if she'd make a good model for 'em. Model!' He snorted. 'What did 'e do? I'll tell you what. Filled 'er full o' drink – so's she wouldn't be shy, 'e said – took a whole pile o' pictures, then gave 'er more to drink. Didn't know whether she was on 'er arse or 'er elbow, she didn't, poor lass. And then that bastard bedded 'er. Bloody well bedded 'er! Our Greta! Didn't use nothin', neither, 'e didn't. Knocked 'er up, 'e did. Seventeen she was. Seventeen!' He paused. 'Daren't tell us, she daren't. Told 'im instead. And wot d'you think 'e did? Said 'e'd 'elp 'er if she'd be in one o' them blue movies, porn, y'know. But she wouldn't, not our Greta. Came and told us instead, thank God. We couldn't 'elp 'er, but in the end we didn't need to. She lost the baby. Best thing as could've 'appened. If you knew what we went through. Specially Inga 'ere, who's more out and about among folk than I am. 'S right, ain't it, Inga?'

Mrs Olesen's fingers twined themselves tighter into her apron. 'He's terrible, terrible he is, terrible. But what he says is perfectly true. Brenner did destroy our child.'

Karsten noticed her careful choice of words. He realized that she seemed to speak better than her husband, but now she was obviously making a special effort to distance herself from him, to talk 'posh'.

'Greta's still living with you, I take it,' he said.

Olesen nodded. 'Yes. Only she's often at 'er girlfriend's. Too often if you ask me.' He shot a challenging look at his wife, who stared down into her lap so as not to have to meet his eye.

'Are you expecting her home today?'

The caretaker shrugged his shoulders. 'Don't ask me, ask 'er.' He gestured towards his wife.

'I don't know,' said Inga Olesen helplessly, continuing to stare down into her lap.

'When was she here last?'

'Thursday, wasn't it?' Olesen looked enquiringly at his wife. She nodded.

'What's her girlfriend's name and where's she live?'

'We don't know,' Olesen replied. 'At least, *I* don't.'

'Nor do I,' said his wife, looking up at last. 'She . . . Greta . . . she likes to live her own life. Doesn't like us to interfere.'

Karsten nodded sympathetically. 'Where's she work?'

'She's what they call a freelance,' Olesen answered. 'She's a model. Photographer's model.'

'Back to that Friday and Saturday . . .' Karsten saw Mrs Olesen go pale and a spasm of pain flitted across her face.

'It's my sciatica,' she said apologetically, biting her lower lip. 'Hits me like a knife sometimes.'

'Either of you notice anything special either of those days?' Karsten continued after first commiserating with Mrs Olesen.

'I spend most of me time 'ere, starin' out at that bloody back yard,' said Olesen bitterly. 'Sometimes a cat crosses the yard. Makes my day, that does. Or a chap with a bottle nips in behind that tree for a quick one. Takes a leak, too, like as not. Only thing that keeps the damned tree alive if you ask me. 'Ardly sees the light of day, it don't. Once I saw a coupla youngsters come in and 'ave it off. Right in front of me eyes, it was. Bangin' away like their lives depended on it. Got all het up myself, I did.'

'Rolf!' his wife admonished him. 'We don't talk like that in front of strangers.'

'Oh, I reckon as 'ow policemen know what it's like when a chap can't do nowt 'imself. Stands to sense 'e's goin' to talk about it when 'e wants and where 'e wants. I've got to be allowed to do something. Or can't a poor bloke even talk about it now?'

Inga Olesen looked as though she were about to burst into tears with shame. 'Do you have to be so coarse?' she said imploringly.

'So ladylike you're gettin' all of a sudden.'

'Did *you* happen to notice anything out of the ordinary Friday, Mrs Olesen?' Karsten asked. 'Or Saturday?'

'Don't think so. Friday? Wait a minute – yes, I saw a widow.'

'A widow?' asked both policemen at once.

'You never said nowt about it to me,' said Olesen accusingly. ' 'Ow d'you know she was a widder, anyway?'

'She was all in black,' his wife explained. 'Wearing weeds, she was. I remember thinking she must have loved her husband very dearly and feeling sorry for her. Had a proper veil, couldn't see her face. Trailed right down her back, too.'

'When on Friday would it be?'

'In the morning. I'd just done all the floors in the china shop and had locked the door and was coming round the corner when I saw her coming out of the main entrance. The entrance of this block, you know. Made me wonder who she was and where she'd been so early in the morning. But what struck me most was that she was hurrying so. She was almost running.'

The two policemen looked at each other. Down here, in this rundown little flat, they'd found corroboration of Evensen's story.

'You realize, I'm sure,' said Karsten, 'that possessing such valuable information as you do, and considering the . . . er, nature of the case, I shall have to ask you to make a formal statement. You're quite entitled to refuse to say anything to the police, but it's your duty to give evidence in court if you're asked to do so.' Karsten watched the couple closely. It was clear that his words had gone home.

'In court?' Mrs Olesen looked fearfully at her husband. She turned to Karsten: 'But *we* haven't done anything wrong,' she said, her hands fluttering.

'I know, that's why I hope you'll come with us to Victoria Terrasse and repeat all you've told us,' he said.

Husband and wife regarded each other in silence.

'Do you mean . . . shall we have to say that Brenner . . . that Brenner . . .' Inga Olesen faltered. She stopped and looked helplessly at Karsten.

'Everything you've told us here,' he replied gravely. 'And anything else you can think of.'

'No!' said the woman defiantly. 'We won't. We don't want to get mixed up in anything, do we, Rolf?' She crossed quickly over to her husband and whispered something into his ear.

'No,' he said. 'We ain't 'avin' it. We don't admit to 'avin' said nothin', so it's no good tryin' to get us to go with you.'

'Well, of course, if you prefer to be summoned to attend, officially –' Karsten began. He got no further.

'We'll come,' Inga Olesen broke in. 'But we're not saying a word about what Brenner's done, just so's you know.'

'Ain't it enough that you two know what 'e's like?' Olesen asked. 'What an 'ard-working couple like Inga and me 'ere, just ordinary folk, 'ave to say don't count when you're up against a chap like Brenner, one of the nobs, like. Even if you did decide that he was guilty, because of what we'd told you and other

83

things as well, 'e'd get away with it, I'll bet.'

'I've said we'll go, Rolf, so there we are,' his wife said decisively. 'Come on, I'll help you tidy up and put on a suit. You can't go into town looking like that.'

'There's no need to change,' Karsten put in quickly. He was afraid that Mrs Olesen wanted to have a few words with her husband in private, to tell him what to say and what not to say. 'He looks quite all right to me, and I'm sure he will to other people too. But before we go I should like to have a picture of the two of you taken fairly recently.'

'We ain't been near a photographer's since we got married.'

'An ordinary snapshot will do fine.'

'We ain't got none o' them neither.'

'Oh, well, doesn't matter,' said Karsten amiably. 'We'll just have to take one down at Victoria Terrasse instead.'

His words produced the desired effect.

'Greta took one when we were out on that island last summer, remember, when that friend of hers drove us.' She looked at Karsten. 'I'll go and get it.'

She was away for so long her husband began to evince signs of impatience: 'Inga! Come on, what're you doin'?'

'I'm looking,' came the reply through the open door. 'Oh, here it is!'

'Thank you. And I'd also like a picture of your daughter,' said Karsten as Mrs Olesen handed him a fuzzy coloured snapshot of her and her husband arm in arm against a line of trees.

'We ain't got none of 'er neither,' said Olesen again, almost before the words were out of Karsten's mouth.

'That's strange, isn't it?' Karsten couldn't help remarking. 'I should have thought you'd have had stacks of them, her being a model.'

In the event he had to content himself with a snap that had been tucked into the frame of another picture. It showed a smiling young girl with tumbling fair hair. He couldn't see her eyes as she was wearing sunglasses. She appeared to be mooring a boat. Fat lot of good this is going to be, he thought morosely.

Dr Moe excelled himself that day. He had determined to treat himself to an evening off for once. Since the death of his wife three years earlier he had tended even more than in the past to devote himself to his work, in an endeavour to assuage his loss. That evening he was going to have dinner with friends. He was looking forward to a good meal, relaxed, intelligent conversation, and a brandy and sofa afterwards before a cheerful log fire. All this was in the back of his mind as he worked quickly and efficiently at his appointed task. It was only just after four when he phone Rudolf.

'You're just sitting there waiting and wondering, aren't you?' He gave a dry chuckle. 'Well, you asked for it, and now you're going to get it. This'll give you something to get your teeth into.'

'What will?' asked Rudolf, unable to share the doctor's good humour.

'My report. The cause of death.'

'It won't if I don't know what it is,' said Rudolf, putting as much sarcasm into his voice as he dared.

'Well, pin your ears back, my lad, and I'll tell you. Your friend Brandt was drowned!'

'Drowned? You having me on?'

'No, not this time. He was drowned. In fresh water. No drugs, nothing like that, but there are clear signs of inflammation round an upper molar; upper left. He must have been in terrible pain, poor chap. Happy release, perhaps.' Moe laughed at his own macabre joke.

Getting callous in his old age, Rudolf thought to himself. Aloud he said: 'When did he die?'

'Friday morning, early. Some time between five and ten. Can't say nearer than that.'

Rudolf thanked the doctor and rang off. A moment later he phoned Records. No, they had no record of anyone on his list, with one exception, Greta Olesen. She sometimes lived in a flat in Madserud Allé, one she owned herself. Called herself Bettina and did a little modelling every so often.

'Probably to have something to put on her income-tax return,' said the cynical voice on the other end of the line. 'She's been picked up a couple of times for possession of drugs.

Amphetamines. Says here that she's friendly with a lot of politicians.' The man laughed. 'Very friendly. Only it's one-way traffic. They visit her, not the other way round. Not the big boys, mind you, the smaller fry lower down. She's down as a possible security risk and they're keeping tabs on her.'

Rudolf had no need to ask who 'they' were. He decided to have Greta Olesen alias Bettina brought in for questioning without delay.

15

From then on it was all go. Interviews, meetings, reports, it never stopped. The press thought at first that the police were trying to pull the wool over their eyes. Drowned – in a dentist's surgery? Making no attempt to disguise their scepticism, radio and television newscasters informed the public of the bare outlines of the case and left it at that. Not so the popular press. Speculation was rife.

Why should the murderer have chosen to drown his victim by holding his head under water? And how had he got him to keep still? Either he must have been exceptionally strong or there were two of them. There were no signs of a struggle or of the rest of the body having been in water. Even the victim's hair had stayed dry. If the murderer had intended in advance to kill it was strange that he had not been armed. But if he hadn't planned the crime, why then had he taken Brandt's life? It didn't make sense.

In the middle of it all Magda phoned to ask Rudolf if what she'd heard on the radio was true. Her husband assured her that it was and took the opportunity to tell her that he'd be late. The whole of the Oslo police force had been alerted. She reminded him that he'd said the same thing when all those drugs were stolen from Ulleval, and wanted to know what he'd like her to do with the dinner she'd prepared – pickle it? That was as far as she got. If only she'd not mentioned food! God, he was hungry! Rather more sharply than he had intended, Rudolf answered that as she'd been dumb enough to marry a policeman, she'd just have to take the consequences, and rang off before he could say something he'd really regret. Round about ten Karsten entered Rudolf's office. Rudolf could see at a glance that his brother was near the end of his tether.

'My brain's at a standstill,' Karsten said. 'I'm thinking of calling it a day. Like to come along, or are you going to spend the night here? There's nothing more we can do now, anyway, you know that as well as I do.'

It was a long time since Rudolf had been at Karsten's, and longer still since he'd been invited. 'Wouldn't say no,' Rudolf replied. 'If you're alone, that is.' His brother assured him that he was. 'He's bound to offer me a drink,' thought Rudolf, 'and my word, couldn't I do with one!'

But Karsten had nothing stronger to offer than the four bottles of beer he still had hoarded on top of his wardrobe. He went and got them and left them for a few minutes in the freezer to chill. Neither he nor Rudolf felt inclined to wait longer. It was only when he was well into his first foaming glass that Karsten recalled his resolution of that morning. Oh, well, he consoled himself, it's too late now. Anyway, this must count as one of the exigencies of the service.

'Everything points to this Brandt having been the male equivalent of a blushing violet, never said boo to a goose, apparently,' said Rudolf out of the blue, reverting to what was uppermost in both their minds. Although they'd hashed and rehashed the case over and over, one never knew when a chance remark might set off a new train of thought or bring sudden enlightenment. It had happened before. 'Loving son, virtually invisible tenant, the perfect shop assistant – if a zombie's perfect – a chap who neither drank nor chased the fillies . . . why on earth should anyone want to kill him?'

'Not so long ago, Rudolf, we were agreed that all that might have been just a front, protective colouring, so to speak. Remember? I find it hard to believe that anyone could be *that* self-effacing.' After a brief interval, an interval which was, however, long enough for him to refill their glasses, Karsten continued: 'But what could he have been wanting to hide if it was a front? Some racket or other, but what? Drugs, like his mother hinted at? Could be, of course, but then someone would have been bound to have seen him together with people

88

known to be in the business. I know we haven't questioned the whole town, how can we, but hell's bells, there isn't a soul in the building that's ever heard a sound from his flat or seen anyone go in or out. And you know what neighbours are like, never miss a thing. Makes him sound like a hermit. And even if he was into something and knew something or had done something that prompted someone to want to get rid of him, why do it at Brenner's? And if it was premeditated, planned in advance, you'd think whoever did it would have had a weapon ready, wouldn't you?'

'Yes, you would,' his brother agreed. 'There's something fishy about that Brenner, you know,' he went on, going off at a tangent. 'He's hiding something, I'm sure of it. First he goes around telling all and sundry that he's off on holiday, then he comes home, goes to his flat the same day Brandt's killed and on top of it all sleeps there. And all that without ever having a look into his surgery. No, he's hiding something all right. His wife's in on it too, I'll bet. Well, I'll have it out of them, you wait and see if I don't! Think it's true that they didn't hear Evensen when he rang because they'd pulled the phone out?'

'Sounds reasonable,' said Karsten mildly. 'After all, officially they were on holiday till Sunday, and they said themselves they didn't want all the hassle of having to explain why they'd cut their stay short. I think it's funnier that Evensen can't praise AK as he calls him highly enough, while the Olesens detest him.'

'Hum,' his brother grunted. 'Brenner's far too clever to have killed Brandt and left him in his own surgery in the hope that we'd be so naive as to believe that he'd never be that dumb. Next time I see him I'm going to ask him about Iversen. I'm having Iversen checked out, by the way. I'm going to ask Brenner why he's got that damned great calendar on the bedroom wall, too. And that clock. Looks like Big Ben! I think we can rely on Evensen, don't you? And from what he says the meeting between Brandt and that widow must have been completely unexpected.'

'Yes, that's the way it strikes me too,' Karsten assented. 'Quite a disguise when you come to think of it. With a veil like that it could just as easily have been a man as a woman.'

'I remember how in the old days, when it was common, I always felt so helpless and uncomfortable when I saw a woman in weeds,' Rudolf said slowly.

'Yes,' his brother agreed, 'same with me. Used to depress me. Reminded me that I was mortal, I suppose. Not that I am, of course,' he added with a smile. 'Funny how simple things like that can set you thinking.'

'If this so-called widow – man or woman, makes no difference – killed Brandt, then it must have been to cover up some other crime – assuming that we accept Evensen's statement that their meeting was accidental and that they didn't know one another. And Brandt did have toothache, so he could have gone on the off chance.' Rudolf seemed to be talking more to himself than to his brother. 'But what sort of crime could it have been? If those weeds were a disguise, whoever it was must have had a damned good reason for not wanting to be recognized. But we don't know of any other crime, do we? You can't call Brenner's missing towel a crime, can you now? And why did the "widow" feel that he or she had to kill Brandt anyway? He couldn't have given a description of her, probably didn't even know what sex she was.'

'Personally I wouldn't have believed in her at all if Mrs Olesen hadn't seen her, too,' said Karsten. 'I've taken quite a liking to Evensen, but he's a sly old fox. Think there's anything in that idea of his about the widow being one of Brenner's girlfriends who didn't want anyone in the building to see her? Because that would mean either that she knew some of the neighbours or that she lived there herself and knew them all. She obviously has all the keys, both of the street door and of Brenner's flat.' He was silent for a moment. 'She must have put on all that black a good way off if she didn't want to run the risk of being seen near the building and recognized. And even if she doesn't live there, she must have got dressed up before she went in, don't you think? Can she have been looking for compromising pictures of herself? It's possible, you know, if Brenner really is involved in porn.'

'But why kill Brandt? That's what gets me.'

'Yes, why? And why doesn't Brenner have a receptionist? He can obviously afford it. As it is now, first he has to release the lock on the street door by pressing a button in his surgery, then he has to drop whatever he's doing and trail all through the flat to let the caller in. Looks as though he doesn't want to let anyone in unless he knows exactly who it is.'

'If he's in the skinflick trade he can just as easily be involved in other shady dealings too, things he wouldn't want anyone else to know about, naturally. His dentist's practice could even be a cover; be a good one, wouldn't it? Lots of people coming and going, but not necessarily to have their teeth done. Seems strange to me that he should have volunteered the information about when he went into the flat. Evensen could have been primed, of course, to provide corroboration. We've no guarantee that he's incorruptible, have we? And why's Iversen so scared? Brandt would never have gone to Brenner if he hadn't known that he started work at seven. I've checked the telephone directory: nine to two it says there, no Saturdays. Brandt was pretty desperate, must have been, so it's a reasonable assumption.'

'I've had a look at Iversen's card in Brenner's file; he's a regular patient all right. If you're satisfied with your dentist, you tend to stick with him. Same with toothpaste, come to that. So it'd be perfectly natural for him to recommend him, wouldn't you think?'

Rudolf nodded. 'The char hadn't a bad word to say about the Brenners.' Then, as the thought struck him: 'That could be another reason why the Olesens don't like him, because he doesn't have Mrs Olesen to clean for him.'

After a moment's silence he added: 'Wonder how long we shall be able to keep the widow under our hats? As soon as the news gets out we shall have half the town phoning to say that they've seen her, here, there and everywhere, and all at the same time. And the devil of it is that we shall have to check out every blasted lead, just in case one might be genuine. Hundreds of hours of work for nothing, and all the time the real trail's getting colder. Isn't that always the way?'

The police were already making extensive enquiries. All concerned, no matter how peripheral their involvement in the case, had been carefully investigated. None of them had as much as a distant relative who had been bereaved in the course of the last year or so or who even knew of anyone who had worn widow's weeds for at least the last fifteen years. The custom had completely died out.

Evensen's impression was that the widow had been quite tall. Mrs Olesen had been so flummoxed and in such pain from her sciatica that she'd no idea of her height; she'd registered the uncommon sight and the flowing veil and that was all. Stout? Evensen had had to think. Finally he concluded that she'd been 'just about middling, the way you'd expect a woman of her age to be' – a description which helped not the slightest. Her age? How could he know, he'd replied, a hint of impatience in his voice. Still, he'd reasoned, widow's weeds had gone out years ago, so anybody who still wore them had to be getting on. Some women became dried up and wizened as they grew older, others put on weight. The widow he'd seen had been like that. 'Like what?' 'Well, middling, you know, middling.'

Karsten lit another cigarette. 'What beats me is how someone all dolled up like that could wander unnoticed through the streets of Oslo. I know you can wear pretty well anything these days without people batting an eyelid, but they're more hippie-style clothes, more way out. I saw somewhere that a chap in Copenhagen had strolled through a shopping mall in his birthday suit. Nobody turned a hair till in the end the police stepped in. But full mourning like that, these days, I mean to say it's different, isn't it? Must have had a car nearby – or turned into a witch and ridden off on a broomstick!' Becoming serious again, he went on: 'She wore gloves, that's obvious. There weren't any fingerprints about in the surgery, apart from the Brenners' and the char's. She's in the clear. Hadn't noticed anything out of the ordinary at all, either.'

Karsten opened the last bottle. Only then did it occur to Rudolf that he was supposed to be on a diet and that beer was full of calories. He sighed softly. 'And why did whoever did Brandt in take that towel?' he asked.

'Perhaps it had his monogram on it,' his brother suggested, 'or maybe Grand Hotel or Oslo City Transport.' He laughed.

Shortly afterwards Rudolf phoned for a taxi and left. For some reason the thought of that missing towel was starting to niggle.

16

Strange, that business of the towel, Rudolf was to reflect many times in the days that followed. Brenner insisted that it was all that was missing. The Friday before he had left to go on holiday he had taken a towel from the drawer beside the washbasin in his surgery. He remembered having debated with himself whether to dump it in the dirty-clothes basket, but in the event he had decided to leave it out as it had been used only that once. Rudolf knew from experience that people tend to notice the most insignificant things at times when one would have thought they would have had other, more important, things to occupy them. Brenner was a case in point. He claimed to have opened the door to his surgery to start the day at seven on Monday, the eighth of March, found the dead man in the chair – and noticed that the towel had gone. Such things were quite commonplace. But was it true in this case?

Another funny thing was that Brenner now seemed to be regretting having mentioned the towel in the first place. 'Forget it, Sergeant,' he'd said. Did he really want him to, Rudolf wondered. Or was it merely a ruse to get him to focus more closely on the towel than he would otherwise have done?

The Brenners had changed their tune entirely after that first encounter. They had even apologized for having acted so boorishly. It had been because they'd still been at loggerheads, they'd explained, but now they were determined to do all in their power to help the police. Brenner couldn't say much about Iversen, except that he was a model patient, came in regularly for check-ups, paid on the nail, and never cancelled an appointment. Blue movies? Brenner had laughed heartily when he had heard what he was accused of; his wife, on the other hand, did not laugh. She had taken her husband's hand. 'How can people be so vile?' she had exclaimed in a hurt voice. 'Who is it, anyway, who says so?'

'The Olesens,' Rudolf replied, watching Brenner closely. 'They say that you were responsible for their daughter's, er – downfall.'

'Well, of all the cheek!' said Inga Brenner vehemently. 'That Greta's been a fast little hussy since she was fourteen. Downfall! I don't know how they dare.'

'Now don't get all worked up, Inga,' her husband said quietly. 'They've probably never heard of slander. Greta must have spun them some cock-and-bull story to get herself out of trouble. Probably told them some smart alec had led her astray, and then when they wanted to know who it was she just took the first name that came into her head. It's no secret that we've had some pretty lively parties in the flat. Greta had to come up once, remember? Asked us to tone it down a bit so's her father could get some sleep. You've not forgotten that, surely? I expect she remembered the parties and clutched at a straw when they backed her into a corner. They're simple people, don't forget, and Greta's not even their daughter, really. They just accepted what she told them, it's no worse than that. I shall insist on a retraction and an apology, though, and if they're not willing to give me one I shall take them to court. But I don't think they'd be prepared to go that far.'

'What about orgies?' Rudolf interposed softly.

The couple exchanged glances. 'What dirty minds they must have!' exclaimed Inga Brenner. 'We've had some wild parties, I admit, as my husband's just told you. But orgies . . . and blue movies . . . how can they? It makes me sick to think of it, to think that they should accuse us of something so – so filthy.'

'There's something I've been wondering about,' said Rudolf. 'That calendar – and the clock. They seem so out of place.' He looked at the couple enquiringly.

Peter Brenner's weak mouth twitched slightly. 'Honestly,

94

Sergeant, do we have to answer for them, too?' he asked in an offended tone. 'We *like* them, both the calendar *and* the clock. You must have things in your own home that you've bought because they took your fancy. You must have. Or do you only buy things you know your family and friends will approve of?' He looked challengingly at Rudolf.

Rudolf had to admit that it all sounded very plausible. Why, then, he asked himself, did he have such difficulty in accepting it? Simply because the two objects were so utterly at odds with the style of the bedroom at large? Good taste, no expense spared – and that business-like calendar and cheap-looking clock. He decided to let the matter drop, however, and told them that both Evensen and Mrs Olesen had seen a person in full widow's weeds in the building early Friday morning.

'Widow's weeds?' laughed Inga Brenner. Rudolf thought he detected a note of relief in her voice. 'I've heard of pink elephants, but widows, that's a new one on me.' No, she wouldn't go so far as to claim that Evensen drank. Probably took a drop every now and again, like most people, but no more. As for Mrs Olesen, well, if she did, who could blame her? It would be a miracle if she didn't drink a bit too much at times with a husband like that and a daughter who had gone off the rails and was such a trial to her.

Peter Brenner ventured that perhaps Evensen was so lonely that he had to dream up all sorts of things just to avoid going up the wall. Almost as an afterthought he added that once or twice he had given him a bottle of whisky when they were going to have a party. After all, he was the one who suffered most from the noise. He couldn't understand why the Olesens should have complained that time; the din was hardly likely to reach all the way down to them. He had a sneaking suspicion that Olesen had sent Greta up in the hope of being bought off with a bottle. 'A sop to Cerebus' was how he put it.

'Olesen tipples, you've only got to look at him to know that,' he said. 'I'm sure most of his disability pension goes on drink. And there's his poor wife working her fingers to the bone to keep a roof over their heads. Evensen told me once that before he had that accident they were reasonably well-off. Nice home they had, too. Mrs Olesen's good with a needle, used to make all Greta's clothes herself, she knitted, embroidered, crocheted, everything. But then Olesen fell off that ladder and did his back in and that was that. Started drinking – not that I blame him. He hit the bottle really hard, though, and it's been downhill all the way ever since. But back to that widow. Did Mrs Olesen and old Evensen really see a widow on Friday?'

'Seems so.'

'I thought full mourning like that, weeds and all the rest of it, had gone out years ago,' said the dentist, looking enquiringly at his wife.

'So it did. Jolly good job too, if you ask me. Terrible custom it was. Barbaric!' She shuddered. 'I don't know what I'd do if I suddenly found myself face to face with someone like that these days.'

'Do me a favour, will you?' Rudolf asked them. 'Don't mention this widow business to anyone, OK?'

'We won't, don't worry,' Brenner assured him, evidently speaking for them both. 'If a story like that were to get about people'd go wild. It's bad enough Brandt being drowned in my surgery.'

Someone turned up the fact that just over twenty-five years ago Iversen had served a prison sentence for having stolen a car while drunk and knocked an old man down – fortunately without causing him serious injury.

Rudolf asked Iversen to come and see him and confronted him with this piece of information. The man looked as though he were about to faint.

'Please don't let it get about,' he pleaded. 'Please. If Lessner got to know I'd be out like a shot. It was a teenage escapade, one I've bitterly regretted ever since. I'd never been in trouble with the police before and I haven't afterwards, either.'

'Have you remembered recommending Brenner to Brandt since I was in the shop?'

Iversen shook his head. 'I can't remember having ever recommended him to anyone, never mind Brandt. The only thing I can remember is once sitting in the staff room –' He laughed sardonically. 'Staff room! That cupboard place, you know. Well, I was sitting there with two or three other people and saying that Brenner was OK and how handy it was to have a dentist who started work so early, at seven. I don't know whether Brandt was there, though, or whether he came in while we were talking. Don't mix me up in this, Sergeant, please,' he exhorted Rudolf. 'If that old story were to come out I don't know what I'd do.'

Rudolf smiled at him reassuringly. 'Don't worry, Mr Iversen, it's all over and done with. Water under the bridge.' He was on the point of adding 'there but for the grace of God go I', but checked himself just in time; there was a limit to how human a policeman could be expected to be!

That damned towel!

If Brandt had been battered to death, knifed, if blood had flowed, Rudolf would have understood the killer's taking it. But he'd been drowned. There had been no sign of violence whatever. And there'd been no scrapings of skin under the nails of the corpse, so Brandt couldn't have clawed his murderer in a desperate struggle for his life. Had the killer's nose started to bleed all of a sudden? Or did he have some open wound, a cut or a sore? Or eczema or something like that?

Perhaps it was his work, thought Rudolf. If he'd dried his hands and knew that there was something on the towel that could provide a clue. But what? Printer's ink? Chemicals? Could he be engaged in some process that left traces on his hands? Could he be a chemist?

He, he, he. He always thought in terms of a man, though he knew full well that it could just have easily have been a woman. 'Stereotyped thinking,' he told himself. 'Got to watch out for that.'

Perhaps there *had* been blood on the towel, the murderer's own, a nose-bleed, a cut, whatever, and if it were of a rare type . . . 'That'd explain it,' Rudolf decided. Or maybe the blood group was a common enough one but the killer suffered from some disease that would show up on scientific examination. In that case he or she would be registered as a patient somewhere.

Rudolf resolved to leave the question of the murderer's sex open, but for the sake of convenience to treat him or her as a he. If he had come with the affirmed intention of killing Brenner it was strange that he hadn't taken steps to make sure that the dentist would be in that day. And if he'd come for some other reason, it was a mystery why he'd killed Brandt. With a disguise like that he could be sure that Brandt wouldn't be able to give a proper description.

It didn't make things any easier for Rudolf that he was always hungry. Sometimes he felt he was going to faint. When that happened he invariably sank down heavily on the nearest chair and asked himself if it was worth all this suffering just to lose a few kilos. Come to that, when would he start losing them? He hadn't seen any signs of it yet when he religiously weighed himself each morning. To make matters worse, not a soul evinced the slightest sympathy, Magda least of all. Wolfing down eggs and bacon and at the same time claiming that she too was slimming! 'You don't want to get hung up on calories, Rudolf,' she'd chided him. 'It's carbohydrates that do the damage. In a normal household people eat up to 400 grams a day, but forty to sixty's enough really. That's what everybody has to have. If you don't, you can get fat even so – or damage your liver and kidneys. You can even eat leaf fat –'

'For heaven's sake, Magda, give it a rest,' Rudolf implored. 'I don't *want* to eat leaf fat, whatever it may be. Just because you insist on stuffing yourself with eggs and bacon, you don't have to justify yourself to me. Nobody's going to tell me I don't have to count my calories. Why, we learnt that at school.'

'Now don't go getting all steamed up,' his wife had admonished him gently. 'I'll go and make you something nice. Something you can eat without fear of getting fat.' She'd disappeared into the kitchen to return some time later with a mish-mash of vegetables which she proudly presented as kohlrabi steak. His one consolation had been that for once Roly-Poly hadn't begged to share his meal; he was left to 'enjoy' it in peace. Even the bloody dog's got the sense not to be a vegetarian, Rudolf thought morosely.

The Olesens were questioned separately and together, not once but several times. Inga Olesen admitted that she knew that Greta had a flat of her own, but she'd kept quiet about it, she said, for fear of what her husband would do if he found out. She begged them not to say anything to him. She didn't change her statement even when she heard that Greta had disappeared. Bettina? No, the name meant nothing to her. A prostitute? A prostitute, her Greta! No, that was too much. Who did the police think they were, saying things like that?

Although the Brenners likewise insisted on sticking to their story, Rudolf began to wonder about their stay at the hotel in Voss, and he got the local police to check. A message came back to say that they had been there, but that they'd left hardly any impression on the staff. 'Part of the wallpaper' was the phrase Rudolf's informant had used.

Strange, Rudolf mused. It did happen that people just popped into the bar at places like that without registering. Was that what had happened? That someone who knew them had turned up without warning and they'd scampered home?

In spite of their assurance that they would do all they could to help, the couple were adamant: they had packed up and come home because of a violent quarrel. But they refused to divulge what the quarrel had been about.

17

Friday the twelfth of March, exactly one week after Brandt had died, Alfred Kristoffersen – AK – declared himself able to see Rudolf. He was still not completely recovered from his bout of flu, but if Rudolf wasn't afraid of catching it . . . He hoped it wasn't going to take too long. Would three o'clock be all right?

The day was no less hectic than its predecessors. What is more, it was the sixth day that Rudolf hadn't sat down to a good meal, so it was perhaps no wonder that he wasn't feeling in the best of humour. Nor did it help when 'Binder' Pearson tottered into his office and proudly announced that he was still on his feet despite the fact that he was running a high temperature.

'You ought to be in bed,' said Rudolf, 'instead of walking around here giving it to half the Force.'

'There's so much to do.'

'That's just it,' Rudolf retorted, 'there is – and we need every man jack we've got to do it. So it's better to have one man in bed, even if it is the king-pin, than have the place deserted.'

Pearson was tall, thin and nothing much to look at, but in his own eyes he was handsome, macho, witty and indispensable. Most of his colleagues couldn't stand him. 'A bumptious ass' was Rudolf's private opinion, 'all puffed up with a false sense of his own importance'.

'Not getting very far with the Brandt case, I hear,' Pearson said.

Rudolf grunted noncommittally: 'And you lot aren't exactly making a lot of headway with those stolen drugs, are you?' he countered.

'No, it's tough going, they both are,' Pearson conceded.

At that moment Karsten came in. 'Hello, still soldiering on?' he said to Pearson with a cheerful grin.

'I'm doing my best,' Pearson replied stiffly. 'That smoke doesn't help, though, you know.'

Karsten pretended not to hear. 'Gunhild's drawn a blank so far,' he reported. 'Checked with every taxi firm and driver for miles around. Nobody's seen hair nor hide of a black widow. I'm beginning to think that theory of mine has something in it after all.'

'What theory?' Pearson wanted to know.

'That she drove off in a stolen car,' said Rudolf quickly before Karsten could say she'd flown off on a broomstick. 'There's plenty about.'

'I've been thinking that for a long time,' Pearson confided.

'I'd've thought you'd have had enough on your plate with Ulleval,' said Karsten tartly, 'without shouldering our problems, too.'

'I was only saying –' Pearson began.

He was interrupted by the appearance of Detective Constable Allan Arvik. 'Hello, what's all this palaver?' he said breezily, surveying the crowded office. 'Big Three in session?' Then, turning to Pearson: 'And how's my favourite flu-zie? As big a drip as ever?' Neither Rudolf nor Karsten could help laughing aloud.

Pearson regarded Arvik sourly. 'Ever thought of going on the stage?' he asked at last. 'You might do better there.' He turned on his heel and stalked out.

Arvik followed him: 'I'll come back later, Rudolf,' he said.

'Old Binder'll be the death of me,' Rudolf muttered. 'Here I am, living on food that wouldn't keep a rabbit alive, and that clot comes in here spraying his germs all over the place. Irresponsible, I call it.'

'You're so crabby these days, Rudolf, I hardly know you,' Magda had complained that morning, the first time they'd really had time to speak to one another for several days. Rudolf had seized on the first excuse that came into his head: 'Sorry,' he'd said, 'I've a lot on my mind. This Brandt case, you know.'

'You've been busy before,' his wife had replied, 'but at least I've been able to talk to you. Now you snap my head off the moment I open my mouth.' With an effort Rudolf wrenched his mind back to the present.

His brother lit a cigarette from the stump of the first. 'The postmen in the area haven't seen anything. They can't remember having delivered any suspicious post, either, anything out of the ordinary, that is. Haven't seen anyone, no widows, no nothing, just the usual daily round. So there we are, sweet Fanny Adams there too.' To his brother's surprise, without being asked he strode across and opened the window.

'My word,' said Rudolf, 'we *are* coming on! Well, we shall just have to keep going, shan't we? Isn't much else we can do. Go round again, perhaps. You know as well as I do how people often remember something afterwards, when they've had time to think. They freeze in their mental tracks when a copper asks them something, then when they get home and get their slippers on and their minds start functioning normally again, it's amazing what some of them come up with. "I'm sure it's not important, but . . ." God, how many times haven't I heard that – and found out that it *was* important? So we shall just have to keep on knocking on doors.'

'I'm checking Brenner's life story back to the womb,' said Karsten, closing the window. 'Nothing at all so far. Nothing on his wife, either. They're a couple of slippery ones if you like!'

'Yes, I feel the same way,' Rudolf concurred. 'They're hiding something, I'm damned sure they are. Seems to me she's just acting. Doesn't come across as genuine as far as I'm concerned. And then there's that blasted towel. And Johansen – I'm thinking of his financial affairs. Looks like a tramp yet owns the building. Find out anything, by the way?'

'Only that he seems to be telling the truth,' Karsten replied. 'We're busy checking out Lessner and the rest of the staff at Harts. Evensen, too. But we haven't come across anything new.' He fell silent, then continued: 'I'm going to have a word with a chap called Gregers Berger today. Knew Evensen when his wife was still alive. Evensen put me on to him, asked me to, in fact. By now he can have primed Berger up to the ears for all I know, but we can't afford not to talk to him even if he has. You never know, he might muff his lines and let something slip.'

'And I'm seeing Kristoffersen at three this afternoon,' said Rudolf. 'Don't suppose it'll help much, but it had to be done.' He paused. 'Can't say I'm looking forward to it very much. First he spent God knows how long telling me how ill he was and made it sound as though by seeing me he was risking a relapse, then he said he'd like to get it over and done with and could I come at three. As I understood it he's still confined to bed, yet the way he came across to me anyone'd think he was booked up every minute of the day. Playing the big tycoon, obviously. I know the type and I'm not very fond of them.'

'We're digging down into his past, too,' said Karsten, getting up to go. 'When you come to think of it,' he said, turning in the doorway, 'in a case like this there's nothing strange about everyone seemingly being in the clear. Hang it all, we don't even know what we're looking for, do we? We shall just have to console ourselves with the thought that it's early days yet.'

It was a poor consolation, but it was all that Rudolf had to comfort him when he stepped out into the cold of a grey afternoon. March, he thought, and full winter still. People hurried past, heads lowered and muffled up to the eyebrows. They looked as though they were ashamed at being on the streets at all; either that, or as if they'd lash out at the first person who delayed them getting to wherever they were headed.

Alfred Kristoffersen's house stood well back in its own spacious grounds and was just as Rudolf had expected it to be. The wrought-iron gates were closed, so he had to get out of his car and open them before he could enter the drive, and then get out again and close them behind him. He noticed that all the lights in the house seemed to be on; there was even a gleam from the windows of the cellar, he saw. 'Looks like a Festival of Light,' he said to himself. 'Still, if he can afford to keep up a place like this I don't suppose he's going to let the electricity bill worry him.'

He found himself wondering what it was like to live in such a house after having once known poverty. Rags to riches with a vengeance, he reflected. Kristoffersen had never made any secret of his humble origins. On the contrary, in every interview he gave he hammered away at his favourite theme: there's only one key to success – sheer hard work. Wasn't he the living proof? His one regret, the tragedy in his life, was that he had lost his wife fifteen years earlier, when she was only thirty and on the threshold of what promised to be a glittering career on the stage. He was currently living with a well-known Norwegian-Italian fashion designer known as Gemma and her daughter Renee, a product of her first and only marriage. She was always referred to as his wife and addressed as Mrs Kristoffersen, but they had never actually married. Rumour had it that the alliance was in the process of breaking up.

Rudolf rang the bell. He'd been half-expecting the door to be reverently opened by a liveried butler. Instead it was flung open to reveal three young girls of eleven or twelve, all standing gazing at him in obvious anticipation. Politely he told them his name and identified himself as a police officer.

'So you're the policeman who wants to talk to Daddy,' said the tallest, slimmest and prettiest of the three. She had dark-brown eyes, flecked with gold, and an elfin face with a turned-up nose. As she danced from one foot to the other she gave the impression of being unable to stand still for more than a minute or two at a time. Her skin was a shade darker than the others'. She was wearing yellow ski trousers and a high-necked green sweater held in at her waist by a brown leather belt with an outsize buckle. Her dark glossy hair hung well below her shoulders. She was constantly fingering it, something Rudolf would have taken as an outlet for her surplus energy had he not seen that her nails were bitten to the quick.

'But why aren't you in uniform?' the girl asked in a disappointed voice.

'You see, we bet,' one of the other girls, a stolid-looking child with red hair and freckles, put in. 'My father's a captain. On board a ship. He says nobody likes wearing uniform, they only do it because they have to. Renee said you were sure to be in uniform, because you're on duty,' she explained, 'so we bet a krone, and now I've won,' she concluded triumphantly.

'I wasn't in on it,' came from a third member of the trio, who was smaller than her two companions and appeared to be more reticent. Her short curly hair outlined the shape of her skull like a cap. In the middle of the curls was a white clip with a floral design. 'You're a murder policeman, aren't you?' the girl said, giving Rudolf a long, unblinking stare. 'That's what my mother said, and she wasn't going to let me be here when you came. Only she gave in in the end 'cos Kari was allowed.' She indicated the red-haired girl. 'Her mother and mine are best friends, you see.' She came to a sudden stop and blushed as though at the realization that she had just made a long speech all by herself.

'Where will I find your dad, then?' Rudolf asked Renee as she handed him a coat hanger. She's going to make a good hostess one day, he thought.

'Let me hang your coat up first,' the girl said, reproachfully it seemed, 'then I'll take you in.' She beamed at him: 'He's really mad at having to talk to you. He doesn't, usually, he only talks to people he wants to. But he can't say no to you, can he, when you're a policeman? He's been like a bear with a sore head these last few days, Mummy says. He's ill, you know. She's ill, too – really ill. Everybody's ill except me,' she declared proudly. 'I'm never ill. It's because they're all ill that I had to let you in.'

'Your father's been in bed, too, though, hasn't he?' Rudolf asked.

Renee shook her head and twined a lock of hair round her finger. 'Only a bit, now and again. He says it makes you lazy, staying in bed. So most of the time he sits in the lounge and reads and drinks hot toddies and sniffs and coughs and makes everybody miserable. He was bad last week as well, but he went out a couple of times even so. Then when he came back he had to go straight to bed because it'd made him worse.'

'So this week he's stayed indoors, then?'

The girl nodded. 'He just went to the office for a bit one evening after the others had left, that's all. He didn't want them to get it, you see.'

And yet Kristoffersen hadn't been able to see him before today, Rudolf thought angrily, following Renee and her two friends through two large lounges and into a smaller one which was evidently where the family gathered to watch television. A deep brown carpet covered the floor; he dared not look back as he felt that his shoes were leaving a trail of muddy depressions behind. The chairs and settee were low and very comfortable-looking. Lamps with brightly coloured shades were scattered here and there, and across one wall, which was all windows as far as Rudolf could judge, the heavy floral curtains were half-drawn. If it had been me, Rudolf thought, I'd have drawn them right across and shut out this awful weather altogether.

'Pardon my not getting up,' said Kristoffersen, 'but I'm still pretty shaky.' He was in his late fifties and life seemed to have treated him well. His grey hair looked as though it had just been trimmed and washed. His eyes, which were also grey, were a trifle glazed, but that could just have easily have been the toddy as the flu, Rudolf decided.

'Thank you, Renee,' Kristoffersen said. 'Now, run along, will you, you and your friends, and leave us to talk.'

When the girls had gone Kristoffersen turned his attention to Rudolf: 'Everyone's ill in this house, everyone except Renee. Nothing seems to bite on her, not even this blasted flu.'

Rudolf nodded sympathetically: 'But I gather you risked going out the other evening,' he prompted.

'You gather . . .' Then, as enlightenment dawned: 'Oh, Renee!' He smiled. 'Yes. No option. Had to go to the office to see how things were going with one of my pet projects. Didn't want the others to get this little lot. If you've any sense you'll keep your distance, too.'

Considerate of him, thought Rudolf, thinking of Pearson.

'To tell you the truth, Sergeant,' Kristoffersen continued, 'I can't see why you've come at all. I know it has to do with finding that chap dead in Brenner's surgery, but there's no way I can help you, I can assure you.'

'It's purely routine, sir, purely routine,' murmured Rudolf.

'Yes, I understand that, of course I do. But how far down are you thinking of digging? The fact that I happen to own the building . . . My affairs and books are in perfect order, and so they damned well should be, the price I pay for all those auditors and lawyers. But here I am, running on when I've been told to spare my voice as much as I can. Doctor's orders, you know. Now, what can I do for you?' he asked briskly.

Because Kristoffersen was sitting down it was impossible for Rudolf to judge his height, but he looked quite tall and well built, even in a dressing-gown. Underneath he was wearing dark-brown pyjamas – to match the carpet, thought Rudolf. His fleece-lined leather slippers were of the same dark-brown. On his wrist he wore a watch with a heavy gold strap.

'How well do you know Mr Brenner?'

'Brenner?' Kristoffersen started to cough. 'Sorry,' he said, 'thought I was over that now.' He coughed again, blew his nose on a large dark-brown handkerchief, took two or three good swallows of toddy, and continued: 'Last week it was awful. Never felt so miserable in my life. But back to Brenner. I go to him. He's all right. That's about all I can say.'

Rudolf stared at him for a while without speaking. Kristoffersen shifted uneasily under his gaze, then burst out: 'Good Lord, Sergeant, how well do you know *your* dentist?'

'We've gone through Brenner's records for the last five years. Those from before that time have been destroyed. How long have you been going to him?'

Kristoffersen wrinkled his forehead. 'Oh, it's been many years. Can't say exactly when the first time was, but it must have been . . . what? Eight, nine, ten years ago, something like that. I took to him straight away. That's why I let him have that flat. He was seriously thinking of moving his practice away from Oslo if he could find somewhere suitable, and I didn't want to lose him. They're not all reliable, dentists, you know, same as other people. I know quite a few who've been led up the garden path by dentists with flourishing practices who wouldn't know a chap had pyorrhoea even if all his teeth fell out. Actually happened to one of my friends, tnat did. Lost all his teeth because his dentist was careless or incompetent, which amounts to the same thing. I was determined that wasn't going to happen to me, and I was happy with Brenner, so I was willing to do pretty well anything to make sure he stayed in Oslo.' He was racked by another bout of coughing and went through the same ritual as last time, first blowing his nose, then taking a long pull at his glass.

'We're not personal friends, if that's what you're wondering. He's never been here – you can check that with your mole if you like, Renee, I mean.' He chuckled. 'I've never been to his place out at Lysaker, either. It's a purely professional relationship, dentist–patient – and I'm his landlord, of course.'

'When you've sometimes visited old Mr Evensen on the floor above – which is something he appreciates very much, I understand – perhaps it's been when you've had an appointment with Brenner? Two birds with one stone, so to speak.'

Kristoffersen's brow puckered for a second time: 'I visit as many old folk as my time permits, Sergeant. I own quite a lot of property, you know, and a lot of the tenants are getting on. I don't know yet what it's like to be old, but I do know what it's like to be poor. Better than most people in Norway, I should imagine. Anyway, I'm a busy man, so if I did combine a visit or two – well, no harm in that, is there?'

'No, of course there isn't,' Rudolf hastened to assure him. 'But back to Brenner. Even if you weren't actually friends you must have a pretty good idea of what he's like after all these years.'

'Naturally. Stands to sense, doesn't it? Fine chap.' After a moment's reflection Kristoffersen went on: 'If I hadn't thought that I'd never have stuck with him so long. I know people. Have to in my business. I don't like people there's anything evasive about, shifty, afraid to meet your eye, you know the type. Integrity, that's what you have to look for. Doesn't talk a lot when I go, Brenner doesn't, but from what little he does say I can tell he's a worker. Conscientious, someone I can trust. I can safely recommend him if you're looking for a dentist.'

'What would you say if I told you he's been accused of making blue movies in his flat?'

'Blue movies? Brenner?' Kristoffersen laughed aloud: 'That's a good one! Who dreamed that one up, I wonder? Blue movies in a dentist's surgery? "The Maiden and the Molar". "Incisor Incest". "Sex under Sedation". Come off it, Sergeant.'

'And orgies. All for one and one for all. Think that's just as ridiculous?'

'Orgies? There, in Brenner's flat? Who on earth's been spreading stories like that? They ought to be had up for libel or slander or whatever it is. And a nice chap like Brenner. I insist on knowing who it is. I'll get my lawyers on to them, they'll soon put a stop to it.' Red in the face, Kristoffersen started to cough again.

'So you're convinced he's all right, that there's no foundation for these accusations?'

'Of course I am. Isn't that what I've been saying? Damn it all, Sergeant, what do you want me to do, spell it out for you?'

'That won't be necessary, thank you, sir,' said Rudolf placatingly. 'Well, I'll be getting along. I've no more questions to ask, not for the moment, anyway.'

'What do you mean, "not for the moment"?' Kristoffersen demanded. 'I can't tell you more than I have already. You can go over the house with a fine-tooth comb if you like, all the rest of my properties, too, offices included. I've nothing to hide, nothing at all. I'm sorry about that chap getting killed, of course I am, but I didn't know him, didn't know him from Adam. What more can I say – or do?'

'I don't know, Mr Kristoffersen,' said Rudolf. 'Stay where you are,' he added, a trace of sarcasm in his voice, as he noted that his host was making no effort to get up, 'I'll find my own way out.'

'Sorry I couldn't help you,' Kristoffersen said in a more conciliatory tone.

'Oh, I shouldn't worry about that, sir. Who knows, perhaps you have,' Rudolf said cheerfully, turning in the doorway. A frown appeared on Kristoffersen's face. He seemed about to say something when Renee came bursting in: 'Daddy, Daddy, Sonja's here! She wants to talk to you. She's in a hurry, she says. Daddy . . . I think she's ill again.'

Kristoffersen's expression changed abruptly. 'Tell her to go up to her room. I'll come as quickly as I can.'

The girl shot off.

'Before you go, Sergeant, I'd like to know what you meant by saying that I might have helped you.'

'Oh, nothing in particular,' Rudolf answered blithely. 'Bits of the jigsaw, you know. Little drops of water, little grains of sand. All mounts up.'

'I meant what I said about Brenner, every word. And I have

some good lawyers.'

'Nice of you, Mr Kristoffersen. I'd like a patient like you if I were a dentist,' Rudolf said, forcing a smile. Resolutely he strode out of the room before he could be asked any further questions. Kristoffersen seemed to have lost interest in Brenner and to be more intent on delaying him. Rudolf wondered why. Renee had been told to tell Sonja to go up to her room after she'd said that she was ill again. Why 'again'? Kristoffersen had seemed scared that Rudolf might see her. He knew Sonja was Kristoffersen's only daughter.

In the hall he found Renee alternately tugging and cajoling in an endeavour to persuade a young woman to go with her. Obviously the woman was refusing to move.

'No,' Rudolf heard her say in a faraway voice, 'I'm staying here till Dad comes out.' Her eyes were glazed and empty-looking. 'I don't see why I can't go in, anyway, even if he does have someone there,' she said petulantly.

'Oh, there you are,' Renee exclaimed as she caught sight of Rudolf. 'I'll help you get your coat.' She lowered her voice. 'Poor Sonja, she's nearly always ill. It's something to do with her stomach. She has to take medicine all the time. Must be awful, always having pains in your tummy, don't you think?'

Rudolf agreed that it must. 'Stomach,' he thought. 'There's more than that wrong with her, I'll be bound.' He resolved to sit in his car for a while and mull things over before deciding on what to do next. One thing he was sure of: he wasn't going to leave before he'd talked to Sonja. He could have done it in the hall, but something, call it intuition, impelled him to wait a bit and see what happened.

18

Ada phoned Karsten at regular intervals. She wanted to meet him and explain why she'd disappeared in such a hurry that Sunday. Karsten protested that he hadn't the time – 'snowed under with work' was the expression he used. He promised to phone her, but never got around to it, and she continued to call him. In the end he agreed to meet her before carrying on to see Gregers Berger.

They met in a tearoom a few minutes' walk from Karsten's office. Although he was right on time, Ada had already had a cup of tea and disposed of an open-faced shrimp sandwich when he arrived. The first thing he noticed was that she had cut her hair; it suited her – her eyes came more into their own, he thought. She was wearing a smart yellow two-piece costume which looked new; at any rate Karsten hadn't seen it before.

'Hello, Karsten,' she greeted him, smiling warmly. 'How nice to see you again.'

He smiled in return. 'Hi,' he said. That was all. Ada had never looked lovelier, but never had he felt so unmoved at the sight of her.

'So you can get away when you want to,' she said. Karsten let the dig pass.

Although it was getting on for four and one would have thought people would have had something better to do, the tearoom was packed. He felt that they were conspicuous, and the fact made him uneasy. Ada would have looked perfectly at home in the lounge of one of Oslo's big hotels, but here she stood out like a Paris model in a second-hand clothes shop.

'I've only time for a quick cup of tea, Ada,' Karsten said. He purposely kept his voice down in the hope that she would do the same; he hated the thought of having to ask her to do so. He felt that they were the cynosure of all eyes as it was, without her providing a floor show for the people at the tables round about. This was neither the time nor the place for an exchange of intimacies. He'd thought a lot about her since that Sunday and there was no doubt in his mind that the time had come to put an end to the affair. A quick, clean break, that was what was needed.

'Give the lady a smile, now,' Ada said, taking his hand in hers.

Karsten wriggled uncomfortably on his chair. He withdrew his hand and leaning across the table whispered imploringly: 'How about not talking so loud, Ada, eh?'

She looked at him, taken aback. Suddenly her face broke into a smile: 'Bit out of sorts, are we? This murder case getting you down, that chap they found drowned in a dentist's chair?' Although she had lowered her voice it still carried through the room. Karsten sensed that conversation at the nearby tables had come to a stop and that people were looking at them.

'Yes.'

'Not been much in the papers about it these few days.'

'No.'

'Was he really found dead in the chair?'

Karsten nodded. 'Ada, listen –'

'Think you'll ever find out who did it?'

Karsten acted quickly and resolutely. He stood up and grabbed her wrist. 'Come on, Ada, let's go. We can talk while we're walking. I've got to get back to the office.' To his relief she didn't protest. Meekly she gathered her things together and followed him out into the wintry afternoon.

How am I going to tell her it's all over? Karsten wondered. He'd never mastered the art of telling a woman that they'd come to the end of the road. It didn't make it any easier, he reflected, that it had been better with Ada than with any of the others he'd tried to kid himself he was attracted to.

112

'What's all this I hear about a widow?' Ada asked. The question was so unexpected that Karsten stopped dead in his tracks.

'A widow? Who's said anything about a widow?' Against all the odds the police had managed to keep news of the woman in widow's weeds a secret from the media for five long days. Not one of those involved had said a word, he knew, at least not to the press; not even the otherwise so talkative Evensen. Yet here was Ada, who had nothing whatever to do with the case, talking about the widow as though it were common knowledge.

'So there *is* something in it,' she said triumphantly. 'You'd never have reacted like that otherwise.'

'Where'd you get it from, Ada?'

'Strange there's been nothing about her in the papers.'

Unable to restrain himself, Karsten seized her by the arm: 'Come on, tell me! Where?'

'Let go, Karsten, you're hurting me!'

He released her arm. 'Sorry.'

'I heard it from a girlfriend. She'd got it from another girl whose brother-in-law's a policeman. But why's there been nothing in the papers? Why's it such a big secret?'

'It's obviously not a big secret if you and your girlfriends all know it,' said Karsten angrily. He swore. 'A bloody policeman! Who is he?'

'No, that I'm not telling you, and you can't expect me to, either,' Ada retorted. 'I'm not going to get anyone into trouble. I was just curious, that's all. Anyway, I promised I wouldn't tell a soul.'

'Fat lot of good that promise did,' said Karsten sarcastically.

'I haven't mentioned the woman to anyone, Karsten, apart from you,' Ada protested earnestly. 'But we haven't seen each other since last Sunday and we ought to have something else to talk about than widows. Don't let's quarrel. Please! It's bad enough with this miserable weather. Tell me you love me – well, that you're fond of me, at least, that you like me, and I'll tell you why I left on Sunday.' Karsten hardly heard her, he was so engrossed in his own thoughts.

'All right,' she said, when she realized that he wasn't going to answer, 'I'll tell you. I woke somewhere around eleven and saw

113

your note. I had an idea you'd not be back for hours.' She looked at him questioningly, but he gave no sign of having heard. 'I'd a splitting headache and I wasn't very happy at the idea of spending the day all by myself. So I phoned . . . you're not listening, are you?'

'Ada,' Karsten said, seriously, 'you don't need to explain anything, really you don't. You see . . .' He looked at her closely, trying to read her face, then plunged on: 'I'm . . . I'm not in love with you any longer. It has nothing to do with your leaving Sunday. It would have happened anyway, sooner or later. Now it's happened sooner. You must realize yourself that we're far too different ever to live together and be happy, year after year. One day you'll thank me.'

'Save it!' Ada's mouth worked, but no sound emerged.

'It hurts me, but . . .'

'You sound so convincing,' Ada said scathingly. 'How many times have you said the same thing? Practice makes perfect, doesn't it? "It hurts me, but . . . " "one day you'll thank me . . ." Bloody hell!' she exploded. Startled, an old gentleman passing by turned and stared. Ada took no notice. 'Is it because I didn't tidy up, is that it? It was as much your mess as mine, more in fact.'

'No, Ada, it's not that.'

'Think I went straight to someone else, perhaps?'

Karsten shook his head wearily. 'No, Ada, the thought never occurred to me.'

'But you can't be in love with me one day and not the next,' she persisted.

'Perhaps I only thought I was in love with you, Ada.'

'But I haven't been pushing you to get married. I said right from the start that I wasn't interested in marriage.'

'I know. It's only that . . . that I can't go on. I don't know why, Ada, but I feel just sort of empty inside.'

'You've met somebody else! That's it, isn't it, you've met somebody else. Who is she, a policewoman?'

Karsten looked at her beseechingly: 'Ada,' he said, 'don't let's spoil it. Don't let's ruin all those happy memories. Because they were happy, weren't they? Let's be sensible, eh?'

'I'm right!' Ada's voice rose, and took on a tremulous note.

'I can tell. You *have* met somebody else.' She stared at him, hard-eyed. All of a sudden her beauty seemed to have evaporated. Whatever did I see in her? Karsten wondered dispassionately.

'My God, you're going to regret this, Karsten!' she spat at him. Then, turning on her heel, without another word she half-walked, half-ran to the entrance of the Underground.

Karsten shook his head in despair and made his way back to his office. It was still some time before he was due at Gregers Berger's. Lying on his desk, however, was a message to say that Berger had phoned to say that he was ill and had had to go to bed. But he expected to be over the worst by Sunday, and if Karsten would phone then they could fix another time. Karsten cursed silently.

19

Rudolf parked his car far enough away from the Kristoffersen house to ensure that he could not be seen, but positioned it so that he himself could keep the place under observation. It was five to four and already dark. As soon as he switched off the engine, and with it the heater, the cold began to seep into the compartment. He shivered and hunched down into his overcoat, turning up the collar for added warmth. When he'd left that morning he'd promised Magda to be home for dinner on time. And so he would have been, he thought bitterly, if Sonja Kristoffersen hadn't turned up so unexpectedly.

He hadn't been waiting for more than a quarter of an hour before a grey Bentley drove up and stopped in front of the gate. A man in a fur coat got out of the car and opened the gate, leaving it open when he drove through and up to the house. Rudolf saw him ring the bell. The door was opened immediately, not by Renee this time but by Kristoffersen himself. Rudolf caught a brief glimpse of his pale face above the dark-brown dressing-gown.

He waited for another quarter of an hour before getting out of his car and locking it. There was no one about. Suddenly, out of the darkness, two boys on bicycles emerged, heads bent against the wind and driving sleet. Must be frozen stiff, Rudolf thought to himself. March is too early for cycling in this country. With the boys' disappearance the darkness and silence returned. In the distance a dog barked. Accustomed as he was to living in a block of flats, surrounded by the 'noises off' of other families, he found the stillness depressing. If this is Millionaire Row, they can keep it, he told himself. Admittedly

116

there were times when he was exasperated by other people's radios and television sets and, worse still, by teenagers riding round and round on their motorbikes, exhausts blaring, but at least he felt himself part of a living community. Here, on the other hand . . . He shook his head. In summer, perhaps, but during the winter? Not on your life.

He had to ring three times before the door was opened. Kristoffersen stared at him resentfully for a moment, then forced a half-smile. 'Oh, it's you, Sergeant,' he said. 'Forgotten something? I've no more information to give you, you know that.'

'No,' said Rudolf, 'I'd just like a few words with your daughter Sonja.'

He saw the man stiffen. 'Sonja?'

'Yes, I saw her when I left.'

'I know, Renee told me. But why? She's not at all well. Dr Haakonsen's with her now.' Kristoffersen was clearly determined not to let him in and Rudolf was just as determined that he should.

'For your own sake I think it would be better to continue this conversation indoors, sir,' he said, gently but firmly.

Reluctantly the man stepped to one side and allowed Rudolf to enter the hall. 'For the life of me I can't see the point of all this,' he said irritably. 'Sonja's fast asleep. Dr Haakonsen's given her a mild sleeping draught.'

He's been jolly quick about it, then, Rudolf thought. 'How long's she likely to be asleep, do you think?'

Kristoffersen exhaled sharply through his teeth with a hissing noise. 'How can I possibly know that? An hour, maybe, perhaps two, perhaps more.'

'In that case I must ask you to allow me to stay till she wakes,' said Rudolf politely. 'In the meantime I'd like to speak to Dr Haakonsen.'

'But we've no guarantee she'll wake after a couple of hours. You might be hanging about half the night.'

'I've nothing better to do at the moment.'

Kristoffersen was clearly getting riled. 'But –'

'I'm only doing my duty, sir,' Rudolf said mildly, 'you know that as well as I do. Why I want to talk to your daughter is

117

because she's on drugs and she might be able to tell me something of value.'

Kristoffersen went ashen. 'I was afraid you might have tumbled to that,' he said. 'When you left the way you did I'd started to hope that you hadn't realized what was wrong with her. What made you go and then come back half an hour later?'

Rudolf hesitated for a moment, then decided to tell him the truth: 'I wanted to wait a bit and see what happened,' he said simply.

Kristoffersen looked at him thoughtfully: 'Couldn't you come back tomorrow instead?' he asked finally. 'She'll be able to talk sensibly by then. Dr Haakonsen's staying the night to keep an eye on her.' Realizing that his words were having no effect he sighed heavily and said: 'Oh, well, have it your way. But you're wasting your time.' Rudolf didn't answer.

Resignedly, Kristoffersen led the way back to the television lounge. He didn't offer to take Rudolf's coat. 'Wait here,' he said curtly, and left. A moment later he was back with the doctor, who was of much slighter build than he had appeared to be outside. Must have been the fur coat, Rudolf thought.

Dr Haakonsen was fair, very fair, with thinning hair, a wispy beard, and almost invisible eyebrows. He had restless hazel eyes and small, feminine hands and feet; on his left forefinger he wore a broad gold ring. His handshake was listless. Damned if I'd put my trust in a chap like that, was the thought that flashed into Rudolf's mind as Kristoffersen made the introductions.

'Miss Kristoffersen still asleep?' Rudolf asked. The doctor nodded.

'I've just told you she is,' Kristoffersen broke in, testily. 'The effect of the sleeping draught depends on what's in her body – what drugs, and how much she's had. Or how little,' he added bitterly. 'Sometimes she only sleeps for a quarter of an hour or so, at other times it can be a couple of hours. More than that, too, one never knows.' Dr Haakonsen again nodded his agreement and moistened his thin lips.

'That's why I said it'd be better if you came back in the morning,' Kristoffersen went on.

'Thank you, but I prefer to wait.'

'Well, that's up to you, but you're just wasting your time, as I told you. It's no good waking her, we know that from experience. She just babbles a lot of incoherent nonsense. Gets quarrelsome, too. It's better to let her wake up in her own good time.'

'I haven't asked anyone to wake her,' Rudolf pointed out calmly. 'All I've said is that I'd like to be allowed to wait till she wakes up. In the meantime I can talk to Dr Haakonsen. Don't worry about me, I've plenty of time.'

'I haven't, though,' said the doctor. Rudolf didn't like his voice, either. 'I have to be with her when she wakes up, so if you'd keep it short . . .'

'You must have heard that a lot of dangerous drugs have been stolen from Ulleval Hospital,' Rudolf began. 'You know we're questioning every known addict, too. We've appealed in the press and on the radio and television for information that might help us. Promised to be discreet, no names, no pack drill. The main thing for us is to get those drugs back before they reach the market. But we're hoping to get the boys behind the theft and some of the pushers, too. *And* to cut some of the supply lines. And then quite by chance I find that your daughter –' he turned to Kristoffersen 'is an addict. And you, Mr Kristoffersen, tried to stop me talking to her –'

'I haven't tried to stop you talking to her,' Kristoffersen cut in angrily. 'All I've said is that you're wasting your time waiting. She's asleep. And while I'm at it, Sergeant, I'd like you to know that I know my rights. I don't need to tell you anything. The reason I'm doing so is that I've nothing to hide. Dr Haakonsen here's advised me to co-operate with the police, but I don't intend to. I've spent a fortune keeping Sonja's, er – problem a secret. And after having done so successfully for four years you can hardly expect me to go to the police and say my daughter's a junkie. I know you've promised it'll all be in confidence, but what if it did get out? Think of what it'd do to my good name and business.'

'If you have any children of your own,' said Dr Haakonsen quietly, 'you'd know what Mr Kristoffersen's been through. And is still going through.'

'I do have children,' Rudolf replied evenly. 'A boy. But as a doctor, you know that if he doesn't help me, if he won't co-operate, a lot more parents are going to suffer. *And* their children.'

'I'm not in a position to comment. I'm a doctor. Professional ethics, you know.' The doctor spread out his hands in a helpless gesture.

Kristoffersen was showing signs of uneasiness. 'Look here, Sergeant,' he said in what was almost an appeal, 'let Dr Haakonsen go back to Sonja so that he's with her when she wakes up. In the meantime I'll tell you the whole sad story. Then, when she's awake, you can talk to her and . . . and do as you think fit. Take whatever steps you feel are necessary. And then you can talk to the doctor as well. How's that?'

'Yes,' said Rudolf, 'that'll be all right.'

'Just let me have a few words with Dr Haakonsen first,' Kristoffersen added, getting to his feet before Rudolf had time to answer. He went out of the room together with the doctor, but was back a couple of minutes later. 'Sorry,' he said apologetically, 'it was a purely personal matter.' He gave an unexpected smile. 'I can see from your face that you're not quite sure whether to believe me. Well, actually all I said was that in the cupboard on the stairs he'll find a bottle of cognac. I told him to take a glass from the sideboard and collect the bottle on the way up. He's staying the night,' he added hurriedly, probably eager to forestall Rudolf's unspoken question, 'so he won't be using his car. That put your mind at rest?' He paused. 'Perhaps you'd like a drink yourself?'

'No thank you,' Rudolf answered. 'I'm driving, even if he isn't. But I *would* like to take my coat off.'

'Oh, sorry, of course. I wasn't thinking . . .'

I'll bet! thought Rudolf grimly. Aloud, he said: 'No need to hang it up. I can just lay it over the back of this chair if it's OK by you.'

'Certainly, certainly,' Kristoffersen replied. He sighed. 'Mind if *I* have a drink? It's been quite a day.'

'Yes, I'm sure it has. Just go ahead.'

Kristoffersen poured himself a stiff whisky from the cocktail cabinet in the corner – no ice or soda, not even water, Rudolf noted – and took two good pulls at it where he was, standing by the cabinet, before sitting down again. 'I suppose for anyone else, well, for lots of people, it'd all be pretty trite,' he began. 'I come from very humble circumstances, to put it mildly. I really started at the bottom, as you know. I've worked hard – for myself, of course, but also so's Sonja could have the things I couldn't dream of at her age. Naturally she was spoiled. All she needed to do was to point at something and it was hers. In the end, of course, there was nothing left to point at. And then in some way, I'm still not sure how, she got in with a crowd who lived a life that was entirely different from what she was used to. She thought it was exciting – probably for that very reason, that it was different. Well, to start with it was fun. She said so herself. "Tripping", she called it. Then, before she realized it, the old, old story: she was hooked. Had to have a daily fix.' He gave a wry smile. 'You get to know the lingo after a while. I never realized what was happening until it was too late. When I did, my first thought was how to help her. And how to protect myself, too – preserve the image I'd built up over all these years. I didn't understand what I was up against. You've more experience, so I don't need to go into detail, I'm sure. In the end I had to face the fact that it was too big for me to tackle alone and I confided in Dr Haakonsen. He was our family doctor, but he'd not seen Sonja for years; she'd drifted away. When he did, he was shocked. He was prepared to help me, but *he* had to watch his step too – it meant covering up somebody he knew was an addict. He had his practice to think of. In the end I decided to make him company doctor, to put him on the payroll. I wasn't being altogether truthful earlier today when I said I'd nothing to hide – that all my affairs were in order. You see, we already had a company doctor. He's the one who sees my employees. But I reasoned that most businessmen have their maids and cars and boats and whatnot on the company, so that it'd do no harm to bend the rules a bit and make our family doctor company doctor.'

'I doubt whether the taxman would agree with you,' Rudolf said, 'but never mind, it's not my pigeon. Go on.'

'No, and I hope it'll stay that way,' Kristoffersen answered. (Always the businessman, thought Rudolf.) 'Anyway, to continue.' He took a drink from his glass. 'So Dr Haakonsen

121

and I sort of went into partnership. Neither of us really realized what we'd taken on, not then. We went to Switzerland, he and I and Sonja. Stayed for three months. Montreux. Sonja was at a – a convalescent home. It's a euphemism, of course. They specialize in curing – well, addicts. Ease them through the withdrawal symptoms. You pay through the nose, but they know their stuff, I'll grant them that. Quite apart from the obvious reason, anonymity – Norway's like a goldfish bowl, as you know – Dr Haakonsen had heard the place recommended. Everything went marvellously at first. Sonja loved it and she co-operated, which is half the battle. She adored one of the nurses, a young girl called Gabrielle. They were about the same age and they became friends, real friends. When we got back things were fine for a while and we thought it was all over.' He sighed heavily. 'God, how naive we were! Then came the first relapse. It took an age for Dr Haakonsen to get here. He lived out at Nordstrand then and had to cross the whole town. That was when I decided I'd have to get him a place over on this side, somewhere near here. I'd realized by then that we weren't out of the wood by a long chalk, and that future relapses could be more serious. It's progressive, isn't it? I wanted him on call all day and every day, ready at a moment's notice. I got him a house at Kolsaas. Nice place –'

'A "company" house?' Rudolf couldn't help asking.

Kristoffersen looked at him askance: 'Dr Haakonsen's not a pauper, Sergeant,' he said reprovingly. 'He can afford to buy his own houses.'

'It can always be checked, anyway,' said Rudolf. 'Never mind. Sorry – go on.'

Kristoffersen drew a deep breath. It was plain that he was fuming inwardly. 'Because he now lives at Kolsaas he's practically on the doorstep,' he went on after a moment's pause. 'We keep a room for him here. He's had to stay the night on more than one occasion,' he explained. He took another drink of whisky.

'So she's had a few relapses?'

Kristoffersen nodded sadly. 'Yes. We got Nurse Gabrielle to come and look after her, and all went well for a time. She was here for two years. But when she had to go back to Switzerland we were stuck again. We didn't know whether to try a Norwegian nurse or to risk it and assume that Sonja was over it all. She seemed to be, you see. In the end we decided to chance it. We thought it might have an undesirable effect if we were to bring in a regular nurse. Thought Sonja might feel she had a keeper, a watchdog, so to speak. Nurse Gabrielle was different: she was a friend. So we took a chance – and there we were, back to square one. She went into town – alone. We let her go. Couldn't keep her locked up; can't now, either. She hasn't a bank account of her own and I never give her any money, not *real* money, anyway, not enough for drugs. And yet she always manages to get them. Time and again Dr Haakonsen's had to come dashing over to nurse her through . . . a withdrawal. And then three weeks ago she met someone, a young man she insisted on my meeting. She was planning to move in with him and they – she – needed twenty thousand kroner for new furniture. I told you she was spoiled. I assumed his wasn't good enough. Well, I hummed and hahed a bit, naturally, but in the end I went to see the man. Nice sort of chap, I liked him. Hansvik his name was, Anders Hansvik. Elementary-school teacher, struggling to pay off the government loan that had financed his studies. What I liked best, though, was the fact that they seemed so happy together. Happy in a normal way, the way I understand happiness, not all hepped up, cloud nine, living on the top note, that kind of thing, but – well, normal. So I let them have their twenty thousand.' He saw the look in Rudolf's eyes.

'Yes, I know what you're thinking. It's a lot of money. It was to me, too, once. But things change, and now – now it's a drop in the ocean. I'm not boasting, it just is. Anyway, that was three weeks ago, as I said. I really was beginning to hope. And then – well, you were there, weren't you? You saw what a shock it was to me when Renee came in and said Sonja was ill again and that she wanted to talk to me. Renee doesn't know what's wrong with her, by the way; thinks it's stomach trouble and nerves. That's what we've told all our friends, too. There have been times when we've had to cancel parties and things – keep people away for a while till she'd calmed down. First thing she told me today was that this fellow Hansvik – might not even be his real name – had left her. Just took off when he realized that she'd no more money left. He's on drugs too, apparently, hooked as badly as she is. I can't understand why I didn't see it when I was there. I ought to have done, I know all the signs. But they seemed so in love, so happy together, I suppose I wanted to believe and . . . well, there you are,' he finished lamely. He was seized with a sudden bout of coughing, and out came the brown handkerchief again. When it was over he drained his glass and poured himself another.

'She came home because she was broke, as usual. And I phoned Dr Haakonsen. As usual. It's a pattern. I wouldn't wish it on my worst enemy. Anyway, perhaps you understand a bit better now why I didn't go to the police and tell them about it.'

Rudolf evaded the question by asking whether Dr Haakonsen didn't have a family, seeing as how he seemed to be on permanent standby for Kristoffersen.

'He's divorced. They never had any children.'

The two continued to talk for a while until Rudolf, glancing at his watch, remarked that it was a good hour since the doctor had gone up to Sonja.

'He promised to come down and say so as soon as she was awake,' said Kristoffersen.

'I know. Still, how about going up and having a look?' Rudolf urged.

Kristoffersen shrugged his shoulders, making no attempt to conceal his annoyance. 'As you like. It's always the way *you* want it, never the way *I* want it.'

Together they left the lounge and made their way through the house and into the hall. On a small landing halfway up the stairs there was a cupboard. Rudolf stopped in front of it. Divining his thoughts, Kristoffersen opened the door. At the back of a shelf stood a bottle of Martell. 'Didn't he take it after all?' said Kristoffersen, a puzzled look on his face. He hurried up the remaining stairs, Rudolf hard on his heels. Outside one of the bedrooms he paused. He tapped gently on the door: 'Harald,' he whispered. There was no reply. Kristoffersen hesitated for a moment, then quickly opened the door. The room was empty. Rudolf strode to the window and looked out. The Bentley had gone.

20

Rudolf immediately phoned Chief Inspector Albrektsen, who agreed to send Karsten and Haraldsen over. 'I'll also put a man on the gate,' he said. 'And then I'll put out a general call. It shouldn't take long before we have them, not with a Bentley.'

Kristoffersen had plenty of pictures of Sonja, but none of the doctor. 'Can't remember ever having seen one,' he said.

'But I've got some,' cried Renee, who had come into the lounge unnoticed. Her father frowned. That didn't suit him, Rudolf thought.

'Don't you remember, Daddy?' the child went on, oblivious to Kristoffersen's displeasure. 'You gave me a polaroid camera last summer. I took pictures of you and Mummy and Sonja and Uncle Harald, all of you. I'll go and get them.' She dashed off, to return a moment later with an envelope full of photographs.

'I've never had time to put them in an album,' she gasped apologetically. She began to sort through them. 'Here you are,' she exclaimed triumphantly, 'here's you and Mummy and Uncle Harald. And here's one of him by himself.' In the end Rudolf selected two photographs, one of the doctor in profile, the other, taken full face, showing him standing on the lawn with a tall glass in his hand.

'Fine, Renee, thank you,' Rudolf said, smiling. Privately he thought: just what the doctor ordered – only he didn't!

'But why's Uncle Harald gone off with Sonja?' the girl wanted to know.

'I don't know, my dear,' Kristoffersen replied. 'I can't understand it.'

Liar! thought Rudolf, not for the first time that day. He was convinced that a person as colourless as Dr Haakonsen appeared to be would never have had the guts or even the initiative to spirit away his employer's daughter without the latter's prior consent. It was Kristoffersen who had put him up to it – and it was he who had kept him, Rudolf, downstairs talking as long as he could to give the doctor the best possible start. Kristoffersen had masterminded the whole set-up, of that Rudolf was certain.

Now Kristoffersen appeared to have reached the end of his tether. Over and over again he declared that he couldn't understand it, wondered why Harald should do such a thing, whatever could have possessed him, what was the point? Rudolf half-expected him to burst into tears. Only they'd be crocodile tears, he decided. About as genuine as that crocodile-skin handbag Magda once insisted on buying in Las Palmas!

Kristoffersen poured himself yet another glass of whisky, his third to Rudolf's knowledge – plus the toddy. He again offered Rudolf a drink – 'Now that your friends are coming one of them can drive you back' – but again Rudolf declined. Wish he'd offer me something to eat, instead, he thought wrily, I'm famished. As Kristoffersen had assured him that he had no objection to his statement being recorded, Rudolf went out to his car to fetch his Pocket Memo, the small tape recorder he used for interviews and to save taking notes. The sleet had turned to a steady downpour. Well, at least it's rain and not snow, so spring's on its way at last, he consoled himself, wishing he'd stopped to put his coat on.

Despite their long and warm friendship, when it came to the point Kristoffersen proved to know surprisingly little about Dr Haakonsen's private life. He didn't even know whether the doctor had another car besides the Bentley. He himself had three cars, a black BMW which he drove himself, a green Peugeot 500 which Renee's mother, Gemma, used, and a grey Volkswagen which the live-in housemaid used for shopping and running Renee about – to friends, ballet classes, after-school activities and so on.

Kristoffersen informed Rudolf that the doctor had a cabin in the mountains, but he didn't know exactly where. 'Somewhere up near Fagernes,' was the nearest he could get. It was hardly ever used, it seemed; nor, apparently, was an old house he'd inherited from a grateful patient some years ago. In the latter case, according to Kristoffersen, the reason was that the doctor thought it was so gloomy – 'It's in the depths of the Finnskogen Forest, right on the Swedish border,' the doctor had explained once. On the other hand he didn't want to part with it because of the way property values were rising.

'Do you happen to know why whoever it was left it to Dr Haakonsen?' Rudolf asked, his curiosity aroused.

Kristoffersen shook his head. 'Gratitude, I should think. Can't think of any other reason.' A few moments later he continued: 'He must have thought he was doing me a good turn, taking Sonja away like that. Must have.' He drank slowly. He looked sad at the thought.

'Something tells me it was a put-up job,' said Rudolf, tired of playing games. 'He was acting under orders if you ask me – yours!'

'Orders? Mine? Careful, Sergeant, don't overstep your authority. I've spent years trying to keep it all quiet, to get Sonja back on an even keel, and then you accuse me of – of, well, I can't say having her kidnapped, but of having her taken away. Papers get hold of a thing like that and I've had it. What possible reason could I have?'

'I don't know,' Rudolf admitted, still unconvinced. 'Business is business; your daughter's private life is something else entirely. No one would blame you. It'd hardly leave a ripple – seven-day wonder and that'd be it.' He asked if Kristoffersen would mind if they went over the house and grounds or if he insisted on their obtaining an official search warrant.

'Do as you like, Sergeant,' Kristoffersen replied in the doleful tone he'd adopted, a tone that was beginning to grate on Rudolf's nerves. 'Do just as you like.'

Rudolf phoned Albrektsen again and informed him of Kristoffersen's consent to a search. 'I've already taken steps to get a warrant,' the chief inspector said, 'but all right, I'll send a team over now.' He rang off.

It was with relief that Rudolf heard the doorbell ring; he'd had just about enough of Kristoffersen. Damn it all, he thought, I've been holding the fort alone since this afternoon. A moment later Renee came into the room, followed by Karsten and Haraldsen. Rudolf had barely made the necessary introductions before the bell rang again. He hurried off to open the door himself. This time it was the three men detailed to go over the house. Rudolf was gratified to note that Albrektsen had sent the Gleaners, a team who had worked together for years and built up an enviable reputation for missing nothing, hence their name.

'Quite a place, eh?' said the youngest of the three. 'Nice to see how the other half lives. We looking for anything in particular?'

'No-o,' Rudolf replied, 'just look, that's all. Anything that strikes you as funny, let me know. OK, off you go!'

Instead of going straight back to the television lounge Rudolf stood in the doorway and beckoned to Karsten to join him. Then, drawing him into the adjoining room, he said: 'Play back this tape, together with Haraldsen, then carry on from there. I'll go and talk to whoever else is in the house – his wife and the housekeeper, I think, and a maid. I've had him,' he said, jerking his thumb towards the room where Kristoffersen was sitting, 'up to here.' He indicated his throat. 'Bloody hypocrite! Should have been a *real* actor – he has the talent.'

'Got it from his wife, I expect,' said Karsten with a grin.

'His wife?' Rudolf repeated.

'Yes, you know, the one who died. She was quite well-known, wasn't she? Astrid something, Astrid Hagen, wasn't that her stage name?'

Rudolf banged his fist into the palm of his hand as a sudden thought struck him. 'Yes, I'd forgotten that. When you get a chance, try to find out if she ever played the part of a widow – one that needed all the trimmings. Don't make too big a splash, you know what the theatre's like, be all over the place in no time. Have a word with Robotten, he's the culture vulture. It's a long shot, but you never know.' His brother was about to agree when Renee appeared on her way to the inner lounge. Rudolf and Karsten followed her. Kristoffersen was sitting

128

where they had left him, staring vacantly into space, a glass of
whisky still in his hand. Rudolf wondered if it was the same
one. Haraldsen was studying the titles of the books in the
bookcase.

'Daddy, are all these policemen here because Uncle Harald's
gone off with Sonja?' Renee asked.

'Yes, Renee.'

'But Daddy, I don't understand . . .'

'Did you hear the car drive off?' Rudolf asked quickly,
before Kristoffersen could send the child away.

Renee shook her head. 'I was down in the playroom. I've
just had a new cassette player. I don't think I'd've noticed it
down there, though, even if I'd not had it on.'

'Go up to your room, Renee, there's a good girl,' Kristoffersen said. 'This is nothing for you.'

Rudolf smiled at her. 'I'd like to have a word with your
mother,' he said, 'so perhaps you'd show me the way?'

The girl looked questioningly at Kristoffersen, who nodded.
'Yes, do, Renee.'

'Just one thing, sir, before I go up,' said Rudolf, turning to
Kristoffersen. 'While my brother and Haraldsen here play back
the interview we had, perhaps you'd try to remember what
roles your wife played when she was on the stage.'

'What roles my wife played? My *wife*? Whatever's she got to
do with anything?'

'Did she ever play a widow's role, one that required full
mourning, weeds, that sort of thing?'

Kristoffersen shook his head unbelievingly. 'Now you've
really got me guessing, Sergeant. A widow? What on
earth . . . ? She's been dead for fifteen years, you know, but –
no, I'm sure I'd have remembered it if she had.'

Rudolf didn't reply. Instead, he motioned to Renee and the
two of them went out. Her mother's room proved to be next
door to Sonja's. Renee told Rudolf that her father's was the
one after that. So they have separate rooms, Rudolf thought.
Well, it had its advantages, he had to admit, and with a child of
Renee's age in the house . . .

Gemma proved to be an older Renee. She too was tall, slim
and dark, with golden specks in her dark flashing eyes. She was

129

wearing an ankle-length blue wool dressing-gown and white bedroom slippers. Her hands were folded calmly in her lap and her well-manicured nails made Rudolf wonder once again why Renee bit hers so.

'I oughtn't to be out of bed really,' she said when Rudolf had explained who he was. 'I'm running quite a temperature. But all this with Sonja and Harald.' She shook her head. 'It's beyond me.'

She had heard the Bentley drive off, she said, but she wasn't sure when. About an hour and a half ago, she thought. She hadn't seen it as she'd been in bed then, reading, so she hadn't seen Sonja, either. 'Reading's all I'm good for at the moment,' she said apologetically.

Alfred – 'Mr Kristoffersen, you know' – had been off-colour for nearly three weeks, she explained. He'd stayed on his feet to start with, but a week last Tuesday he'd had to give up and go to bed. Dr Haakonsen had been to see him and given him some pills. Wednesday she'd fallen ill and had to do the same. Thursday it had been the turn of their housekeeper, Mrs Moberg. And in the end even their housemaid, Anna, a Danish girl – 'from the country, strong as a horse' – had gone down with it. 'We were like a row of dominoes,' she said. Only Renee had escaped. Dr Haakonsen had been kindness itself: he'd come in every day, taken their temperatures, and given them pills.

'And he brought me chocolate,' Renee put in gleefully. 'Uncle Harald's awfully nice. He nearly always brings me something.'

Her mother gave her a weak smile. 'I don't know how he can stand us all. I'd have been fed up ages ago, what with Sonja and her dr–.' She caught herself just in time. 'What with her nerves and tummy problems and all that means, turning out at odd hours of the night, sleeping here. I mean, doctors don't do that any longer, do they? Not after their first few years, anyway.' She gave Rudolf an enquiring glance to make sure that he was with her.

'And Friday, what happened then, to go back a bit?'

'Nothing, nothing at all, except that we were all ill. Renee had to look after herself. She was going to her friend's – winter holiday last week, you know.' Rudolf nodded. 'She'd arranged to be there at nine, Lord knows why, I mean – on holiday, and that early. And you remember what the weather was like! Anyway, she borrowed an alarm clock, but she never heard it. I didn't, either, but we saw afterwards that it must have rung. I've never known her sleep that deeply before. She got to her friends just in time, but she had to go without breakfast. Just put her head in my door and said she was off. I was still half-asleep myself. I didn't worry about the breakfast, I knew she'd get something where she was going. She said Alf had a sign on his door to say that he shouldn't be disturbed.' She smiled. 'Some years ago we pinched a couple from a hotel. You know, it says "Please do not Disturb" on one side and "Ready for Cleaning" or words to that effect on the other. It happens that one or the other of us feels like a lie-in and then we use the signs. Normally Anna or Mrs Moberg, one of them, brings us in a cup of coffee before we get up; that's why we need the signs. We're both "B" types, can't get up in the morning. Still, he didn't need his sign Friday – there was no one well enough to bring him coffee. If Dr Haakonsen hadn't come and given us both coffee and a bite to eat, all we'd have had would've been pills and a glass of water. Thank heaven he came early! He came very early, in fact, just after Renee had left. She didn't come home till the next day. That was all right, we knew in advance. It was all arranged, only it made it a bit awkward. Would have done, anyway, if it hadn't been for the doctor.'

No, she didn't know Brenner. She'd heard of him, of course, but never met him. She went to the same dentist she had always done, having seen no reason to change. She volunteered the name in case Rudolf wanted to check it – not that he had any reason to doubt her, as he was quick to assure her. To him she seemed a pleasant, straightforward type of person; nothing devious about her at all. He wondered what she saw in Kristoffersen. Admittedly, he was a fine figure of a man, but he was still a rough diamond underneath and she was so – so what? Refined? Cultured? They were very different, that was certain. Could it be security for her and her daughter?

Saturday had been a better day. Renee had come home fairly early and she had looked after the four of them. 'She's very

131

good considering she's only twelve,' her mother said proudly, beaming at her daughter.

Sunday had been another quiet day. Apart from Kristoffersen they'd all stayed in bed, as miserable as ever. Dr Haakonsen had come in, however, and dispensed comfort and good cheer. Regular Florence Nightingale, thought Rudolf sourly. Kristoffersen had gone down and made himself a toddy and sat for a while in the television lounge. She didn't actually say so, but somehow Rudolf felt that she was confirming what her daughter had said about his being in a disagreeable mood. What was it Renee had said her mother had described him as – a bear with a sore head?

Monday Kristoffersen had been up practically all day, wandering around in his dressing-gown. Same thing Tuesday. Wednesday evening he'd gone to the office to do something or other together with Dr Haakonsen. He was running too much of a temperature and had had too many toddies to dare to drive himself, so the doctor had driven him there and back. (He never mentioned that to me, Rudolf reflected.) They had left about six and were back by nine. She couldn't say exactly because she had quite a high temperature herself and had dozed a lot. The trip to the office couldn't have done him any good because Thursday he had had to stay in bed again. The day had been well advanced before he'd ventured down to the TV lounge for a sit and a toddy. The household was still not functioning properly, apart from Renee, but she understood both Mrs Moberg and Anna were on the mend, and the former had managed to make up a tray for each of them. 'But she still has a temperature, so she shouldn't really be up,' she added. 'You wouldn't think it possible, would you, four grown-ups, flat on their backs, all because of one tiny virus?'

Alf – Kristoffersen – had talked a lot about his wife Astrid over the years, but she couldn't remember his ever mentioning a role that required dressing up in widow's weeds. She looked searchingly at Rudolf: 'What a funny question.' When she saw that he wasn't going to elucidate she went on: 'Alf has kept all sorts of things that belonged to her. They're all in boxes up in the loft. I've no idea what's in them; I'm not interested in knowing, either, as I'm sure you understand. Perhaps there *are* some old costumes, I wouldn't know, though I should think it would be more likely to be letters and pictures, wouldn't you? Anyway, your men will go through everything, won't they, so you'll soon know.' She shook her head. 'I don't understand anything of all this,' she said. 'Nothing at all.'

Her husband, Renee's father, had been a well-known racing driver in Italy. He'd been killed on the track. There had been talk of sabotage, but nothing had ever been proved. She had collected a handsome sum in insurance, however, though she didn't put it quite so bluntly. Her Norwegian father, now retired, and her Italian mother lived in Italy. 'Renee and I visit them quite often,' she said. 'I do quite a lot for an Italian fashion house, so I'm able to combine business with pleasure.' He realized that she must be quite comfortably off, so it couldn't be security, after all, that bound her to Kristoffersen.

Nurse Gabrielle? 'Wonderful person! Kind, sensible. Speaks fluent Italian as well as French. Renee and I – Renee speaks Italian like a native, of course – we used to have a lot of fun talking to her in Italian, because Alf doesn't understand it. Gabrielle's English wasn't all that good, but Alf's isn't much better, so that didn't matter. The main thing was that they could communicate.' Rudolf had the impression that things had been easier all round while Gabrielle was there, not least because Sonja had been exceptionally 'well'.

'These relapses of hers are a terrible strain on us all,' Gemma said, looking Rudolf squarely in the face. 'Sometimes I've been tempted to leave Alf because of her and all the trouble she causes. But it's not his fault, and I feel dreadfully sorry for him, so I've stayed on.'

Before he left Gemma's room Rudolf asked Renee to take him to Mrs Moberg and then to Anna.

'You'd better go in first,' her mother said to her. 'Don't frighten them, but tell them it's a policeman.' She turned to Rudolf. 'Mrs Moberg might not mind so much, but I don't think Anna would be very happy if you didn't give her a chance to freshen up first.' She smiled. Rudolf smiled back.

'And then I think this young lady's done her duty for today,' he said with a twinkle. 'And very well, too, I may say. Thank you, Renee. And thank you, too, Madam,' he said, adding gallantly: 'I hope you'll soon be back on your feet again. Good night.' Despite her illness Gemma was so bright and vivacious, ever-ready to smile and laugh, that Rudolf found it quite a wrench leaving her.

On their way to the other side of the house, to what in former times would have been known as the servants' quarters, they met Detective Constable Haraldsen, who was able to inform Rudolf that the Bentley had been found unlocked outside Dr Haakonsen's garage and that the neighbours were certain that he had only one car. Several of them remembered having seen other cars in the drive at times, especially a red Volkswagen driven by a young woman, but no one had any idea who she was.

Rudolf resolved to go back and ask Gemma. Being a woman, he reasoned, she'd know, even if Dr Haakonsen had never told her more than he'd apparently told Kristoffersen, whether he was having an affair with anyone at the moment for example, a young woman in a red Volkswagen who might be prepared to lend him her car. He could have saved himself the trouble. Gemma had no knowledge of a red Volkswagen. Nor had she ever heard or sensed that there was a woman tucked away in the doctor's life.

21

Mrs Moberg was in her mid-sixties. Dumpy and exuding good nature, she was the prototype of an old-style housekeeper. She made no bones about the fact that she loved her work and that she was furious because, as she herself put it, she'd been 'out for the count' when she was needed most; and because she had fallen so far behind with the things she had to do. She told Rudolf that she was a widow and that she had been Kristoffersen's housekeeper for eight years. He had the impression that she was fonder of Gemma than of her employer, and it was clear that she adored Renee. Rudolf chatted with her for a good quarter of an hour, but concluded that she had no information of value to give him, and he left her to see what Anna had to say.

The housemaid, buxom, apple-cheeked and flaxen-haired, came from a small village near Odense. She loved Norway, she said, and had been with the family for almost four years. She was feeling a good deal better and was hoping to get up the next day and start giving Mrs Moberg a hand. However, she had nothing to add to Gemma's statement, either, so Rudolf gave up and went back down into the television lounge, where he found Kristoffersen still sitting slumped in his chair. It was obvious that all the alcohol he had consumed was beginning to catch up on him.

He fixed Rudolf with an unsteady eye: 'I've come to the conclusion that I can avert a scandal,' he said ponderously, slurring his words slightly, 'and not only that, I can turn this business with Dr Haakonsen to my own advantage. Everyone'll know about Sonja now, anyway, so why shouldn't I come out and tell the truth, eh?' he demanded belligerently.

Rudolf looked enquiringly at Karsten: 'What's he on about, do you know?'

'He wants to offer a reward of a hundred thousand kroner to whoever brings the girl back alive or provides information that leads to the same result.'

'Never allowed myself a day off, slaving away, year in, year out,' Kristoffersen suddenly burst out, as though Karsten had never spoken. 'I know lots of journalists. I'll tell 'em how I've worked – and how I've struggled to save Sonja. Spent a fortune, I have, a fortune. And I'm prepared to spend another to get her back. After all, it's not her fault she's hooked on drugs. Why don't the police do more to stop supplies, eh? That's what I'd like to know. And why don't they concentrate more on the people who sell them?' He looked accusingly at Rudolf and Karsten. 'I'm not the only one who's suffered . . . who's suffering. I shall appeal to the people of Norway, to the ordinary people. They know me. They know I like to help wherever I can, that I give large sums to charity, visit people who're old and lonely who live in my flats . . .'

'If you wouldn't mind, sir,' said Rudolf at last, feeling slightly nauseated. He could have saved his breath. Kristoffersen continued his monologue as though he was the only person in the room.

Ignoring him, Rudolf turned to his brother: 'Anything new?' he asked.

'Hardly,' said Karsten with a grimace, rolling his eyes towards the man in the chair.

'All right, then, I'll push off, back to the office. You can take over here, OK?' He picked up his overcoat. 'Good luck!'

'Thanks, I'll need it,' came the laconic reply.

Renee accompanied Rudolf to the front door. 'Do you think Sonja will come back to me?' she asked anxiously.

Rudolf looked down at her and smiled reassuringly: 'I'm sure she will. You're very fond of her, aren't you?'

The child nodded: 'Oh, yes, yes. And I feel so sorry for her because she's ill so often.'

Out in the chill March air Rudolf stood for a moment and drew in several deep draughts before setting off down the drive towards his car. The dog he'd heard earlier was still barking; idly, he wondered why no one bothered to do anything about it.

Awaiting him at his office was a message to say that the girl who had been taken in to Ulleval some days ago in a coma had died. Her name was Kari Gundersen. She was twenty-two.

Rudolf phoned Chief Inspector Albrektsen, who told him that just before the girl died she had regained consciousness for a moment. She never opened her eyes, just mumbled a few words. All the policewoman by her bedside could catch was something that sounded like 'Biggy'. 'That's what it was,' said Albrektsen. 'We've checked the tape. The policewoman saw that the girl was coming to and managed to record it. "Biggy". Mr Big, do you think?

'Could be,' said Rudolf. 'What did she actually die of?'

'Usual story – alcohol and drugs. Amphetamines. An overdose. Could have been an accident, or it could have been suicide, of course. You like to take it from there?'

'Yes, all right,' said Rudolf, not that he had any option. 'I'm going down to the canteen to get myself something to eat. Can't remember the last time. I'd like to hear that tape, though. Perhaps you'd send someone in with it in the meantime?' Albrektsen said he would.

On his way back from the canteen Rudolf called in at Narcotics, but no one there had ever heard of a Biggy. They all knew Kari Gundersen, however, as Rudolf was already aware. She had been on the streets for the last three years, a regular behind the Town Hall. The other girls knew she was on drugs, though they didn't know what they were. She didn't seem to have a pimp; the girls who knew her maintained that she was a loner.

As soon as she had been taken to hospital and news of her identity had reached the police, Rudolf, armed with a search warrant and accompanied by two tried and trusted colleagues. Robotten and Pedersen, had gone to see her father. It was only ten in the morning, but the man was already dead drunk. He declared himself shocked to hear that his daughter was in hospital, suspected of attempted suicide.

'She wouldn't do a thing like that,' he'd insisted thickly. No, he wouldn't go to see her – too ill. (But you're not too ill to go out every day to buy a bottle of booze, Rudolf thought indignantly.) He was unemployed, living on social security.

While Rudolf talked to Gundersen, who strenuously denied that his daughter was 'on the game', as he put it, Robotten and Pedersen searched the mean little flat. It didn't take long, consisting as it did only of a kitchen and two bedrooms, the girl's and her father's. There was no living-room, it probably having been converted into the larger bedroom. The toilet was downstairs, out in the yard.

The two policemen returned with a few amphetamine pills, of which Gundersen disclaimed all knowledge, the girl's passport, and a gold bracelet. She had clearly travelled a lot, as the passport was filled with entry and exit stamps. In it lay a restaurant bill from a town called Caux and a sales slip from a department store in Clarens. Caux? Clarens? Where were they? Rudolf wondered. France? Switzerland? Luxembourg? Neither of the other two policemen knew, either. The bracelet had been lying together with a lot of trashy trinkets in one of Kari's drawers. Stolen? A present in happier days? An heirloom? Gundersen hadn't the faintest idea.

She'd been working in a laundry, but had been given notice because she was so often off work without cause. Rudolf wondered if it had been that that had tipped her over and prompted her to take her own life, if that was what she had done. But he was at a loss to understand why she had struggled to hold down a regular job at all. None of the girls she associated with had ever bothered. Had she really wished to lead a normal, decent life and not succeeded?

Her background, too, differed completely from that of the other girls. She had been one of the brightest in her class all through elementary school and had afterwards gone to a business school from which she had also emerged with flying colours. She had started work with an engineering company, who had nothing but praise for her, but had left five years ago on the death of her mother, giving as her reason that she

138

wanted to see a bit of the world while she was still young. The impression where she had worked was that her mother's sudden death had been a hard blow and that she wanted to escape from her memories and her drunken father. Her passport revealed that she had been in Germany, Italy, Greece, Turkey, Switzerland, England, France, Spain and the Canary Islands, and her father confirmed that she had also been in Sweden and Denmark, where she did not need a passport. Three years ago she had returned to Norway, and immediately found a niche among the whores who operated in the Town Hall area, turning a trick in the cars that constantly cruised the streets there. She herself had had a room, other than the one in her father's flat, to which she took her pick-ups. What had caused her to fall so deep? And how had she come to be on drugs? When did she start, and where? Questions, questions, questions, all seemingly unanswerable.

Rudolf had gone through a batch of photographs from the time when her mother was alive. They all showed a healthy, smiling young girl, right through from when she was a toddler up to the age of about seventeen. And now, five years later: possible suicide.

All this flowed through Rudolf's mind while he was on his way to Gundersen's to tell him that Kari was dead. He found him, if possible, drunker than ever. Rudolf wondered if he ever spent anything on food. The television was blaring away and Gundersen made no move to turn it down. To make sure that the man understood what he had come to tell him, Rudolf strode across the room and switched the set off. 'Your daughter's dead,' he said bluntly.

'Oh?' Gundersen mumbled, trying to focus on Rudolf.

Rudolf had a sudden idea. It was probably a waste of time, but he decided to give it a try. 'Just before she died she said something about "Biggy". Did she ever call you Biggy?'

Gundersen looked up. 'Do I look big to you? Nah, she called me a lot of names, but not that one!'

Rudolf turned and left, glad to get out. Biggy. The strange thing was, he reflected, that on the tape it sounded like a term of endearment.

22

Saturday morning saw Victoria Terrasse invaded by a horde of reporters. Late Friday night the capital's leading newspapers, as well as the radio and TV, had been tipped off that the police were on the look-out for a 'widow' in the Brandt case. Resignedly, Deputy Commissioner Tygesen had confirmed that it was indeed so. Karsten fumed inwardly. Damn her eyes, he thought, thinking of Ada. Well, she's had her revenge, but she's had me, too, the bitch!

He wasn't allowed to ponder on his betrayal for long. Rudolf came storming into his office. 'Come on, get your coat. Greta Olesen or Bettina or whatever she called herself has just been found drowned down by the docks.'

Together with Dr Moe and a number of other policemen the brothers dashed down to the seafront. The girl's clothes suggested that she'd either been out on the town or was intending to go out. Apart from black suede ankle boots she was dressed entirely in red – red dress, red coat, red scarf, still knotted about her throat, red gloves, one of which was missing – the police had even recovered a red knitted woollen cap caught on one of the piles near where the body had been found.

'Another drowning, only in *salt* water this time,' said the doctor in his clipped voice. Rudolf didn't think much of his sense of humour, but forbore to say so.

To Karsten fell the unenviable task of breaking the news to the parents. The mother broke down completely and had to be taken to hospital. The father, on the other hand, got dressed with surprising alacrity and hurried off to the wine and spirits store on the corner, although in theory he could barely walk. Neither of them could be drawn on the subject of Brenner: tight-lipped between her sobs, Mrs Olesen declared that they had made their statements and that was that.

The press had a field day over the widow, *Dagbladet* taking the cake with an execrable pun: KILLED BY THE WIDOW'S MIGHT? Harassed though he was, even Rudolf couldn't help smiling.

Shortly before lunch he realized that he had left the sandwiches Magda had packed for him at home, so he went to fetch them. 'Thought it was a shame to waste them when you'd gone to so much trouble,' he explained to her, giving her shoulder a friendly squeeze. He told her about the finding of Greta Olesen's body. 'I wish I knew why the Olesens insist on lying,' he said. 'Because they are, I'm sure of it.'

'Perhaps they're simply plain scared,' his wife suggested. 'Where could they go if they had to leave? How could two people live on his disability pension, can you tell me that? Just because she has some cleaning jobs there, where she's known, it doesn't mean that she could get work somewhere else. You have to think a bit with your heart, too, Rudolf, not just with your policeman's head.'

To his amazement Rudolf realized that she was actually quite angry. 'But Brenner doesn't own the flats,' he said, puzzled. 'It's not he who decides who's to be caretaker.'

'But Brenner's the great Kristoffersen's dentist, don't forget. They may not be bosom pals but they're on the same social plane. Remember how Kristoffersen closed ranks when you ventured to suggest that Brenner might be making blue movies and having orgies in his flat? Threatened to put his lawyers on to whoever had made the accusation, didn't he?'

'Yes, you could be right, of course you could,' Rudolf replied thoughtfully. There were times when it did him good to talk things over with Magda. With her combination of woman's intuition and a down-to-earth approach she had more than once cut a mental Gordian knot for him.

When he got back to Victoria Terrasse it was to find that no

141

one had so far been found who could cast any light on Greta Olesen's death. He went into his office and put the packet of sandwiches in a drawer. Shortly afterwards he took them out and unpacked them. He stared at them moodily. Magda had done her best: they were tastefully got up, but were they *food*? Rudolf asked himself. One thing was certain, they weren't what he felt like. Suppressing a feeling of guilt, he rewrapped them and put them back in the drawer.

He thought over what his wife had said. But even if Brenner and Kristoffersen were social equals, he reasoned, the latter had made it quite clear that theirs was purely a professional relationship. God, he was hungry!

It was only a quarter past two when Dr Moe phoned. Greta Olesen had had an abortion and it had been botched, meaning that she could never have had children. Moreover, she was full of amphetamines and alcohol. She had drowned some time between Monday and Wednesday. His report was being typed and an unsigned copy would be in Rudolf's hands within a couple of hours or so.

'Why unsigned?' asked Rudolf.

'Because I'm off for the weekend,' laughed the doctor, pleased that Rudolf had walked into his little trap. 'Destination unknown. But I'll tell *you*: it's Shangri-la!' Rudolf could hear him still chuckling as he put the phone down.

There it was again, amphetamines and alcohol, just like Kari Gundersen, Rudolf thought to himself. Karsten came in and picked up the newspaper lying on Rudolf's desk. He scanned it quickly, then tossed it aside.

'Can't be much of a family man – or woman – this widow, this X,' he said. 'I mean to say, it was so early in the morning, wasn't it? What plausible explanation could anyone give for being out at that ungodly hour? Because he, she, was already there when Brandt arrived, poor chap.'

'Oh, lots of people are up at the crack of drawn,' Rudolf replied. 'People work shifts. Policemen, for example. Up all night one day, sleeping like a log the next.'

'Until they're rooted out by their brothers,' Karsten put in with a grin.

'Come on, now,' said Rudolf, 'you'd have missed half the fun

142

if I'd not got you out of bed. Anyway, the family could have been in on it. Or away. School holiday that week, remember.'

It had already been quite a day, but more was to come.

At exactly twenty-five minutes to three a nurse from the Surgical Department at Ulleval Hospital, Elvira Anker, was reported missing. Last seen about midday Wednesday, the report said. Born 11 December 1947, in Oslo. She was 171 centimetres tall, with a slim build, reddish-blonde hair, narrow features, blue eyes, white, even teeth, cultured East-Norwegian speech. When last seen she had been wearing a yellow coat with a black mink collar, a black mink hat, black gloves and black calf-length boots. She had been carrying a black handbag. A general alarm was sent out urging all personnel on duty to keep their eyes open for someone answering to the girl's description.

The nurse had been reported missing by a girlfriend who used to stay with her occasionally and who had the key to her flat. They had been together earlier in the day and had agreed to meet again in the evening. When Elvira failed to appear the friend had gone to the flat and found no one there, but she had noticed that Elvira's street clothes were missing. Mystified, she had hurried back to the original rendezvous in case her friend had been delayed, but she wasn't there. Thursday came and went without a sign of her, Friday too. The girlfriend had checked that Elvira had not been at work, and when Saturday came and she had still not put in an appearance, she had decided to notify the police.

'But I know Elvira Anker!' WPC Gunhild Mortensen burst out on hearing the news. 'It's not long ago since I met her in the street, quite by chance. We hadn't seen each other for years, so we stood and chatted for a bit, brought each other up to date on what we'd been doing. You know the sort of thing.' Rudolf thought he did, and he nodded condescendingly.

'Don't look so smug,' said Gunhild pointedly. 'It was facts, not gossip. Anyway, she was with a girlfriend, so we couldn't really talk, not about personal things. Elvira introduced me, but I didn't take any special notice of her name. We talked about the drugs that had been stolen from Ulleval – naturally, her being in the Surgical Department and me being in the police. She told me she'd been questioned; they all had. And then she said couldn't we meet some time and have a real good natter? She sounded as though she really meant it, that it wasn't just because her friend kept looking at her watch – made it obvious, in fact. I thought it was jolly rude of her. So I gave Elvira my phone number, both of them, here and at home, and told her to give me a ring when she had time. I said we could meet either at my place or in town. She said she'd phone me and that we could meet at her place, too. Apparently she'd inherited a big, rambling flat from an aunt. But you know how these things are. You mean it at the time, but when you haven't seen each other for donkey's years it takes a bit of initiative. One tends to keep putting it off. I'm no better myself, so I didn't think anything of it when I didn't hear from her. I could've phoned her, of course. I didn't have her number, or her address, either, for that matter, but I could have phoned her at the hospital. But – well, I never got around to it.' She shrugged.

'And you never said a word to me.'

'Why should I have? I never gave it a thought – not in connection with my work, anyway. And certainly not with this case. We were good friends, once, and it was just a chance encounter, no more.'

'What did her friend look like?'

Gunhild Mortensen wrinkled her brow. 'Ordinary, neither very pretty nor the opposite. Medium height. Blonde hair, I think. Nicely dressed, smart, in fact. I didn't get the impression that she was a nurse, like Elvira, though I can't for the life of me say why. She worked for a living, I'm sure, but I don't think she was in nursing.' She paused, thinking. 'I remember, now: she had a small mole on the side of her nose. Unless it was part of her make-up, perhaps that's why I didn't think she was a nurse – she had it plastered on pretty thickly.'

'Your description's about as good as Evensen's of the widow,' said Rudolf. 'Apart from the mole, that is. Always assuming that it was a real one.'

23

Elvira Anker's family background proved to be rather strange, to put it mildly. Her father was an engineer. When Elvira's elder and only sister married a Canadian and went to Montreal to live, her parents moved to Canada too, to be near her, despite the fact that they had a son who was not only diabetic but also suffered from epileptic fits. This boy they left Elvira to care for and nurse. She had been more of a mother to him than a sister, right up to the time some two years ago when he had met a girl whom he'd fallen in love with and married. With no other ties Elvira could then have followed her sister and parents to Montreal, but she had chosen to remain in Oslo. The friend who had reported her missing, Anne-Marie Randen, claimed that Elvira's contact with her family in Canada was limited to an exchange of Christmas cards.

Rudolf put Robotten on to the task of questioning Elvira's other friends and fellow nurses, but asked him to enlist the aid of WPC Gunhild Mortensen as it was plain that she had taken her one-time friend's disappearance very hard. He himself set off for 'Rosemullion' to have a word with old Mrs Brandt. She *must* have had a purpose in mentioning drugs, he reasoned.

Johanna Borg herself opened the door to his ring. She was wearing a knitted russet-coloured dress and sensible square-toed walking shoes. She explained that as it was Saturday everyone was having coffee. 'It's just a little custom we've adopted,' she said. 'Breaks the monotony. Would you like a cup, by the way? I can get one of the maids to bring it up to you in Mrs Brandt's room. She didn't want to come down, but she'll be glad of a bit of company, I know. She's taken her son's death very stoically, I think. I admire her, I must say.'

Rudolf gratefully accepted her offer of coffee and made his way alone upstairs to Mrs Brandt's room, while Miss Borg disappeared into the back of the house where the kitchen was. Mrs Brandt was playing patience, a thing Rudolf couldn't remember having seen anyone do for years. Her Bible lay closed on the shelf beside the radio, under the photograph of the clergyman. It looked as though she was careful to segregate the sacred and profane, the Holy Scriptures and the pack of cards.

'I'm glad you've come,' she said when she saw who her visitor was. 'If you'd not, I'd have asked you to. You see . . .' She hesitated. 'I've not been altogether straightforward with you, and that's been worrying me, because you've been so nice to me. Only why I didn't say anything before was because I didn't want to do anything that might – well, harm my son's reputation in any way.'

Rudolf groaned inwardly. How often hadn't he heard those words? 'I haven't been altogether straightforward with you', 'I haven't been completely honest with you'. He ought to have become used to it by now, but to hear them from the little lady seated opposite him left him strangely disappointed. It was small consolation to know that he wouldn't have been sitting there in the first place had he not felt that she was holding something back.

'I've lain awake at nights, thinking . . .'

He let her talk.

'You see, about four years ago Georg got to know an air hostess. I don't know her name or where she lives, or even which airline she worked for, because I never met her. And Georg never said. He just called her Nip. She can't have been all that tiny, though, otherwise she wouldn't have been an air hostess, would she? Perhaps it was just because she was smaller than he was. Or maybe her name was, well, Nipdahl or something like that. Anyway, he was awfully happy, Sergeant, and I was happy too, of course, on his behalf. He was intending to bring her to see me and then – it's terrible, only –' She fell silent.

'Only?' Rudolf prompted.

'Only – he discovered she was bringing in drugs, smuggling, you know, from the Far East somewhere. I don't know how he found out, but I think it was quite by accident once when he was at her place. When he tackled her about it she said she earned more just bringing in a few small packages than she ever could as an air hostess. It was a terrible shock to Georg. He ended the – the relationship immediately, of course, though she did all she could to persuade him not to. She told him she had an account in Switzerland that couldn't be traced because it was only a number.'

Rudolf conjured up the stock vision of an air hostess, smart, pretty, long-legged, exuding glamour and charm, and wondered irreverently what it was that Brandt had had that could catch and hold such an ethereal being. It all seemed highly improbable.

'That was four years ago, Mrs Brandt,' he said. 'Do you happen to know whether he'd met her recently? By chance, perhaps. Seen her, at least, even if they'd not talked with one another.'

The old lady thought for a moment before answering. 'No-o,' she said at last, 'but even so I felt that there was something last time he was here. You see, it was just as though something died in him when he found out what she was doing, because she meant a lot to him, I know. I think it was the first time he'd really been in love since he was a young man. But – well, last time he came . . . though perhaps I'm making this up without knowing it – usually I only make things up if I'm bored – the Wednesday before he . . .' She swallowed. '. . . died . . . I . . . I thought there was something strangely, what – radiant? Yes, radiant. There was something radiant about him. He seemed to have recovered his zest for living. Well, I put two and two together and assumed that he'd met someone, a girl. The thought that it might be this Nip never occurred to me. I don't mind admitting that I was very disappointed when he left without saying anything. Not much happens here, you know, so Georg's visits were the highspots of the week. He always had so

147

much to tell me about the shop and customers and Johansen and his nephew. You'd be surprised at some of the customers. Kept me in fits, he did. But he never said a word that Wednesday about a woman friend. It wasn't till he didn't come on Saturday that I began to wonder if he'd taken up with Nip again but didn't want to say so because he was ashamed. After all, he never hesitated as soon as he found out what she was up to, he broke it off immediately. He knew what I'd say if I found out he was together with *her* again, I thought. Well,' she said, looking up at Rudolf a trifle anxiously, 'now you know why I mentioned drugs.'

At that moment there was a knock at the door and a maid came in with a tray. While Mrs Brandt was pouring the coffee Rudolf's mind was working overtime. An air hostess. And all he knew about her was that she was called Nip. Why? Nipper? Nipdahl, as Mrs Brandt had suggested? Nippon, because she was on the regular Tokyo run? But it was four years back, and he'd no guarantee that Brandt really had met her again. Or that she was still flying, for that matter. Nevertheless, he had to follow it up. Brandt's photograph would have to be distributed to all the airlines and everyone who was an air hostess or had been in the last few years would have to be asked whether they knew him or had seen him together with another hostess, and if they knew anyone who went by the name of Nip. God, Rudolf sighed, thinking of the hue and cry in connection with the disappearance of Dr Haakonsen and Sonja, we've more than enough on our plates as it is.

The doctor and the girl had obviously gone into hiding somewhere or managed to flee the country – no great problem with miles of virtually unguarded border between Norway and Sweden. They might well have had false passports, which would suggest that they had long been prepared for just such an emergency getaway. But why? he wondered. What was it they had to hide? Kristoffersen had been asked to surrender his passport 'just as a matter of form, sir, if you wouldn't mind', and had done so with bad grace. 'Just as well he was in pretty much of a trance because of the whisky,' Rudolf had said to Karsten afterwards, 'because we've absolutely nothing on him, nothing at all.' The house was still being watched, but nothing

148

untoward had been observed. Interpol had been alerted and the Swiss police were busy checking out the clinic and Montreux, Nurse Gabrielle, the hotel at which Kristoffersen and Dr Haakonsen had stayed, and as many details as they could gather of Sonja's three-month-long term of residence at the clinic – as well as the doings of the two men.

'I wasn't trying to hide anything, it wasn't that,' said the old lady, tears welling up into her eyes. 'But being his mother . . .'

Rudolf jerked his mind back to the present. He took her frail hand in both of his. 'I understand you perfectly, Mrs Brandt,' he said soothingly. 'Now don't you worry. Forget all about this girl, this Nip. We'll take care of everything. In all the time I've been working on this case I haven't met anyone who's had an ill word to say about your son. I'm sure he was a fine person.'

'He was, Sergeant Nilsen, he was,' Mrs Brandt said fervently. 'I'm not saying that just because he was my son. It's a fact. That's why he was so shocked when he found out about that girl and the drugs.' She sat for a moment as though to collect her thoughts, then went on. 'I've reconciled myself to the fact that Georg is dead. I'm coming to the end of the road myself, and I know that when I do we shall meet again in the hereafter. And I shall be reunited with my dear husband and all the other wonderful people I used to know on this earth. But I'm afraid I shall also meet a lot of people in Heaven whom I detested when I knew them here, the kind you get everywhere.' She gave a derisive snort. 'The kind that go around looking as though butter wouldn't melt in their mouths, yet who are really as corrupt as they come. Hypocrites, the lot of them! Whited sepulchres!'

Rudolf couldn't help but smile. My word, he thought to himself, if she hadn't been so ladylike she'd've spat! Wonder who she has in mind? He patted her comfortingly on the shoulder. 'Now, now,' he said, 'no point in getting all worked up.' He laughed: 'Anyway, I'm sure no one can cheat anyone else in Heaven.'

'This blessed patience isn't going to come out,' said Mrs Brandt, abruptly changing the subject. 'Sometimes *I* cheat, you know. Just a bit.' She gave Rudolf a disarming smile. 'I think an old lady like me ought to be allowed to, don't you?

149

Although he was close to his home Rudolf decided to go back to Victoria Terrasse to see if there had been any new developments. He found the section humming. WPC Gunhild Mortensen had resolved to start by door-to-door questioning of all the tenants in the block of flats where Elvira lived, and had started with the flat next door. The door had been opened by a sprightly old lady in her late eighties, a Miss Laura Hansen, who'd informed her that she had seen Elvira as late as Wednesday evening.

'And do you know what she said?' Gunhild asked excitedly, switching into the reedy voice of an old lady. 'I opened my door to take in a paper my friend on the floor above lets me have after her, but never until just before the seven o'clock news is about to start on the telly, and I saw Elvira coming out of her flat with a lady. She was crying so, she never even noticed me, sobbing away, she was, and I remember thinking that perhaps her brother was dead, he's been ill for years, you know, otherwise she wouldn't have been crying like that. She could hardly walk, stumbling along she was, and the woman was helping her. Do you know, I didn't go off till nearly two that night, the sight made such an impression on me. It's such a long time since I've seen a woman in deep mourning that I couldn't help thinking of all the funerals I've been to. And then I started to think about death and that we're all mortal and that . . .' Only then did Rudolf realize that Gunhild herself had been crying.

'A widow, Rudolf! What do you think of that? Miss Hansen said that her black veil covered the whole of her hat and face and hung right down to below her waist. That means Elvira's dead!'

'No it doesn't,' said Rudolf reassuringly. 'Not by any means. Now you go on home and take a couple of sleeping tablets or something and try to get some sleep. You've absolutely nothing to blame yourself for, you've done jolly well. Go on, off you go!'

The policewoman stood her ground, thinking. 'But supposing this girl, this woman she was with when I met her, is somehow connected with the stealing of all those drugs from Ulleval, and that she got the wind up when she heard that

Elvira was thinking of meeting me. Wherever it was, there'd just have been the two of us, and with me being in the police . . .' her voice trailed miserably away.

'Even if this widow *has* turned up again it doesn't necessarily mean that Elvira's been killed, does it now? Perhaps she's just been taken to a cabin somewhere, God knows, there are thousands of them, or somewhere else, maybe. Taken out of circulation for a while, so to speak.'

'You don't believe that yourself.'

'No,' Rudolf had to admit. 'But let's hope so, eh? Now come on, you get yourself home. You've done your bit for today.'

The young policewoman left, and Rudolf sought out his brother. 'We were wrong, you know, Karsten,' he said. 'We should never have kept quiet about that blasted widow. We should have given it to the press right away, let them splash it all over the front pages, then Elvira would never have opened the door. I expect she had a peephole, living mostly alone, or at least a chain on the door.'

It was something of an anticlimax when Detective Constable Arvik came in with a copy of the relevant pages of the register from the hotel where the Brenners had spent their amputated winter holiday. The local police had done the copying, but it had taken several days because their copier had broken down and they hadn't been able to get it repaired till the previous day. 'Sometimes you'd think we were living in the middle of the Gobi Desert,' Arvik said with a grimace. 'Couldn't get it repaired! Couldn't they have borrowed one somewhere?' He gave a disgusted snort and left.

While the Brenners were there fifteen Danes, nineteen Swedes, seven Americans, one Canadian, three Dutch people, and fifty-seven Norwegians had been staying at the hotel. All had arrived the preceding Friday or Saturday: no one had checked in on the Thursday the Brenners had suddenly taken it into their heads to return home.

'Now *I'm* going to return home,' said Karsten, stifling a yawn.

'You do,' Rudolf replied absently. He found the file on Kari Gundersen, took out her passport, and studied the receipts from the restaurant and department store that were still inside

151

it. They couldn't possibly check everything, and no one had thought of following up the two old bills. 'Any idea where Clarens is?' he asked. 'Or Caux?'

'I've gone,' said Karsten from the doorway.

'Before you do, find me an atlas, there's a good lad. I think Albrektsen has one.'

Rudolf picked up the phone and dialled the reception desk in the main hall. He knew Sergeant Antonsen, the crossword fiend, was on duty. 'Ever heard of a town called Caux?' he asked. 'Or Clarens?'

'You started solving crosswords, too?' the sergeant wanted to know.

'Not on your life. I leave that to people like you who've got nothing better to do. Caux's with a "c", by the way.'

'You don't say?' came the sarcastic rejoinder. 'I thought it was with a "k", like Cannes! Let's see, now, Caux, Caux. It's in Switzerland, I think, though I can't say exactly where. If I remember rightly, it's the headquarters of some big international organization. Don't know where Clarens is, though. Somewhere round there, perhaps – or maybe it's in France. Could be Luxembourg, too.'

Rudolf thanked him and rang off. Switzerland? That was interesting.

Shortly afterwards Karsten returned with an atlas.

'Hang on a sec, Karsten,' said Rudolf, laying a hand on his brother's arm. 'I think we're on to something here.' Quickly he turned to the map of Switzerland. He peered at the small print. 'Didn't bring a microscope, too, did you?' He rummaged in a drawer and produced a large magnifying-glass. 'Ah, that's better. At least, it would be if I knew where to start looking.'

'How about the index?' his brother suggested with a sly smile.

'Brilliant! We'll make a policeman of you yet.' Rudolf turned to the rear pages and ran his finger down the list of names. 'There we are! Caux.' He turned back to the map of Switzerland. 'Ah, so that's where it is. I don't think you know, but we found this hotel bill and sales slip in Kari Gundersen's passport. The bill's from Clarens and the sales slip's from Caux. Well, you can see for yourself. And look where they are. Both

152

of them near Montreux. So it shows that Kari Gundersen was in Switzerland three years ago. That's when Kristoffersen and Dr Haakonsen were there. How's that for a turn-up for the books, eh? First thing tomorrow, copy the visa pages of Kristoffersen's passport. We'll see if their visits coincided exactly, and where else he went. And she. Getting warmer, do you think?'

'Looks like it, doesn't it?' said his brother. 'Getting tireder and hungrier, too. How about calling it a day, huh, and pushing off home?'

'Yes, we may as well,' Rudolf agreed. 'My brain's ticking over and that's just about all. Come on, home sweet home.'

He found Magda on the point of going to bed. 'Hello, home already?' she greeted him. 'I'd given you up. Lars is out and Roly and I have had an exciting evening together in front of the telly, like we often do on a Saturday night.'

Rudolf thought it rather strange that she was taking it so lightly and only teasing him. She seemed to be quite elated. Luckily, before he could ask if she and Roly had had a drink or two, too, she went on: 'Do you know, if I continue to lose weight at this rate, all my old clothes'll be too big for me.'

'What, with all *you*'ve been putting away?'

'Yes. I've been watching the carbohydrates, see. I keep trying to tell you it's the carbohydrates that do it, but you're so hung up on calories. I shall soon be needing some money to buy a new outfit for the spring and summer.'

'Can't you alter the ones from last year?' Rudolf suggested tentatively.

'Don't be so practical!' She grew thoughtful. 'Well, perhaps I could – only then I'd have to have a new sewing-machine.' She looked at her husband archly. 'My old one's ready for the antique shop. Strange you should mention it. I saw a lovely one just the other day. Only four thousand kroner.'

Not for the first time Rudolf marvelled at her unconscious wiles. '*I* didn't mention it, you did,' he said mildly. 'Four thousand kroner. Gold-plated, is it?' He suddenly grew serious. 'I'm just about dead on my feet, Magda. How about hitting the hay, eh?'

'Have you eaten?' his wife asked, suddenly solicitous.

'I've eaten my sandwiches, if that's what you mean. Four carrots, half a what was it, kohlrabi? And a tomato. A whole one!'

'Let me make you something proper, Rudolf,' Magda said sympathetically. 'How about a chop? There's one in the fridge. Won't take long. I can fry up the potatoes left from my dinner.'

'No, it's all right Magda, really it is,' he assured her. 'Just a cup of tea. Slice of lemon and no sugar.'

'Oh, Rudolf, that's not enough!'

But her husband refused to let himself be tempted.

24

Ten o'clock in the morning on Sunday the fourteenth of March found Rudolf back at Victoria Terrasse. He had slept badly, waking several times in the course of the night. His stomach felt as if it were filled with lead. Magda said it was because he always insisted on eating the wrong kinds of food. She herself had tucked into a plate of egg and bacon for breakfast with undisguised relish while he had sat dejectedly munching a slice of crispbread. But she wasn't eating bread, she was careful to point out. 'Do you know,' she said earnestly, looking up from her plate for a moment, 'in a single slice of bread there are twenty-two grams of carbohydrate? What d'you think of that? And carbohydrate ends up as fat.'

It had been a fine start to the day, Rudolf thought sourly. On his desk lay a photocopy of Kristoffersen's passport. All of it. A study of the entry and exit stamps showed that Kristoffersen had been in Switzerland not only at the same time as Dr Haakonsen and Sonja, but as Kari Gundersen as well. Pausing only long enough to pick up a photograph of the dead girl and to say where he was going, Rudolf got into his car and drove out to Kristoffersen's. Mrs Moberg opened the door. Recognizing him, she said that Kristoffersen was still not well and that he was in bed and couldn't see anyone.

'He can see me,' said Rudolf in a tone that brooked no denial, and marched into the hall. 'Just tell him Sergeant Nilsen would like to have a word with him, will you?' he instructed the somewhat flummoxed housekeeper. 'It won't take long. I can go up unannounced if you'd rather,' he added, seeing her hesitate.

'He's hung up his "Do not Disturb" sign.'

'I shan't keep him for long, Mrs Moberg.'

'Oh, well, in that case . . .' Reluctantly the woman began to ascend the stairs. Rudolf remained standing in the hall. It was raining again and his heavy overcoat felt cold and exuded a smell of wet wool. He felt sure he had a cold coming on; just as long as it wasn't flu! And he was hungry. My God, he was hungry! But he was damned if he was going to leave without having seen Alfred the Great.

Mrs Moberg came back down the stairs. 'Mr Kristoffersen asks if you'd wait in the television room,' she said, helping Rudolf off with his coat. Rudolf could see from her expression that Kristoffersen hadn't taken kindly to the interruption. He had to wait for more than a quarter of an hour before the great man put in an appearance.

'What's all this about, Sergeant, coming barging in at this hour on a Sunday morning?' he demanded belligerently. 'I've worries enough as it is with Sonja. If you have news of her, couldn't you have phoned? It'd've been quicker.'

Playacting again, Rudolf thought grimly, not deigning to answer; the question had been purely rhetorical, anyway. He showed Kristoffersen the picture of Kari Gundersen. Admittedly, she'd been only seventeen at the time it was taken, but she hadn't changed much in the meantime, despite the life she'd led. 'Know her?' he asked.

Kristoffersen studied the photograph intently. 'No,' he said at last. 'Ought I to?' He handed it back. 'Who is she, anyway?'

'A girl called Kari Gundersen. Died at Ulleval last Friday.'

'But what made you think I might know her? I don't quite see . . .'

'She was in Switzerland at the same time as you and Dr Haakonsen and your daughter.'

'And I thought Sonja was the only Norwegian girl in the whole country,' said Kristoffersen, his voice heavy with sarcasm.

'Were you ever in Caux or Clarens?'

Kristoffersen wrinkled his brow in thought. 'It's possible. We hired a car in Montreux and travelled about a bit. We had to do something to pass the time. I don't know French, so it was a bit boring, day after day.'

'You said you stayed at the Hotel de Paix. Ever stay anywhere else? Overnight, for instance?'

'Once or twice, yes.'

'Could you have stayed in one of those towns? Or both?'

'I really don't know. Could have, I suppose. Harald did most of the driving and made all the arrangements. He speaks French. Made life a lot easier.'

'Does the name "Gros Bonnet" mean anything to you?'

Kristoffersen shook his head. 'Not a thing.'

Rudolf gave the name of the shop in Clarens, but all he got was another shake of the head.

'Am I allowed to ask exactly where these towns are and why you're so interested in knowing whether I was there?'

'They're both near Montreux.'

'And?'

Rudolf looked at him for a moment before replying. 'Kari Gundersen's dead, Mr Kristoffersen. She was twenty-two. That's all, twenty-two. She died of an overdose of amphetamines and alcohol.' He continued to look Kristoffersen steadily in the eye. 'The last thing she said before she died was "Biggy".'

'Biggy? That's a strange thing to say, isn't it? Who's Biggy? Or what?'

Am I imagining it, Rudolf wondered, or is he forcing himself to ask?

'That's just what we're trying to find out. But I shan't keep you any longer, sir. Sorry I had to drag you out of bed. I'll let myself out.'

On his way back to Victoria Terrasse Rudolf was seized by a sudden urge to look in on the Brenners. The police had their passports, too, as a precautionary measure, and their home was under constant observation. It was approaching noon when, after having exchanged a few words with the two policemen in what was outwardly a commercial van parked near the house, he rang the bell. The policemen had informed him that the

157

house was surprisingly quiet, and the men they had relieved had reported the same thing.

It was Mrs Brenner who opened the door. She was wearing a well-worn bathrobe and her hair was in curlers; her head was covered by a yellow silk scarf, knotted under her chin. She made no attempt to hide her displeasure at seeing Rudolf.

'My husband's asleep,' she said in a low voice before Rudolf could open his mouth. 'We sat up rather late last night. Didn't feel like going to bed, either of us. Had a drink instead and played cards.' She paused. 'All these deaths . . . This talk in the papers about a widow . . . It's enough to get on anybody's nerves.' She looked at him helplessly.

'Perhaps we could talk inside,' said Rudolf as a gust of wind set his coat-tails flapping. Standing in the open doorway as she was, thinly clad, Mrs Brenner was shivering with cold, but she had made no move to invite him in.

Reluctantly she moved aside. 'Of course, only is there any need to wake Peter?'

'I'm afraid so,' said Rudolf apologetically.

The woman gave a deep sigh. 'Well, in that case perhaps you'd like to take off your coat and go into the lounge. I'll nip up and get him.'

In the lounge cards lay spread out on the table by the fire. An overflowing ashtray and two empty glasses suggested that neither of them had had the energy to clear up. The dentist looked as though he'd just run his fingers through his hair and thrown a dressing-gown on over his pyjamas. He barely said hello to Rudolf before slumping into a chair.

'What's it about this time?' he demanded truculently, fishing a packet of cigarettes out of his pocket. He took one, put it in his mouth and lit it without offering the packet to Rudolf. Although he'd stopped smoking a good three years previously Rudolf still felt slightly piqued every time someone deprived him of the chance to say: 'No thanks, I've given it up.'

'In any case we shall be checking your passports,' Rudolf began, 'but to save time I'd like to ask you a few questions now. We shall know the answers soon anyway. Were you by any chance in Switzerland three years ago?'

The couple exchanged glances before Peter Brenner

answered that they went to Switzerland at least once a year, so they'd undoubtedly been there at some time three years ago too. 'But why're you asking?'

Instead of replying, Rudolf asked if they could remember exactly when, and after a bit of umming and ahing it transpired that they had been there at the same time as Kristoffersen, Dr Haakonsen and Kristoffersen's daughter, which coincided with the dates of the receipts Kari Gundersen had kept. Pressed to say where they had stayed, Mrs Brenner said that it was where they always stayed, at the Metropole in Geneva. She added that they'd hired a car and spent a week driving about the country.

Had they been in Caux or Clarens at that time?

Again they looked at one another. 'We were in both places, in and out, not staying. We've friends in Montreux and they've friends of their own in places round about who they take us to visit.' This time it was the husband who replied. 'But two small towns like that, why the sudden interest?'

'All in good time, Mr Brenner,' said Rudolf. 'But back to Caux and Clarens. How can you be so sure that you were there three years ago and that it wasn't two, say, or four? After all, you go to Switzerland so often.'

'I remember it very well now,' Mrs Brenner answered. 'It was the year I had my tonsils out. All right for children, but it's no fun at my age, I can tell you. I was ill for so long afterwards that we were in two minds about cancelling our holiday. But in the end we went and we had a wonderful time – and that was thanks not least to these friends of ours in Montreux. They really did all they could to make sure that we enjoyed ourselves.'

Rudolf named the department store in Clarens. 'Do you know it?' he asked.

'Know it? I'll say we know it!' Brenner replied with a hollow laugh. 'We spent a small fortune there. It's twice as expensive as anywhere else, maybe more. You pay for the name – through the nose.' He stubbed out his cigarette among the remains of the others lying cold in the ashtray. 'But if there's a point to all these questions, I'd appreciate knowing what it is. I should like to get back to bed. Neither I nor my wife got much sleep last night.'

Rudolf decided to try a long shot: 'What I'd like to know is whether it was you who recommended the Gros Bonnet in Caux to Kristoffersen or was it he who recommended it to you?'

'As it happens it was I who recommended it to him,' the dentist replied. 'My wife and I know Switzerland far better than he does. The Gros Bonnet's the best restaurant in Caux. We'd discovered it when we were there some years earlier, and when I heard that he was thinking of going to Switzerland, and to Montreux at that, and would be staying there for a while, naturally I recommended a place that both my wife and I myself liked such a lot.'

'So you're quite sure that it was you who recommended the restaurant to Kristoffersen and not the other way round?' Rudolf realized that his suppressed emotion was beginning to show in his voice, but he was finding it difficult to control his rising excitement.

'Of course I'm sure, Sergeant. But what's it matter, anyhow? The main thing is that we both know the place well.'

'Would you mind if I recorded your answers?'

'Not at all. Be my guest. But . . .' Rudolf took his recorder from his pocket and switched it on.

'Does Kristoffersen say that it was he who recommended it to me?' Brenner asked. 'If he does, his memory's failing him. It doesn't worry me, though; if he wants to claim the credit for having discovered the Gros Bonnet, let him.' He shot a wary glance at the recorder. 'I'm beginning to wonder, Sergeant. Perhaps he's right after all and it was he who recommended it to me. It could have been another restaurant I recommended to him. My wife and I know so many good hotels in Switzerland.'

'Hotels? Is the Gros Bonnet a hotel, too?'

'Yes, didn't he tell you?'

'No,' said Rudolf thoughtfully. 'No, he didn't. Well, thank you, Mr Brenner, Mrs Brenner. It won't be necessary to record more of what you have to say. I can manage OK without.' He showed them the picture of Kari Gundersen and asked if they knew her. They both shook their heads, but Rudolf thought they had paled.

'Who is she?' Elsa Brenner asked at last.

'Her name's Kari Gundersen. She died at Ulleval on Friday – of an overdose of amphetamines and alcohol. She was twenty-two.'

'How terrible!' the woman exclaimed, holding a hand to her temple.

'But what made you think we might know her?' asked her husband in what seemed to Rudolf to be rather a strained tone.

'Nothing in particular. I just wondered. She was in Switzerland at the same time as you were – and Kristoffersen and his daughter and Dr Haakonsen. We found a bill from the Gros Bonnet, the restaurant, in her passport and a sales slip from the department store in Clarens. If she kept them they must have meant something to her; she didn't leave much otherwise. I thought perhaps you might have run across her. Not necessarily spoken to her, but at least noticed her. She was quite a good-looking girl. Were you ever at the Gros Bonnet with Kristoffersen, by the way?'

'How about asking him?'

'I intend to, Mr Brenner. All in good time. Now I'm asking you.' Rudolf looked at the dentist expectantly.

'I'm too tired to think,' Brenner said after a while. 'We *were* with him somewhere, but I'm hanged if I can remember where.'

His wife shook her curler-festooned hair vigorously. 'I'm not sure, either, Sergeant. Have you any news about Sonja and Dr Haakonsen?'

'We shall find them, don't you worry,' was the bleak answer she got.

'It's incredible that something like that could happen,' Brenner put in. 'After all, the man's a doctor – he has his career to think of. It's beyond me.' He lit another cigarette. Rudolf noticed that his hands were unsteady, though whether it was from nervousness or the after-effects of the alcohol he'd consumed the night before it was impossible to say.

'How well did you know Dr Haakonsen?'

'We don't know him at all, except by hearsay. Kristoffersen's talked about him sometimes when he's been for treatment,' the dentist replied. He was clearly becoming increasingly ill at

161

ease. 'They're such close friends, you know.'

'Yes, well, I shan't need to keep you any longer,' said Rudolf, getting to his feet. He paused in the doorway, striking a nonchalant pose for effect. (Too much TV, he thought to himself. I'm getting more like Colombo every day.) 'I wonder if I could have a picture of you, the two of you? I can use your passport photos, but a more natural pose would be better. Besides, they'd have to be enlarged. So if you have a fairly big one . . .'

'But what do you want a picture of us for?' Brenner wanted to know.

'We need it for our investigations,' Rudolf answered. 'We're working together with Interpol and the Swiss police.'

'But what wrong have *we* done?' Peter Brenner demanded, his voice rising. 'All we did was to go away for a week's holiday. I'll grant you that we had a bit of a tiff and packed up and came home early, but that's our business. It's not my fault that someone decided to kill a man I'd never seen in my life and leave him in my surgery. And I'm sure you know by now that there's nothing in those malicious tales about my making blue movies. As if I would! Damn it all, I've a first-class practice and I'm earning better than most dentists in Oslo. You can check that easily – just ask the tax people. I don't need to risk my name and neck dabbling in pornography. I'll admit to pinching apples when I was a kid, but since then I've stayed strictly on the straight and narrow. Both here and in Switzerland. Everywhere else too, come to that. So why're you hounding us the way you are? You're turning us into nervous wrecks, both of us. That's why we couldn't sleep last night, why we stayed up half the night playing cards and drinking. Because that's what we did. A whole bottle of Dawson's between us – *and* started on another. No damn' wonder we're not thinking straight.'

'Yes, it's all very sad,' Rudolf agreed sympathetically. 'Now, what about that picture?' Realizing that further protest was futile, Mrs Brenner went out and returned a moment later with a good snap of the two of them. Rudolf thanked her politely and took his leave. He was in no doubt that they were afraid. But of what? He would have given a lot to know.

He decided to go back to Kristoffersen's instead of returning

162

to the office. Once again it was Mrs Moberg who opened the door. Her lips tightened when she saw who it was.

'I'm awfully sorry, Mrs Moberg,' Rudolf said, forestalling her, 'but I need to see Mr Kristoffersen again.'

Without a word the housekeeper turned on her heel and marched up the stairs. Two minutes later she was back. 'The sign's still on his door,' she said. 'I knocked several times, but he didn't answer. He must be fast asleep, and it'd be more than my life's worth to wake him.'

'I'll risk mine, then,' said Rudolf cheerfully, stepping into the hall. 'You don't need to come up, even I know the way.' But he received no reply, either, when he knocked. He rapped harder. There was still no response. No wonder, he thought, when he turned the handle and went in: the room was empty.

Well, it was Kristoffersen's house, Kristoffersen's room, and Kristoffersen's door. If he wanted to leave the sign hanging on the handle when he left, that was his privilege. Or he could quite simply have forgotten to take it off. Rudolf went down to Mrs Moberg and told her that Kristoffersen wasn't in his room. 'Any idea where he might be?' he asked.

'But the sign . . .' the housekeeper faltered.

'It's still there. He may have forgotten it. He can't be far away, can he? Perhaps he's still in the lounge, where we left him. Would you see if you could find him, please?'

Only then did he realize how big and rambling the house actually was, and how easy it was to come and go as one pleased. The discovery led his thoughts back to Friday the fifth of March. Gemma had told him that Kristoffersen had had the sign on the door then, too – quite unnecessarily, as she had pointed out, as everyone was laid low with flu and no one was thinking of serving him morning coffee in bed. Dr Haakonsen had been in Thursday evening and given them all some pills, apart from Renee, who said herself that she'd had chocolate. And that particular Friday Renee had overslept and nearly been too late getting to her friends. If everyone was fast asleep, or at least more or less out for the count, mused Rudolf, it would have been a simple matter for Kristoffersen to have sneaked out of the house, killed Brandt, and slipped back in again without anyone noticing.

'Now you're letting your imagination run away with you,' Rudolf admonished himself. Why on earth should a man in Kristoffersen's position want to do away with a seeming nonentity like Brandt? In any case there was not a single thing to link Brandt to the others. Dr Haakonsen's house had been thoroughly searched, but without result. There wasn't anything there to connect him with Kristoffersen, even; no scribbled notes, no receipts, nothing, despite the fact that he was on the company payroll and must have been drawing a handsome salary. And all Kristoffersen's suits were tailor-made, which meant that he'd hardly know where Harts was, let alone have seen a humble shop assistant like Brandt. 'No go,' Rudolf admitted sadly to himself, 'that one's a non-starter.'

Kristoffersen turned out to be in the playroom, together with Renee, who was listening to pop music on her cassette player. They both looked up when Mrs Moberg showed Rudolf in, and a look of annoyance fitted across the man's face. 'Making a habit of it, Sergeant, saying goodbye and then coming back half an hour later?' he said.

Rudolf smiled equably. 'I'm sorry to disturb you again, sir, but I've just been talking to the Brenners. Mr Brenner says he actually recommended the Gros Bonnet to you. And that both he and you liked it. Yet when I asked you you said you didn't know it. Now, how do you account for that? Before you answer I ought perhaps to point out that we intend to contact the Swiss police and get them to find out if you're known at the Gros Bonnet. That's why I came back – to ask if I could have a better photograph than the one in your passport. I can always get a press photograph, of course, but it's Sunday and – well, I thought I'd see if you had one first.'

Kristoffersen had gone white. 'Did Brenner really say that I know this place – the Gros Bonnet, was that what you called it? I think he's got it round his neck if he does, because I can't remember ever having been there.'

'But weren't you there together with the Brenners one evening?' Rudolf asked archly.

Kristoffersen shot a quick glance at Renee, and Rudolf couldn't help smiling inwardly when he realized that Kristoffersen thought that he, Rudolf, had expressed himself so

164

discreetly because she was listening. So there *had* been a special evening . . .

'I don't understand what you're getting at,' Kristoffersen said at last. 'You couldn't explain yourself a bit, could you? Renee, you run up to your mother, there's a good girl, while I talk to Mr Nilsen.'

Obediently the girl rose to her feet. She swallowed hard. 'You – you haven't heard anything about Sonja, have you?' she blurted, looking up at Rudolf with a plaintive expression.

'No, I'm sorry, Renee, I haven't,' Rudolf said kindly. 'But it won't be long now, you'll see.'

'Yes,' she said doubtfully, and left, closing the door behind her.

'Let me ask you something else, Mr Kristoffersen. And think carefully before you answer, will you? Are you sure that Kari Gundersen, the girl whose picture I showed you this morning, wasn't at the Gros Bonnet that evening? That you not only saw her, but that you know her well, very well?' That was a very long shot indeed, but it seemed to find its mark.

'I'm not saying another word until I've talked to my lawyer,' said Kristoffersen pompously.

'That's perfectly in order, sir,' Rudolf assured him. 'Just let me have a photograph, would you, and I shan't disturb you further today. And while you're at it, sir, if you don't mind my saying so, I should think up a good reason for not telling me that you were good friends with the Brenners.'

Kristoffersen opened his mouth to speak, but evidently thought better of it.

As Rudolf got into his car he wondered why Brenner hadn't phoned Kristoffersen immediately he, Rudolf, had left and tipped him off. Perhaps he thought his phone was tapped, or Kristoffersen's. Must be Watergate, he smiled to himself. It's an ill wind . . . But doesn't he know that we don't do that here?

25

Instead of going straight back to the office Rudolf decided to get another job out of the way and drop in on the Lessners. They didn't have passports, either of them, professing to be interested neither in sun-drenched beaches nor the opportunities for comparatively inexpensive shopping offered by London. All they wanted to do in their holidays was to drive around and see their own country. And they had a cabin on the eastern shore of the Oslo fjord where they spent their summer weekends and part of the annual holiday. Plus a farm, which went with the woods and sawmill they owned. They were content. Rudolf knew therefore that there was no chance of their having met Kari Gundersen in Switzerland, but he had the glimmerings of another theory. Maybe Lessner . . . He resolved to give it a try.

It was Lessner himself who came to the door. Rudolf explained why he'd come, and showed him the picture of the dead girl. Lessner flinched.

'How . . . however did you know that I . . . that I . . .?' He threw a frightened glance over his shoulder, and instead of asking Rudolf in stepped out on to the porch and pulled the door almost to behind him. 'But I've never done her any harm, Sergeant. On the contrary, I've always been generous towards her, very generous, even though I say it myself. There's nothing wrong, it's not breaking the law or anything, is it, er – knowing her?'

Another bit of the puzzle in place, thought Rudolf, all on the strength of a hunch. That's a hat trick this morning.

'You see . . .' Lessner lowered his voice. 'Margit, my wife,

166

you know, she's no longer . . . er . . . interested in that side of marriage.'

Rudolf nodded and gave him a sympathetic man-to-man look. 'Did she call you Biggy?'

Lessner's eyes threatened to pop out of his head. 'Biggy? No, she called me Erik. That's what I told her my name was. It's all in the past, anyway. It was only sort of now and again, even while it lasted. Not regular, you know, nothing like that.'

'Erik?'

'Yes. I couldn't very well tell her my real name, could I? She knew neither my name nor where I lived, what I do, nothing. I was careful about that, of course I was. Stands to reason.'

'Did you ever talk about other things, or was it only . . . business?'

'Oh, yes, we talked about all sorts of things. She had a room near Vestheim School. Quite nice. You'd be surprised. She's well spoken, nothing common about her at all. I asked her several times how she'd come to be doing what she was, but she'd never tell me.'

'Did she ever mention Switzerland?'

'Switzerland? No, I don't think so. She told me quite a lot about what she'd seen and done abroad, where she'd been and that, but I can't recall her ever saying anything about Switzerland.' He looked questioningly at Rudolf for a while before going on, the words tumbling out as though he was eager to salve his conscience. 'I know that at one time or another there'd been a man in her life who really meant a lot to her. Older, I gathered, sugar-daddy style of thing, took her to all the smart places, bought her lots of nice clothes and jewellery and stuff. You know how it is. He was really kind to her, apparently, and she was genuinely fond of him. But don't ask me who he was. Or perhaps you know? Was he Swiss, is that why you asked me if she ever said anything about Switzerland?'

'Do you know whether she called *him* Biggy?'

Lessner looked puzzled. 'As a sort of nickname, you mean? Something private, between the two of them?'

'Exactly.'

'No. All I know about him is that there was a time when he

167

made Kari happier than she'd ever been in her life before – or since, for that matter, I should imagine.' He looked anxiously at Rudolf. 'You're not thinking of saying anything to my wife, are you?'

'I'm investigating a murder, Mr Lessner, not judging morals,' Rudolf replied evenly.

At that moment a woman's raucous voice, slurred with drink, came through the partly open door. 'Daddy, Baby's getting cold. Why don't you come in and sit with me? Who're you talking to all this time?'

Lessner looked both fearful and sheepish. 'You won't tell Kari who I really am, will you?' he implored.

'I'd have a job,' said Rudolf heavily. 'She died at Ulleval Friday evening. Drugs and alcohol.'

'Died!' Lessner gasped. 'Kari's dead?'

'Yes,' said Rudolf shortly, turning to go. As Lessner hurried through the door Rudolf heard the woman's voice again: 'Come on, Daddykins, Baby's frozen.'

'Poor devil,' Rudolf said to himself. 'Who's to blame him?'

'Where on earth have *you* been all day, Rudolf?' asked the sergeant at the desk in the hall when Rudolf finally reached Victoria Terrasse. 'We've been trying to get hold of you for hours.'

'Can't understand that,' Rudolf replied. 'I've certainly been away from my car a lot, but I've done a fair amount of driving, too. I shall have to get my phone looked at. It was on the blink last week, but I thought it was OK again. What's up, anyway?'

'Just after you left a report came in that some youths had found a woman's body near Skogen. They were out with their dogs, Greenland huskies, but as docile as they come, apparently, and the dogs suddenly went belting off into the woods and – well, they followed and there you are. They found the body.'

Rudolf looked at his watch. It was a quarter to two.

'Don't bother,' said the sergeant, whose name was Svendsen, 'Albrektsen's just phoned in. He'll be back soon.'

'Is Karsten with them?'

'Half the force, Rudolf, half the force. Getting a bit much, isn't it? All these murders, I mean. What do we do, blame it on television?'

'Not this time, I don't think,' said Rudolf. 'All right, I'll go up to my office, then.'

'OK, I'll tell them.'

'No, hang on! I'll check my phone first.' Rudolf ran out to his car – trotted would be more accurate. Since he'd started trying to get his weight down he had also tried to move faster, but without conspicuous success. He lifted the phone. It was dead. 'Damn!' he said aloud. Still, he consoled himself, it had been a rewarding morning's work, phone or no phone.

Elvira, he thought to himself, it's Elvira they've found. His mind made a sudden leap to WPC Gunhild Mortensen. Perhaps she had been a kind of catalyst after all. He was writing a report on his morning's investigations when Chief Inspector Albrektsen came in.

'Where've you been? Spent half the morning trying to get hold of you,' Albrektsen exclaimed.

'Blasted phone's packed up. I hear some boys have found a woman's body. Elvira Anker?'

Albrektsen looked gloomy. 'Looks like it. Nothing on her to identify her, but she had reddish-blonde hair and the age is about right.' They'd finally managed to get hold of Anne-Marie Randen, her friend, and she was now on her way to the mortuary to identify her. They hadn't made any attempt to inform Gunhild; that could wait till they knew for sure. Dr Moe had promised to start his examination right away.

'Moe has?' said Rudolf in surprise. 'Crafty old devil. Only yesterday he told me he was going away for the weekend. Said he was just leaving. "Shangri-la" he said when I asked him where he'd be.'

'Must be the name of his house,' said Albrektsen with a laugh. 'You ought to have known better than to fall for that one, Rudolf. He never goes anywhere. Said it just to be sure of a bit of peace and quiet – and went to work, I shouldn't wonder. Writing another book, isn't he? He wasn't expecting another body to turn up this soon, though. Still, who was? No one took the phone when I rang him, but I just sent a couple of the boys round and he opened the door himself. Took it like a lamb.'

Rudolf chuckled. 'Yes, he's not a bad old stick at heart. Well, I've picked up a few bits and pieces myself that might come in useful.' Quickly he gave the chief inspector a brief rundown on his morning's activities. Half an hour later confirmation arrived that the dead woman was indeed Elvira Anker.

At seven o'clock that same evening Dr Moe appeared at Victoria Terrasse in person. Chief Inspector Albrektsen hurriedly convened a meeting in his office. Surprisingly, many of those involved in the case turned up, despite its being a Sunday evening.

'This is getting to be too much of a good thing,' Dr Moe said when all eight present were settled in their seats. 'Believe it or not, but this one too died from drowning. *And* in fresh water. I happen to know that part of Skogen pretty well, and there are no ponds or anything, not just there, not even a tiny stream. And even if there were, up there at that height they wouldn't be open yet. Nor would they have Zalo in them!' He looked at his audience like a conjurer about to produce a rabbit from a hat. 'Yes, Zalo. There was Zalo in the water in her lungs. I know some lakes and rivers are full of detergents, but not up there in those woods. And there were traces of alcohol and drugs in her body, too. The mixture as before – amphetamines. Getting to be an epidemic. I'm not going to get technical.' He gave a dry chuckle. 'I'll try to explain it so that even a policeman'll understand it. Drowning is actually suffocation – the lungs get filled with liquid, usually water, and the person concerned can't breathe properly. If nothing's done to prevent it, after a couple of minutes breathing stops altogether and whoever it is becomes unconscious. The heart continues to beat for four or five minutes, sometimes for much longer. During that time the person is to all intents and purposes dead, but can be brought back to life by means of various methods of resuscitation. You all know them – the old one you learned in first aid when you were scouts and the new one, mouth to mouth, the kiss of life. That's worth giving a try even an hour

170

later. Well, now, Brandt's head must have been held under water long enough to make sure that he was dead, or as good as. Greta Olesen had been in the sea for quite a while. It's only when someone's been in the water for several days that it's possible to see straight away that the cause of death was drowning: the blood runs into the skin and produces a sort of mottled effect, all mauve patches. In the case of Elvira Anker, her head must have been held under water, too, in a receptacle of some kind, I should think, perhaps a bucket, one that had had detergent in it – Zalo. I wish it had been something else; every other bucket in Oslo's had Zalo in it. Kari Gundersen seems to have committed suicide, but we don't know for certain. Somebody could have got her to take an overdose. Without knowing it. She was on drugs, we know that, but she wasn't so far gone that her natural defence mechanism, her mental brakes, if you like, wasn't still functioning. She must have known intuitively where the borderline was. People don't usually take their own lives when they're reasonably happy, they do it when they're desperate, despairing, can't see any other way out. Let's have another listen to that tape. I'm sure you've all heard it before, but listen very carefully now. Not so much to what she says but to the way she says it.'

Detective Constable Haraldsen pressed a button on the tape recorder by his side.

'Let's have it again,' said the doctor.

Six times they sat in silence and listened to Kari Gundersen's dying whisper: 'Biggy'.

'Hear it?' the doctor asked finally. 'That's not despair, is it? It sounds to me more like a term of endearment. Love, in fact. Or am I having auditory hallucinations? After all, I'm not used to doing post mortems on people who've drowned in a dentist's surgery or in the middle of a wood without so much as a brook for miles.'

He stopped and looked expectantly at the men gathered around him.

Chief Inspector Albrektsen was the first to speak: 'Now that you come to mention it, yes, I think you have a point. In any case it won't do any harm to work a bit along those lines. OK, Rudolf, your turn now. Tell them what you told me – what you found out this morning.'

Rudolf did so, concluding by saying that the photographs he had secured had already been telefaxed to Switzerland and Interpol and that enquiries were already being made there.

'So this chap's been having a bit on the side, eh?' said Karsten to his brother, falling into step beside him when the meeting broke up. He followed Rudolf into his office and without being asked dropped into a chair. 'Can't say I blame him. You've never seen her, have you, his wife? Looks like a heap of dough – the baker's kind.'

'No, only heard her, and that'll do for starters. Finishers, too, for that matter. What about Gregers Berger? Anything of interest?'

'Only that he confirms every word Evensen has said. Evensen's had quite a day, too. Both *Aftenposten* and *Dagbladet* have been at him to hear what the widow looked like. I shall be interested to see what their articles have made of her tomorrow. But how about calling it a day now? I've had enough, and I'm sure you have, too. Wasn't there a film called *Sunday, Bloody Sunday*? Now I know where they got the title from!'

Rudolf agreed and reached for his coat.

Deputy Commissioner Tygesen had gone straight from the meeting to give a press conference. What neither Rudolf nor Karsten knew, but what Tygesen was discovering at that moment, was that Alfred Kristoffersen had called a similar conference at five that afternoon and promised a reward of one hundred thousand kroner to anyone who could supply information that led to the return alive of his beloved daughter Sonja.

When he got home shortly after nine Rudolf found his wife engrossed in a television thriller.

'Shush,' she admonished him before he could say a word. 'It's so exciting. I'll make you something in a moment. Just let me see how it ends. It won't be long now.'

Resignedly Rudolf sank into an armchair. It occurred to him that that was how he himself felt, that the threads were starting to pull together and the end was in sight, though he couldn't for the life of him guess what it was going to be. He realized that although he was off duty his unconscious mind was still

172

wrestling with the problem, sorting, sifting, reviewing, shuffling all the bits and pieces. He sighed and went into the bedroom. There he undressed, and after a shower returned in his dressing-gown and slippers. Magda switched the television off just as he entered.

'There,' she said breathlessly, her eyes shining. 'That *was* good. Now, dear, what would you like? How about that chop you didn't have yesterday?'

Almost without realizing it her husband ran his hand over his stomach. Still plenty there, too much, in fact. 'No, thanks. Just a cup of bouillon and a couple of slices of crispbread'll do. No butter.'

'Don't overdo it, Rudolf,' Magda urged. 'Man shall not live by crispbread alone.'

'I know. That's why I'm having bouillon as well.'

'A bit of real meat wouldn't do you any harm.'

For a moment Rudolf wavered. 'No,' he said finally. 'Another time. A snack's all I feel like now.'

'All right, have it your own way. Only don't you go fainting on me.'

In an endeavour to make a meal out of his oblongs of crispbread and cup of steaming bouillon Rudolf ate slowly, chewing and swallowing each piece before taking another bite. In between he told Magda of the day's events, concluding by asking himself, rather than her, why Kristoffersen should be so adamant that he didn't know the Gros Bonnet. 'As far as I know *gros* means "big, thick, fat, heavy", something like that and *bonnet* has something to do with "good", hasn't it? No, that can't be right. No hotel would ever call itself fat or heavy.'

'How about good and fat?' his wife laughed. 'Wouldn't it be easier to look it up?'

'I will, it's just that I haven't got around to it.'

'I'll do it for you. *Gros*, that's g-r-o-s, isn't it? And *bonnet*'s the same as in Dubonnet, I take it. I know what it means in English, it's a kind of hat.' She leafed through the pocket dictionary that had stood unopened in their bookcase for years. 'Here we are, *bonnet*. Well, we were wrong. *Bonnet*'s a hat, a cap, in French, too. But do you know what *gros bonnet* means? It's a person of importance, a bigwig.'

'A bigwig? Well, I'll be damned! A bigwig. Mr Big. Biggy. But surely a girl wouldn't breathe her last with the name of a hotel on her lips?'

'Must have been something to do with the hotel – or the restaurant,' said Magda. 'Didn't you say they were both called the same? A man she stayed there with, could that be it?'

A picture of Lessner floated into Rudolf's mind. Lessner, who had taken such care to ensure that Kari never learnt his true identity. Nothing new in that; it was a natural precaution. He allowed his mind to wander at random. Kristoffersen. Supposing that Kristoffersen had been Kari Gundersen's sugar daddy. That sounded more feasible. Lessner had had the impression that it was an elderly man who had made her so happy. Three years ago she would have been nineteen and Kristoffersen would have been, what? Mid-fifties? Somewhere around there. Elderly, at any rate.

All right, he thought, so the pair of them had lived it up, one evening together with the Brenners, perhaps. But Kari Gundersen would have had no idea of who Kristoffersen was. She must have called him Mr Big, and eventually Biggy, because someone had told her that Gros Bonnet meant bigwig, and because he was obviously well-to-do. But then had come the parting of the ways. No more shopping to her heart's content in Clarens's leading department store where, according to Brenner, everything cost twice as much as anywhere else. No more gourmet wining and dining and staying at places like the Gros Bonnet, either. Life must have suddenly become very dull for her. She'd continued to rake around Europe, but her thoughts were obviously full of Mr Big, Biggy. And in Las Palmas she had decided to go back to Norway.

No, thought Rudolf, there's something missing: there had to be a reason why the girl had started working the Town Hall beat, which was where those who'd been at it for years usually finished up, the last stop before East Station and the docks. He couldn't think of a valid reason, and decided to go on with his theorizing.

Kari Gundersen had still not known who Biggy was. She wasn't the type to read newspapers or to keep up with events in the world about her. She'd just lived from day to day, week after week, month after month, apathetic and oblivious, gradually sinking deeper and deeper but still hanging on, tooth and nail, to her job in the laundry. And then, supposing – one day, three years after their parting in Switzerland, she'd suddenly found herself face to face with her Biggy again! She'd greet him by that name and the man would have the shock of his life. What would he do? Invite her somewhere quiet? But where? It would have to be somewhere where there was no chance of their being seen together, and where could that be? It was then Rudolf recalled Lessner's faltering voice telling him about the girl's room behind Vestheim School. He hadn't seen it himself, but the men who had searched it shortly after Kari Gundersen had been taken to hospital had reported that it was just a dingy little bed-sitter that appeared to have been furnished with things from a junkyard. All they'd found to link it with Kari Gundersen had been a pair of tights, rolled off with a panty still inside them, a grubby bra, and a cheap dressing-gown in shining red sateen. Was it likely that she would have invited the man she adored to such a place? Or that he'd go?

OK, thought Rudolf, let's assume that he not only went but decided to dispose of this ghost from the past for good. He'd hardly be likely to have a bottle of booze and a supply of amphetamine tablets ready to hand in his pocket or briefcase. So what would he do? Make a date for later and come prepared?

He began to visualize the scene. Kari Gundersen would be over the moon at having found her long-lost love again, her adored Biggy. Her critical faculties would be in suspension. That's how it had happened. Moe was right. It hadn't been suicide at all! Surmise, surmise, surmise, he told himself. Come on back down to earth. And where's your evidence? Another thing: how did Brandt get into the act?

That night Rudolf lay awake, tossing and turning, his brain racing. In the end Magda climbed out of bed and fetched a mild sleeping tablet.

'Here,' she said, 'take this. You may not need to eat and sleep, but I do.'

Obediently her husband swallowed the proffered tablet. Shortly afterwards he was sleeping like a child.

26

Monday came, the fifteenth of March. Along with Elvira Anker's death Alfred Kristoffersen's 100,000-kroner reward was front-page news in all the papers. Evensen's version of the widow as reproduced by various artists proved as fanciful as Rudolf had feared. A flowing veil covered the old-fashioned hat she wore, with its high crown and broad brim, and her coat reached nearly to her ankles. On her feet were heavy black walking-shoes with thick laces. ('Looks as if she plays for Arsenal,' was Karsten's comment.) She was depicted carrying a capacious black bag of the type once associated with midwives.

Without exception the papers asked the same question: when can we expect an arrest? No wonder people were worried, was the cry. *Dagbladet* succumbed to the temptation of linking the fact that all the victims had been drowned with the widow (who now, of course, was being reported as having been seen all over the capital, including up at Skogen) and dubbed her the Water Widow. 'When will the Water Widow strike again?' the paper asked its readers.

'If for some reason a person didn't want to use his own car – I'm thinking both of the drugs that were stolen from Ulleval and all these murders – what would he do?' asked Karsten, pitching *Dagbladet* on to the pile of newspapers on Rudolf's desk. 'Perhaps it wouldn't be a bad idea to do the rounds of the cab-hire firms. That container was pretty big, so whoever stole it – and don't ask me how they did it, unless it was those

176

brothers-in-law, and we've no reason to believe that it was –
must have had a van or a station wagon. Or a car with a hell of a
lot of room.'

Rudolf chewed thoughtfully on the end of a red pencil before
answering. 'It's worth a try, but I doubt whether it'll get us
anywhere. To hire a car whoever it was would have to prove his
identity, show his driving licence, sign for it . . .'

'But was it such a risk? After all, we've only just thought
about it – two weeks after the haul.'

'We? You were the one who thought of it, Karsten,' said
Rudolf magnanimously.

'Yes, well – perhaps I'll get a medal,' Karsten grinned. 'Or a
lollipop. But I'll be honest. I'd never have thought of it either if
I hadn't happened to see a damn great sign with "Rent a Car"
on it on my way to work this morning. It seemed to stare me in
the face, as if it had been put there just for my benefit. And
then I thought of the Ulleval heist and all those killings, and
then, well – bingo!'

'I'll have a word with Albrektsen,' said Rudolf. 'Can't do
any harm to give it a whirl. Though where we'll find a spare
bod . . . Still, we'll see.' He got up and strode out of the office,
shaking his head gloomily.

A few minutes later he was back. 'It's on,' he said. 'He's
sending Olberg. We agreed on hirings from the first of
February through to today, or as near as we can get. That do
you?'

Karsten nodded. 'Nothing ventured . . .' he said. 'You never
know your luck.'

At half-past nine a message came in to say that Mrs Olesen
wanted to see 'those two policemen who'd visited them that
time'. She wished to change her statement and Karsten and
Haraldsen hastened off at once. A certain Nurse Andersen on
the ward where Mrs Olesen had been taken reported that the
woman – the patient, as she called her – had been so well when
she woke up that morning that there had seemed no reason why
she shouldn't be allowed to go down and buy a newspaper, as
she'd asked to. 'Afterwards she seemed awfully put out,' the

nurse explained apologetically, almost as if she were expecting the two policeman to reprimand her. When they remained silent she led them into a room where Mrs Olesen was lying in semi-darkness with her eyes closed. She appeared to be asleep, but at the sound of their footsteps she opened her eyes and jerked upright. The nurse plumped up her pillows and smoothed down the bedclothes with practised hands, then went out, whispering to Karsten as she passed that she'd be just around the corner. 'Anything you want, just ring,' she said.

'I didn't tell you the truth that time,' Inga Olesen said as soon as they were alone. 'I know Rolf'll just about kill me if he ever finds out, but I saw the paper this morning and –' She broke off and asked if she might have a little water. Haraldsen, who was nearest as, with Mrs Olesen's permission, he was recording the proceedings, silently handed her the glass standing on the bedside table. The woman took a sip, then went on: 'Ever since Rolf's accident my life's been hell. Sheer hell. Greta and I were friends more than mother and daughter. That's what we were, friends. It was I who helped her get an abortion. It wasn't legal then, but I knew a woman . . . She's dead now, so you can have her name if you want. We told Rolf Greta had had a miscarriage. What else could we say: Greta was a fun-loving girl. I knew she used to go into town occasionally, just to meet boys. Stayed the night too, sometimes. No harm in that. You're only young once is what I say. It's not like it was in my day.' She sighed. 'It doesn't mean a thing to them now, take their fun where they can find it, they do. Anyway, because we were such good friends and she knew how I felt, she told me about Brenner's proposition. He'd offered her a nice flat in Madserud Allé and said she'd have a marvellous time. All she had to do was to be nice to some gentlemen – respectable men they'd be – he sent along.'

She paused again and looked from Karsten to Haraldsen as though daring them to contradict her. 'Well, it's no worse than an eighteen-year-old girl, married and happy with her husband, so she says, advertising for a girlfriend, is it?' she demanded truculently. 'I saw an ad like that only the other day. "Girlish get-together", it said. She needed "teaching". What do you think of that, eh? Isn't it awful?'

178

Haraldsen looked away and Karsten muttered noncommittally. 'Back to Greta, Mrs Olesen,' he said.

The woman waited a moment before replying. 'Greta told me the Brenners were millionaires and she said she was going to be, too. Said she'd have to work for it, but that didn't worry her. So Brenner rigged up this camera in that flat where his surgery is.'

'There's no camera there now,' said Haraldsen.

'Then he must have taken it away,' said Mrs Olesen without hesitation. 'If Greta said there was one, then there was.' She fixed him with a challenging eye. 'He even taught her how to operate it. And he installed a tape recorder. Taught her how to operate that, too. All by remote control, you know. Brenner saw to the rest, took the films out and got them developed and printed. Afterwards he sold them to the men who were on the film. He used to make films, as well, movies, you know. Bring in more girls and men and they'd all sort of, well, play around. Only that was "official" – they knew they were being filmed. Had to – they had all the lights on. Greta said the other camera was a special one that didn't need much light, it could take photographs almost in the dark. When Greta said OK Brenner opened an account for her in Switzerland, one of those with only a number, you know, no name. Greta told me all about it. She was a clever girl, our Greta. She knew what she was doing was risky. And she knew something might happen to her one day. Car accident, anything. She wanted to be sure that the money didn't just stay there for ever. She wanted me to have it.'

Karsten felt a bit sick. He'd thought that as a policeman he'd pretty well seen it all, but this was the first time he'd heard a mother calmly telling how she'd encouraged her own daughter to take up prostitution. And Switzerland. There it was again! But was the woman so naive as not to realize that what Greta had been engaged in was not primarily the making of blue movies, but downright blackmail? And that the law cracked down heavily on blackmail, even today?

'Why did you go on buying toothpaste and things for your daughter when she was making so much money?' he couldn't help asking.

179

'We had to pretend everything was the same as ever. Because of Rolf, because of my husband.'

'And when you got so heated over the Brenners –'

The woman never gave him time to finish. Impatiently, as though speaking to a child, she said: 'Don't you see, I had to pretend, of course I had, with Rolf there.'

'But how did your husband find out –'

Again he was not allowed to finish. 'What happened was that before I could get her to this woman who – helped her, Greta was so unhappy that one day she, well, drowned her sorrows in drink, so to speak, and let slip about what the Brenners were up to.'

'The Brenners? Is his wife in it, too?'

'She's his agent. When the films were developed, the movies, that is, she used to go over to Sweden – a shopping trip to Arvika – and hand them over to a man there who sent them abroad somewhere. She used to come back with sugar or liquor or something, whatever happened to be cheaper there at the time, same as all the housewives do, to make it look natural. You know how many people cross the border just to shop. But what Rolf can't forgive Brenner for is that Greta never knew whose child it was. Brenner wasn't the only one who – well, you know. There were others, too. All very respectable and well-to-do, mind you, not just anyone off the street. They never knew that they'd been photographed. Brenner was in on it himself, sometimes. Has his girlfriends, he has. He has a big calendar on the wall above the bed, and a clock, so there's never any doubt as to when the pictures were made. You can imagine: a chap tells his wife he's got to go to a meeting on, say, the twelfth of April, and she believes him. Afterwards Brenner shows him a picture of himself in action with both the date and the time on it and threatens to show it to the man's wife unless he pays up.' (So she *does* know, thought Karsten in disgust.) 'And the wife would remember that her husband was going to a meeting, so he wouldn't be able to say that it was taken before they were married or anything like that. You can see how well thought out it was. Clever devil, Brenner. Same applies to his own girlfriends, of course – most of them were married.'

'But why was your husband willing to tell us about Greta's

miscarriage and then a few moments later retract the whole story?' asked Haraldsen, mystified.

'Because he knew that if Brenner once found out what we'd said, he'd go straight to Kristoffersen and we'd be out on the street in no time. When I think of what good friends they are, thick as thieves, we wouldn't have stood an earthly. So I told Rolf the risk he was running and at the same time promised him half a bottle of whisky. You mustn't go thinking badly about Greta. She was a good girl, wouldn't harm a fly. I used to phone her every evening when she wasn't home, either from one of the offices where I clean or from the box on the corner. We're not on the phone ourselves.'

'Did you phone her after we'd been to see you?' Karsten asked.

' 'Course I did. Had to tell her what had happened, naturally. She wasn't very pleased, I can tell you. She said she'd try and sort it out and she asked me to convince Rolf that he had to say that the Brenners were nice people. If he didn't, it'd be goodbye to our flat *and* her.'

'They know what you and your husband accused them of the first time we came. Said they'd take you both to court if you didn't withdraw your accusations.'

'To court?' Inga Olesen gave a scornful laugh. 'He can get us thrown out, yes, but to court – that's a good one! Just let him try, that's all I say.' She grew suddenly serious.

'Greta's gone and nothing I can do will bring her back. We were friends, partners if you like, but how am I going to get hold of the money she earned when I don't even know which bank it's in? I'm tired of scrubbing and slaving for a drunken layabout – he's not that crippled that he couldn't give me a hand now and again. I know Greta would have wanted me to have that money . . . '

Karsten refused to be drawn. Instead he brought the conversation back to Kristoffersen and Brenner. He'd never realized, he said, that they were so close.

'If they're not, then he must have awfully bad teeth,' said Mrs Olesen with a bitter laugh. 'He just about lives there. There was one morning not so long ago when I wondered if he was thinking of moving in for good. It was a Saturday, I

181

remember. Humping two great suitcases, he was. Looked real put out when he saw me. Had a row with his wife, I thought. Only she's not his wife, is she? Still, it wasn't my business. I just mentioned it now to show what good friends they are.'

'Do you happen to remember which Saturday it was?'

'Happen to? I can't help it, it was Greta's birthday – the twenty-eighth of February.'

'What about the time? Approximately.' Karsten threw Haraldsen a quick glance. The drugs had been stolen on the twenty-sixth. Could it be . . . ?

'I know that, too. I'd just finished my work and I remember looking at my watch and thinking that it was two hours till the liquor store opened, and if Rolf doesn't get half a bottle a day he's impossible. Saturdays I always have to buy a half for Sunday and hide it somewhere he can't find it, otherwise he'd drink it and that'd be Sunday ruined. You've no idea.'

'So on Saturday the twenty-eighth Brenner was there and let Kristoffersen in?'

'I didn't say Brenner was there. He didn't need to be. Kristoffersen has his own key.'

When, some time later, the two policemen were preparing to take their leave, Mrs Olesen stretched out a hand and grasped Karsten's arm: 'Talk to Kristoffersen,' she said. 'Tell him what I've told you about the Brenners. I'm sure they're behind his daughter's disappearance. And he's promised a hundred thousand kroner to anyone who can help find her. And don't forget that money of Greta's is mine . . .'

When they finally got out into the corridor Haraldsen turned to Karsten with a dazed look on his face. 'I've come across a few,' he said, 'but honestly, she takes the cake. Her own daughter. Greedy bitch! Like a bloody vulture, can't wait for the pickings.'

Karsten looked at him in amazement. Was this the Scout? He'd never heard him so vehement before, never mind swear.

'Yes, bit of a shaker, wasn't it? She's had a rotten life, I don't doubt that, but . . .'

'Let's forget her,' said Haraldsen. 'When did you last have lamb?'

Karsten stopped in his tracks. 'Lamb?' he repeated stupidly.

Now it was Haraldsen's turn to look surprised. 'Yes, lamb. Roast lamb.'

God, thought Karsten, I nearly put my foot in it there! Aloud, he said: 'Can't remember, really I can't. Must have been ages ago. Why?'

'We had it for dinner yesterday, Sunday joint, you know, and we'll be having it again today, cold. I thought you might like to come to dinner as soon as we can get away. My parents would be happy to see you and – well, I thought perhaps you could have a look at something I've written. Poetry. I'm rather pleased with it, actually, but you know so much more about these things. I've only just started.'

Karsten couldn't help but feel flattered. It was the first time he'd ever been asked to offer an opinion on somebody else's work. And all this on the strength of one slim volume, years ago. He was careful not to mention that he'd started to pick up the threads of his own writing again. Time for that when he saw what came out of it.

'That's very kind of you,' he said. 'If you're sure your parents won't mind.'

'They'll be delighted. I'll let them know when we get back to HQ.'

'There wasn't a camera or a tape recorder in Greta Olesen's flat, either,' said Karsten reflectively, his thoughts reverting to the case in hand. 'So where've they gone? And where did Brenner get his films developed? Had to be somewhere, because there were no signs of developing trays and a darkroom around, and I don't think Mrs Olesen was making it up.'

'Even if *she* was, her husband isn't bright enough to,' said Haraldsen decisively. 'I believe her. And I think that whoever drowned Greta drowned the evidence as well.'

27

On Tuesday the sixteenth of March Rudolf found himself laughing heartily for the first time since the case had started. It was his brother who was the cause. On the preceding Saturday he had had the bright idea of advertising in the personal column of *Dagbladet* 'on the off chance', as he'd put it. His *cri de coeur* appeared under a box number on the Monday and urged the blonde with a mole on her nose who had been in the company of a tall, slim girl to contact 'the well-dressed gentleman in his late forties who had smiled at her on Kirkeveien at about three o'clock on 1 March' and to give a phone number if possible. To Karsten's chagrin and his brother's amusement Tuesday brought a whole sheaf of replies.

'You'd better answer them in alphabetical order,' said Rudolf, laughing till he had to wipe his eyes.

'But they can't *all* have a mole on the side of their nose,' said Karsten in mock despair. 'And if they all smiled at a middle-aged man on Kirkeveien at three o'clock on Saturday afternoon, all I can say is that the street must have been pretty crowded.'

'It's a long street, remember,' said Rudolf helpfully.

'It's all very well for you,' his brother replied, 'but what am I going to do?'

'Well, how about sitting down and going through them? You mightn't find the one you're after, but perhaps your dream girl's hidden somewhere in that pile.'

But his laughter was shortlived. Anne-Marie Randen, Elvira Anker's friend, had recovered sufficiently from the shock she had sustained to call on him and insist that the dead girl's reputation be cleared. 'Publicly,' she said firmly. 'Elvira never touched anything stronger than sherry. I should know, I stayed with her a lot. Neither of us drinks – drank – not really. And as for drugs . . .'

Rudolf promised to do his utmost, a promise he had to repeat three times before she was convinced that he really meant it. No, she said, she didn't know of any friend of Elvira's who had a mole on her nose. As far as she knew she herself was her only close friend. She had no idea who the young blonde woman who had been with Elvira could be. Another nurse, perhaps? But she'd met several of her friend's colleagues, and not one of them had a mole on her nose as far as she could remember. Male friends? Anyone in particular? No, she was sure Elvira hadn't been going with anyone special at the time she was murdered. She'd been very much in love with a chap but the affair had finished as quickly as it had begun, and Elvira had taken it very hard. She'd no idea who he was, only that his first name was Raoul; nor did she know what he did for a living or why the two had broken up. All Elvira had said was that never again would she trust a man: even the best of them weren't averse to a bit of fun on the side. They hadn't been her exact words, but that was what it boiled down to, according to Miss Randen. Beyond that, Elvira had refused to talk about it.

Anne-Marie Randen had only just left when Chief Inspector Albrektsen came in to say that the financial experts had gone through Alfred Kristoffersen's accounts and that they showed that the three months he had spent in Switzerland had come to only 20,745 Norwegian kroner.

'Got away cheaply, didn't he?' said Albrektsen with bluff good humour, 'considering that it costs a small fortune at the Paix for a single room with a private bathroom. To that could be added countless meals – not even breakfast was included in the price of the room. Then there was car hire for three months, overnight stays at other hotels (with both Kristoffersen and Dr Haakonsen retaining their rooms at the Hotel de Paix), not to mention 3,000 kroner a week for Sonja at the clinic. Plus the trip down to Switzerland and back. 'I'd like to know the

185

secret for my own holidays,' the inspector concluded.

'So it's back to numbered accounts, is it?' said Rudolf. 'And Kristoffersen claims his accounts are perfectly in order. Well, I suppose they are in a manner of speaking. Depends what you match 'em against, doesn't it?' He thought for a moment. 'How long do you think we should give him? And the Brenners? Don't you think we should bring 'em in and –'

'No,' Albrektsen broke in quickly. 'Let them be. Give 'em all the rope they need to hang themselves. That's Tygesen's view, and I'm inclined to agree with him. When you have a big one on, you have to play him carefully. We've a lot of circumstantial evidence, but we've nothing concrete, nothing we can prove, apart from the financial wheelings and dealings, and even then we'd be a bit pushed. Swiss banks are like oysters, you know that as well as I do. And where's your proof about the Brenners? We'd never get off the ground. No, leave them to sweat. They can't get away, anyway.'

'Haakonsen and the girl did.'

'Then, yes, but they wouldn't have managed it now. Not with what we know about the lot of them and with a watch on their houses.'

When the chief inspector had gone Rudolf took out the copy of the hotel register from Voss and rechecked it. There was no getting away from it: the Brenners *had* checked in on Friday the twenty-seventh of February. That meant that if Mrs Olesen was telling the truth about seeing Kristoffersen lugging two suitcases up the stairs on Saturday the twenty-eighth, he must have had the key to the dentist's flat.

Reports began to come in from the airlines and from the policemen charged with the task of checking out serving and former stewardesses, those who had been flying four years previously. Nothing. The switchboard was almost choked by people phoning in to say that they'd seen the widow. There was even a call from Copenhagen. And there was a lot of fishing after Kristoffersen's reward. As if we haven't got enough to do, thought Rudolf irritably.

Detective Constables Arvik and Haraldsen went to interview Kristoffersen again, but he refused to see them. Instead they spoke to Gemma, Mrs Moberg and Anna, the maid. None of them could say anything about what Kristoffersen had done on

Saturday the twenty-eighth of February. All they could say was that the 'Please do not Disturb' sign had been on his door then, too, of that they were all three convinced. Gemma remembered having looked for an umbrella which she thought she must have left in Kristoffersen's BMW. She had rummaged around in the back seat and the trunk without finding it and driven into town in her own car without it.

'Just because his car was in the garage it doesn't necessarily mean that he was at home,' said Rudolf when this was reported to him. 'Someone could have fetched him – Dr Haakonsen, for instance. Or someone we don't even know exists.'

The Swiss police were both helpful and efficient. They reported not only that Monsieur Kristoffersen and his daughter, together with Dr Haakonsen, had twice stayed at the Gros Bonnet in Caux, but also that they had spent three days at a place called Le Perroquet in Clarens. His daughter? thought Rudolf. That's strange. He compared the dates given with that on the bill from the Gros Bonnet restaurant that Kari Gundersen had so lovingly preserved and with the sales slip from the store in Clarens. They matched – not that he was surprised. So that's how he got round the passport problem, he mused. Used Sonja's, while she was at the clinic. God, how simple it all was, with hindsight!

It transpired that some of the other tenants in the tumble-down block of flats where Kari Gundersen had had her bed-sitter, a block scheduled for demolition, had noticed Kristoffersen when he was there. Much of their lives consisted in watching what their neighbours were doing. Dr Moe's findings showed that the girl had drunk a considerable quantity of alcohol shortly before she was taken to hospital. Kristoffersen had probably taken a bottle with him, Rudolf surmised. But had he had amphetamines with him, too?

Mrs Olesen had said that Brenner had seen to the developing of the films himself. But where? And where were the cameras and the recorder? The list of unanswered questions was endless. Rudolf sighed.

Could a man as prominent in public life as Kristoffersen really have concealed his identity from Kari Gundersen for so long? Wouldn't the hotel staff have addressed him as Mr Kristoffersen, or would it simply have been sir, or monsieur?

187

Perhaps he had bribed them not to reveal his name. Because if the girl had known who her Mr Big, her Biggy, was – assuming that it really was Kristoffersen, and all the evidence pointed in that direction – surely, Rudolf reasoned, the first thing she would have done on her return to Oslo would have been to contact him. She would hardly have waited till they met by chance. Or had their meeting actually been by agreement?

He knew they used Zalo at Kristoffersen's as he'd seen it in the kitchen, but that didn't mean much. His own wife washed up with it, as he himself did whenever he was able to give her a hand, and so did half Norway.

Wearily Rudolf put on his coat and left the office. It had been another hard day. He reached home just in time for the bi-monthly cookery lesson. The woman on the screen seemed to be looking directly at him. 'It would be a shame to throw away the water you've boiled the tongue in. Use it as stock to make a stew,' she said. 'Peel a suitable number of potatoes and dice them. Parboil them in the stock. Add diced carrots, a slice or two of turnip, perhaps, a little onion – not too much, it can give the stew a very strong taste – in short, whatever you happen to have to hand. Season to taste . . .' Her voice droned on. Rudolf looked away. He was just about dying of hunger. His wife shot him a quick glance, sized up the situation in an instant, and considerately switched the set off. Again she insisted on getting him a proper meal, but he was adamant: 'No, thanks, just tea and a slice or two of lemon,' he said.

'I know – and no sugar. But you can't keep this up for long.' Magda went into the kitchen to put the kettle on.

Rudolf settled himself into an armchair. Kristoffersen had himself volunteered the information last Friday that two days earlier he had looked in at the office, after everyone had gone. That meant that he'd been out of the house Wednesday evening, the evening Elvira Anker had met her death, and perhaps also Greta Olesen.

He picked up the paper and scanned the evening's programmes. Anything to take his mind off the case. The more he wrestled with it, the more involved it became. 'I'm not watching the play, Magda,' he said. 'It's another of those Finnish kitchen-sink things, all rapes and knifings and booze by the bucketful. Get enough of that kind of thing at work. Can't understand a word they say, either. Norway probably gets them free – nobody else'll have 'em.' He grimaced. 'I'll have an early night instead.'

'I think that's a jolly good idea,' his wife replied understandingly. She paused for a moment. 'Have you talked to Karsten lately? Really talked, I mean, not just shop.'

'Have I? I may have done, can't really remember. He seems to be pulling out of it, anyway, looks better altogether. More cheerful, too. And he seems to be off the hard stuff as well.' Rudolf recounted the story of his brother's ad in *Dagbladet*. 'Sprat to catch a mackerel and he landed a whole shoal! Ought to be in clover.' He started to laugh, but the laughter died in his throat. He suddenly thought of Magda's remark the morning the case broke. What was it she had said? 'When do you ever have time for trifles like that?' Where had she put the emphasis, he mused, on the 'you' or on 'time'? Hell! he thought, suddenly anxious. I hope Magda isn't on the way to becoming a new Wendy. But why had she asked if he'd talked to Karsten lately? She didn't usually pry into his relations with his brother. Was it a gentle hint that the same fate might befall him?

Magda wanted to watch the play, so Rudolf decided to go to bed without her. First, however, he treated himself to a long, hot shower and then, in his pyjamas and with his teeth brushed, stepped blithely on to the bathroom scale. He peered at the dial. The pointer had moved all right, but in the wrong direction. He checked the adjustment. It was correct. 'Damn it!' he said aloud. 'After all that I've *gained* weight.' Vaguely he recalled having read somewhere that it was often some days before the results of a change of diet manifested themselves in the shape of lost weight. He braced himself: it was just a matter of perseverance; the body tended to retain liquid. But what did 'some days' mean in practice? Were all his sacrifices to be in vain? And how come Magda tucked in like nobody's business and still lost weight?

He sighed and climbed into bed, to fall asleep almost as soon as his head touched the pillow. His last conscious thought was of the woman on television explaining how to make a stew. He had an uncanny feeling that she had said something that would help him solve the widow case. But what?

28

On Wednesday the seventeenth of March Rudolf woke early after a restless night. He squinted at his watch in the half-light. Just gone five. Beside him Magda slept like a child. He felt a sudden urge to reach out a hand and stroke her cheek, but restrained himself. One doesn't wake one's wife at five o'clock on a wintry morning without a good reason, and he had none. It wasn't that he didn't want to, it was just that he knew all too well that he couldn't. What he couldn't decide was whether it was his being overweight, his desperate effort to slim, or pressure of work. Perhaps it was a bit of all three?

Resignedly he climbed quietly out of bed, padded through to the bathroom, showered, dressed and went into the kitchen. There he made himself a cup of coffee and slowly munched and chewed his way through yet another slice of crispbread, again without butter. Going back to the bathroom he cleaned his teeth, ran a comb through his hair, frowned at his reflection in the mirror, and returned to the kitchen. He scribbled a note to Magda – 'Gone to the office. Have a good day. Love, R.'– and propped it up against a vase on the table. He determined to buy her some flowers on his way home; he couldn't remember the last time he'd done so.

What could Brenner have done with the camera and all the rest of the equipment he'd used in his sordid trade? Where would one hide a fish on shore? Rudolf asked himself, and the answer came pat: in a fish shop, among a lot of other fish. But they didn't have the manpower to trawl all Oslo's photographic shops on the off chance. Besides, even if that were the answer,

Brenner could just as well have used a shop somewhere else.

And what had become of those two heavy cases Mrs Olesen claimed that Kristoffersen had dumped in Brenner's flat the day after the Ulleval heist? Was it to collect them that Brenner had gone to his flat on the evening of Friday the fifteenth? Could that also be the reason why the couple had left Voss earlier than planned? Rudolf resolved to find out whether they had phoned anyone from the hotel or, if possible, whether they had received any calls while they were there, but first he had to check with Albrektsen. Perhaps he had already looked into it.

He hadn't been long at the office when he was informed that Elvira Anker's parents in Montreal had sent a cable – not to their son, Elvira's brother, who had cabled them the sad news, but direct to the police. The son had probably not felt up to the task of phoning after not having had anything to do with his parents for so many years. Rudolf scanned the printed form quickly. It was in English, brief and to the point: they were deeply shocked but could not come to Norway just now. Rudolf made a note to inform the son later in the day.

Then he took out Dr Haakonsen's register of patients and began to study the names. It must have cost the doctor dear, having to leave his records behind, he reflected, but he had doubtless realized that to have destroyed them or taken them with him would have revealed that he had had them with him in his car and that the flight had been premeditated. Rudolf compared the names with those on Peter Brenner's register and suddenly found one that appeared on both. It was still early, but hoping that WPC Gunhild Mortensen was already in, he phoned her. She was, and he asked her to find out more about the man concerned.

There was a knock at the door and Detective Constable Robotten entered. He had a paper in his hand. 'Here's a list of all the roles Astrid Hagen ever played,' he said. 'None of them required her to dress up as a widow. But – funny thing, chap I know, an actor, small-time, Kurt Krosby, perhaps you know him –?' Rudolf nodded. 'Well, he was at school with her. He told me that not long after they left school several of them had got together and put on a play. She was in it. It was one of those obscure, way-out things by a French author whose name he couldn't remember. Doesn't matter, anyway. What does matter is that it was called *The House of Death* or *The House of the Dead* or something cheerful like that, and everyone in it, both men and women, had to wear black. Full mourning. It only ran for a couple of nights. People refused to take it seriously, apparently, and laughed in all the wrong places. I asked him what the women wore and from what he said it sounded like the widow's weeds we're looking for. Long black dress, long black coat, and a long, heavy black veil. Kristoffersen said he had all his wife's costumes, but there's nothing like that on the list Paulsen and Larsen made of the contents of those trunks in the attic. Krosby was positive that Kristoffersen had been at those two performances. How about that, eh?'

'Well done,' said Rudolf, and meant it. 'He conveniently forgets things at times, friend Alfred does.' He looked at Robotten's list. 'He told me he'd seen all her plays, been there night after night, but he could name only four or five when I pressed him. If they were amateurs who did your *House of the Dead* or whatever it was they'd all know one another well, don't you think? And he'd know them and they'd know him. Think Krosby would remember the names of the others?'

'I asked him that and he said he'd try,' Robotten replied. 'But it's a long time ago now and he's lost touch with them. Naturally enough.'

'Keep at him,' said Rudolf. 'There could be a name that would ring a bell, though I doubt it.' The constable left and Rudolf returned to his study of the two lists of patients. While he worked his mind wandered to Greta Olesen who had evidently sealed her own fate by phoning – yes, to whom? Brenner? Kristoffersen? Dr Haakonsen? – and telling whoever it was of her mother's phonecall.

Both Karsten and Haraldsen were adamant that Mrs Olesen hadn't been the least worried when they told her that Brenner had threatened legal action if they didn't withdraw their allegations. It seemed almost as though she wished he would.

Rudolf cast his mind back over the situation. Peter Brenner and his wife, in common with Kristoffersen and his entire household, were being kept under constant surveillance – at no little expense to the taxpayer, Rudolf reflected wrily. Kristoffersen had made two journeys into town, simply going up to his office, then returning home. Brenner had visited his surgery every day, but only for a couple of hours each time. Rudolf wondered what he did there, because he'd clearly cancelled all his appointments. On the door he had put up a notice: 'Closed owing to illness'. Mrs Brenner hadn't been out of the house. Neither had Gemma, but she'd been hardest hit of them all by the flu, so it was understandable that she should wish to take things quietly. Mrs Moberg hadn't been out, either. Anna, the maid, on the other hand, went out regularly to do the shopping in Gemma's car, and one evening she had met one of her Norwegian boyfriends. They had gone to a cinema and afterwards to a small restaurant for a meal. She'd gone up to his flat, but two hours later had reappeared and taken a taxi home. Renee had seemed a bit depressed. She went regularly to school, visited what were clearly her best friends, and stayed the night with one of them. None of her friends came to see her, probably because they were not allowed to by their parents. Rudolf felt genuinely sorry for the child. If he had had a daughter he wouldn't have minded her being like Renee, apart from the nail-biting. He was still thinking about her when the phone rang. It was Robotten.

'Can you spare five minutes?' the young constable asked. Rudolf had barely put the phone down before Robotten came in. He had another list in his hand.

'I didn't need to remind him,' he said. 'He phoned and actually apologized for taking so long, only he'd had to confer with some of the others and he couldn't get hold of them at first. Here you are. And you know what?' he said excitedly. 'Albert Linderud was one of them. You know him, he was mixed up in that sex-club scandal a few years back. Norway's first, wasn't it? Created quite a stink, remember? Well, we've had a few since then, haven't we?' He smiled ruefully. 'If he hadn't had such a smart lawyer he'd never have got off like he did.'

'Yes,' said Rudolf, 'I remember. Nasty piece of work all round.'

'He's going straight now, though, it seems,' said Robotten. 'Runs a photographer's studio and photographic shop in

Kongens Gate.'

'A photographer's?'

'Yes. Well, so Krosby said. He laughed when he told me. Tickled him to think of Albert Linderud going straight. "Born a bad 'un," he said. "Couldn't trust him an inch, even as a kid." '

'Come on,' said Rudolf, springing to his feet. 'Let's go and see Albrektsen. I have an idea.'

Twenty minutes later Rudolf was on his way home in his car, together with Robotten, to change his clothes. His car phone had been replaced the same day it had been found to be defective, but Chief Inspector Albrektsen had insisted that no one engaged on the 'Widow Case' was to use his phone for fear of the conversation being picked up by outsiders. Karsten had immediately christened the chief inspector's ban 'Operation Silent Night'.

'It's a shot in the dark,' Rudolf explained, 'but Linderud's always sailed close to the wind, and as we now know that he knows Kristoffersen, and with Kristoffersen and Brenner being such close friends – "thick as thieves", wasn't that what Mrs Olesen said? – it's quite possible that that's where all Brenner's equipment is. I've only seen Linderud once so I shall know him when I see him, but he didn't see me, so he won't know me from Adam. And dressed in sporting tweeds, and if I'm discreet . . .' He laughed. 'If I realize he's clean we'll take no further action. Save us a lot of bother afterwards, apologies and all that. You know how it is if it's official.'

Magda was not a little surprised when her husband turned up in the middle of a working day and proceeded to change into sportswear, but he offered no explanation and she was too experienced to ask for one. Instead she made coffee and sat down and chatted with them while they drank it. Rudolf gazed at her fondly, again making a mental note to buy her some flowers. 'I *mustn't* forget,' he told himself.

A quarter of an hour later the two policemen were on their way back into the centre of the city. It took them an age to find a parking space in the vicinity of the shop, but eventually they succeeded.

194

'Now try to behave like an ordinary customer,' Rudolf instructed his companion. 'It shouldn't be too difficult. I don't know how I shall get on as the villain of the piece, but at least I can give it a try. Might finish up on the stage yet.'

'Have you thought what you're going to say?' asked Robotten curiously.

'More or less.' Suddenly Rudolf thought of Lars, his son. Absently, he wondered what he thought of his father. That he was all right, but a bit square, a bit of a stick-in-the-mud? A plodder, set in his ways? Unconsciously he straightened his back and squared his shoulders. For some reason it had suddenly become important to him that Lars should look up to him. And that he and Magda should recapture their easy relationship of former years. When this lot's over, he promised himself, we'll treat ourselves to a long weekend somewhere. Take the boat over to Copenhagen, live it up a bit. The family that plays together, stays together! He shook his head vigorously. This wouldn't do. He had to concentrate on the job in hand.

'Give me a couple of minutes before you come in,' he said to Robotten.

Robotten obediently slowed down and started to gaze into the nearest shop window. Rudolf quickened his pace, then, as he neared the shop, peered furtively over his shoulder, as though he were afraid he were being followed. The shop looked very smart and prosperous; Rudolf realized he'd passed it many times without having the faintest idea who owned it.

The bell on the door gave a subdued 'pling' as he entered. Albert Linderud was fiddling with a camera at one end of the long counter and two assistants were busy dealing with customers.

'Good morning,' Linderud said, giving Rudolf an ingratiating smile. 'What can I do for you?'

'Do you have somewhere at the back where we can talk?' Rudolf asked in a low voice.

Linderud looked at him warily. 'What's it about?' he asked.

Rudolf waited a moment before replying. Then he leaned across the counter and whispered in a low voice: 'Left luggage.'

'Left luggage?' Rudolf could see that the man was genuinely

baffled. 'I'm not here to answer riddles, you know. What do you mean, "Left luggage"?'

'A place where you can leave . . .' Rudolf cast a quick glance at the others in the shop. ' . . . *special* photographic equipment.' He looked around again, an expression of puzzled innocence on his face. 'Don't tell me you don't keep things for people, special equipment they're afraid to leave lying about.' He paused again. 'Come on,' he continued in a sharper tone, 'you're not that dumb, surely? You don't want me to say it out loud, do you, in front of the other customers?'

'Pling!' went the bell behind him. It was Robotten, right on cue.

'Come with me,' said Linderud hastily, beckoning Rudolf in behind the counter and leading the way to the back of the shop. Rudolf was just in time to see one of the other customers leave and to hear Robotten ask for a carton of flashbulbs. Linderud led Rudolf into a back room and carefully closed the door behind them. 'Now,' he said, 'let's have it. What's it all about, eh? I'm a busy man. What do you mean, "left luggage" and "special photographic equipment"?'

Rudolf didn't answer. Instead, he simply stared coldly at Linderud. The man shifted uneasily from one foot to the other.

'Well,' he said at last, 'can't stand here all day. Either tell me what you want or get the hell out. If you don't, I'll call the police.'

'Oh, that won't be necessary, Mr Linderud,' Rudolf said evenly. 'I'm a police officer myself.' He proffered his identity card. 'Detective Sergeant Nilsen.'

The man before him blanched and sank into a chair.

'Now perhaps you know what I mean,' said Rudolf. He crossed to the door and opened it. To the astonishment of the assistant who was just giving Robotten his change, he beckoned his companion in and closed the door. 'This is Detective Constable Robotten. If you don't want to talk here we can go up to Victoria Terrasse. We shall probably have to go there anyway to take a statement. But it would save a lot of time if you'd talk now.'

Linderud buried his face in his hands. 'I knew it,' he sighed. 'I knew it. I knew it'd end like this. Oh, my God!'

196

'That what would end like this?' asked Rudolf sharply. 'Come on, out with it!'

'I had to, Sergeant, I just had to. They made me.'

'They? Who're "they"?'

'The Brenners. The pair of them.'

'Never mind the equipment for now. How about the . . . er, end products?'

Dejectedly Linderud crossed to a row of shelves behind him and came back with two cardboard boxes, which he placed on the table in silence. Rudolf lifted the lid of one. In the box was a pile of photographs. He picked up the top ones. They were very similar – middle-aged women, beyond the first bloom of youth, writhing in apparent ecstasy beneath the muscular body of a younger man with his back to the camera. The other box contained similar pictures, only this time they were of flabby-looking middle-aged and elderly men locked in the embrace of a slim young woman; her face was either half-turned away from the camera or hidden by her hair. In every case the date and exact time were shown by the large calendar and clock above the bed.

Both Rudolf and Robotten had been in Brenner's flat. They recognized the bedroom immediately. Involuntarily Rudolf found himself thinking of an enlargement of an amateur snapshot, a photograph of a girl with tumbling fair hair, smiling up at the camera. A girl whose eyes were hidden behind large sunglasses, a girl who seemed to be mooring a boat. He shook his head sadly.

Linderud cowered abjectly in his chair. 'It's not my fault,' he whined. 'I'm innocent, I am, really I am. I'll tell you all I know.'

'I sincerely hope you will, not least for your own sake,' said Rudolf. 'But not here. Get your coat and you can make a proper statement in my office.' He could feel his pulses throbbing. This won't do, he told himself. I'm getting too involved. Turning to Linderud, he said: 'Ready? OK, let's go.' He indicated the two cardboard boxes. 'I'd like to burn them here and now,' he said, 'but we shall need them as evidence. *You* carry them!' Meekly, Linderud did as he was bade, and the three men marched out.

29

Rudolf had barely got back to Victoria Terrasse and handed over to Robotten the task of taking a statement from Albert Linderud when a call came from the duty sergeant in the hall to say that a Miss Anne-Marie Randen wished to speak to him. Immediately she entered his office the girl formally shook hands with him, but instead of releasing his hand, she continued to hold it while she rather sheepishly confessed that she had doubted very much whether he really would clear Elvira Anker of any stain on her character. But she had read all the Oslo papers, she said, and without exception . . .

'Oh, that's all right, Miss Randen, glad I was able to help,' Rudolf said, almost as embarrassed as she was. He wasn't accustomed to people coming to express their gratitude.

'I've been thinking,' the young woman said, finally letting go of his hand. 'If Elvira died because she'd got involved in something . . . well, it *could* have been something to do with the fellow she was so in love with. So if you're looking for a man, I should imagine he'd be of the quiet, unobtrusive type – probably fairly well built. And she usually fell for fair-haired men . . .' Her voice trailed dispiritedly away. There was no trace of the woman who, not many days earlier, had almost hammered on Rudolf's desk. It was plain that she was very badly cut up over her friend's death. Rudolf found himself liking her much better than he had before.

'It's also occurred to me that perhaps whoever took those

198

drugs from Ulleval thought she knew something she didn't. That that's why –' She stopped. Rudolf could see that she was fighting back her tears. 'There must have been a reason, mustn't there? Obviously it didn't have to be Raoul, but perhaps it's worth following up. He's like I told you, and probably also a good deal older than Elvira was. She wasn't very keen on men of her own age, too childish, she said. I don't know whether I'm being silly saying this, but I sometimes used to wonder if she wasn't unconsciously looking for the father she never had. One thing's certain, she wanted security – and by that I don't mean money. Elvira wasn't like that. What I mean by security is that she wanted someone who understood her sufficiently to enable her to dare to be herself when they were together. Someone she knew would stand by her, care for her if she was ill or depressed or anything.'

She rose. 'I've not put it very well, I'm afraid, but I'm not thinking straight, either. Not where Elvira's concerned, anyway. We were such good friends, you know. Perhaps it was because we were always attracted by different types.'

When Rudolf asked her what she meant by men who were 'a good deal older' she replied that Elvira was quite happy if they were eight, ten, even twelve or more years older than she was. Rudolf thanked her, and a little later she left. She seemed so young and so overcome by the terrible fate that had befallen her friend. Understandably, he thought. His heart went out to her. Raoul . . .

A thought struck him. He leafed quickly through the bulging file on the theft from the Surgical Department at Ulleval Hospital. There it was! One of the two who had taken the container over from the Dispensary was named Raoul. Raoul Hansen.

Rudolf himself hadn't spoken to the man; he had been questioned by someone from the Narcotics Division proper. He found the report and read it, slowly, thinking hard. Satisfied, he closed the file, grabbed his coat, and set off for Ulleval. At the Dispensary he was informed that Raoul Hansen was off ill. Konrad Lassen, the head dispenser, told him, 'strictly between ourselves', that Hansen's nerves had been in shreds for a long time and that he had repeatedly urged him to see a doctor.

Hansen had had trouble with his nerves before, the dispenser said, but ever since early February he had been in such a bad way that he had been virtually useless at work.

'I feel sorry for him,' Lassen explained. 'He's pretty big, you know, but as meek as a lamb when it comes to the point. You know the type: conscientious to a fault. The mere thought that he might be suspected of complicity . . .' The dispenser spread his well-manicured hands in a theatrical gesture. 'Well, you can imagine.' He smiled. 'We all feel a bit helpless, a bit Lilliputian, when we think the police are after us.'

Rudolf gave him an understanding nod. 'How long's he been off work?'

'Since Monday.'

Monday was the day the story of the discovery of Elvira Anker's body had appeared in the papers.

'If's he's away for more than three days he'll need a doctor's certificate,' Lassen added helpfully. 'Not that that'll be any problem in his case. A doctor's only got to look at him to give him sick leave until further notice. To tell you the truth, I rather wish one would. There's a lot to do here and Hansen's not been pulling his weight lately. Falls on the rest of us, naturally. We can't go on doing his work indefinitely, though.'

Rudolf drove to Hansen's bed-sitter, part of a large, rambling old flat close by in Ullevalsveien. The flat was owned by an elderly widow, a Mrs Rustad, who informed him that her tenant was staying with his sister at the moment because he wasn't well. No, she said, she didn't mind his having a look round.

Rudolf asked her if she'd care to leave him alone for a while, and somewhat reluctantly she left him to it. As soon as she had gone he picked up one of several wooden figures lined up on a shelf. It was beautifully crafted, every detail clearly carved with loving care. Rudolf hefted it thoughtfully in his hand; it was perfectly balanced and a pleasure to hold. It was evident that Hansen employed most of the room as a workshop; the other half was his living-room and bedroom. A low table with an easy chair at each end, a studio couch, a reading lamp, a bookshelf filled with westerns and books on woodcarving, a tall chest of drawers – that was all the furniture there was. Rudolf searched quickly through the chest of drawers. In the bottom drawer, tucked away in a pile of underclothes, he found a letter which appeared to have been read and reread many times. Holding a corner of the envelope gingerly between thumb and forefinger, he eased the letter out and teased it open. He read it with narrowed eyes:

Raoul, dearest,
   I'm so down. I don't understand a thing. We seemed to be so good for each other. What's made you stop loving me – so suddenly? And what makes you say I'm too good for you? If you don't love me, why can't you come right out and say so? But what have I said or done? Darling Raoul, phone me – please! I can't stand it much longer, this not knowing.

The letter was dated 10 February. It was signed: 'Yours as ever, Elvira'. Rudolf carefully replaced the letter in the envelope and slipped it into his pocket. Outside the door he ran into Mrs Rustad. Ignoring her questioning look, he thanked her and left.

Half an hour later he was on his way to where Raoul Hansen's sister Svanhild lived with her husband, Jon Valberg. The Valbergs lived in an old house on the outskirts of the city. He had to ring the bell twice before Mrs Valberg came to the door.

Rudolf gave a start. Svanhild Valberg was neither pretty nor ugly, simply plain. Of medium height, she had blonde hair and was wearing an electric-blue dress that was in glaring contrast to the dingy appearance of the house.

'Yes?' she said, sizing him up with veiled eyes.

Rudolf introduced himself. 'I'd like to have a word with your brother Raoul, if I may. I gather that he's staying with you.'

The woman wrinkled her brow. 'Why?'

Instead of answering her question Rudolf fixed her with a cold eye: 'And with you, too, Mrs Valberg,' he said.

'With me? I don't understand . . .'

'It's about Elvira Anker,' said Rudolf. Reluctantly the woman stepped aside and ushered him in.

As he crossed the threshold Rudolf was tempted to add:

'And about your mole.'

When he got back to Victoria Terrasse Rudolf found the Brenners in Chief Inspector Albrektsen's office; also there were Karsten and Haraldsen.

'Linderud hasn't stopped talking since you left,' said Albrektsen. 'He just goes on and on.'

'You strike me as being a sensible chap, Sergeant,' said Peter Brenner before Rudolf could reply. 'These others here . . .' He made a dismissive gesture. 'How many times do I have to say that we've occasionally let our flat for a while without knowing what it was going to be used for? We thought a few lads, men about town, you know, were going to have a bit of a party with their girlfriends. Can't be too narrow-minded these days, can one? But we'd no idea . . . And as for these filthy pictures! Do you really think, Sergeant, that we'd be party to such a thing as blackmail?'

'You took money when you let your flat out, though, didn't you?' Albrektsen put in.

'Of course we did.' Brenner's face took on a pained look. 'Why shouldn't we? It's a fine place for parties, better than some of the reception rooms I've been in. We've had a few noisy dos there ourselves. Out at Lysaker it's like living in a monastery. We're surrounded by a lot of decrepit old fogies who complain if you laugh aloud.'

'The walls are as thin as paper,' said Rudolf. 'But I suppose the people in the other flats are too afraid of their landlord to complain. Linderud claims it was you who took the camera and things to his shop and that you used to hand in the films in person.'

'Quite true,' the dentist replied. 'Both my wife and I were in the shop several times. But I swear that we hadn't the faintest idea what kind of films we were dealing with. We wouldn't have dreamed of helping to get them developed and copied if we'd known what they were.' He glanced at his wife. 'The truth is – and I'm sure this isn't against the law – we used sometimes to take a few . . . er, intimate pictures of ourselves. But then I developed them myself. I'd never have dreamed of letting a

202

photographer do it.'

'But what did you think they were, then, these films you handed in?' asked Albrektsen, who was having difficulty in concealing his loathing of the couple.

'We never really thought about it, either of us. Didn't connect it with letting out the flat. Just thought we were doing a good turn.' He paused. 'We keep on hearing this accusation about our having orgies in the flat, but if I had, or we had, I, we . . .' He again glanced at his wife, who was looking increasingly pale and worn. 'We'd have been on the pictures, wouldn't we? But we're not. Not on a single one. If there really were orgies, proper ones, I mean, and somebody filmed them, that's not our fault.'

'But didn't it ever occur to you to ask why it should always be you who handed in the films? Didn't you ask whoever it was who gave them to you why he didn't do it himself?'

Brenner shook his head. 'It was always Dr Haakonsen who gave them to me and asked me to put them in for developing.'

'Why didn't he do it himself?'

'He said he was too busy. And he always gave me something for my trouble, as he was at pains to point out.'

Albrektsen was getting impatient. 'It's no good, Mr Brenner,' he put in at last, unable to restrain himself any longer. 'You must realize yourself how feeble it all sounds. You, a dentist with a flourishing practice running errands for – for peanuts.' He gave a snort of disbelief.

The dentist made no answer.

Rudolf turned to the chief inspector. 'Has Linderud said how he got involved?' he asked.

'He says that Brenner here threatened him. He'd been, er . . . enjoying the favours of a certain Bettina and she'd recorded some of their conversations and, er . . . get-togethers.' He permitted himself a tight smile at the euphemism. 'Says Brenner knew her – intimately, not to put too fine a point on it. And that she confided in him what she'd done. Brenner got hold of the tapes and threatened to send them to Linderud's wife.'

'It's a lie,' Brenner protested vehemently. 'He's made it all up. I don't know anything about his private life. He can do what he likes with as many women as he likes, what do I care? I've never known any Bettina, intimately or otherwise. I haven't the faintest idea who she is even.'

'But you knew Greta Olesen.'

'*Intimately?*' He swore, then apologized. 'You must realize that he's lying. I hadn't the faintest idea what the films were I was handing in to him, so why should I have threatened him? I gave them in to be developed and printed and I always got them back in a sealed envelope. He didn't want me to know what they were, I suppose.'

'So you collected them, too?' said Albrektsen.

'Yes. Never said anything different, have I?' Brenner looked aggrieved. 'Dr Haakonsen game me the exposed film and he got the finished pictures back from me – all wrapped up and sealed, as I said. It was *his* friends who borrowed the flat, not mine. But who's going to believe me, now that he's done a bunk?'

'Just one small point,' said Karsten, speaking for the first time. 'Mrs Olesen doesn't seem a bit worried by your threat of legal action. Why do you think that is?'

'Don't ask me,' Brenner replied irritably. 'You can tell her from me, though, that unless she retracts her stinking allegations I shall take her to court. I mean it! If she thinks she has proof, then let her produce it. She's not playing cat and mouse with me. I'll soon settle *her* hash!'

'You *knew* that Bettina and Greta Olesen were one and the same person, Mr Brenner,' Rudolf said. 'You slipped up there, you know.'

'Yes, I noticed that,' said Chief Inspector Albrektsen. 'I've been careful to talk about Bettina all the time without saying she was Greta Olesen. Yet when I said that he knew Greta Olesen, what was his reply? "Intimately?" That's what he said. Then he swore. Instead of asking what *she* had to do with it, which would have been natural.'

'For heaven's sake stop talking as though I weren't here!' Peter Brenner burst out. 'Of course I know she's one and the same person. So does everyone else in Norway who can read or has a television.'

'Not long ago you said you didn't know her.'

'*Know* her, not know *of* her, who she was. Bettina, I mean. Greta I've known since she was a kid.'

Albrektsen passed a weary hand across his face. He turned to Karsten and asked him to take them out. Rudolf then reported briefly on the day's events, while Albrektsen and Haraldsen listened in silence. When Karsten returned, Rudolf gave him a quick rundown on what he had said. While he was doing so the door opened to admit Detective Constable Arvik with a handful of lists from Oslo's car-hire firms. He laid them on the chief inspector's desk. When Rudolf had finished speaking Albrektsen thanked him and phoned for WPC Gunhild Mortensen. Quickly, he brought her up to date on all the new developments. 'And I think I can assure you,' he said kindly, 'that your friend Elvira would have been killed whether you'd been in the police or not. So don't go blaming yourself.'

'Poor Elvira,' Gunhild mumbled, her eyes filling with tears. 'Sorry,' she said, blinking them back. 'Shows how little one knows about one's fellows, doesn't it, even one's friends. I'd always thought that Elvira had her sights set on a sister's job, or even higher, that marriage wasn't anywhere in her plans. And now I find . . . ' She fished a packet of cigarettes out of her tunic pocket and lit one with the match Karsten obligingly proffered.

'Thank you,' she said in a low voice. Her gaze wandered from Albrektsen to Rudolf, and back to Karsten. 'I've made quite a discovery,' she said. 'The only name that's on both Dr Haakonsen's list of patients and on Brenner's is – well, it's quite interesting, really. He stopped going to Brenner four years ago, but according to Dr Haakonsen's appointments book he went to see *him* three months ago. And I find that rather strange, because – well, quite simply he died four years ago!' She looked expectantly about her, pleased at the bombshell she had dropped.

'Died?' asked Rudolf incredulously. 'Yet . . . '

'That's right, Rudolf, he's dead. I've checked with Central Registry, the Probate Office, you name it, I've checked it. And once I was sure, I started on the other names in his book. I'd begun to have my suspicions by then. They're all dead, every single one of them. So we haven't got his real register of patients, if he had one. Means he'd been planning his getaway for a long time.'

'Clever,' said Karsten, 'real clever. He must have been carrying it about with him for just such an emergency. Perhaps there was someone on it who could have given us a lead to where he is now or what he's been up to.'

'And how about this?' said Rudolf, who had been quietly scanning the list of rented-out cars. 'Order placed on February the sixth for the twenty-sixth. For a large station wagon – for one day only. And who by? Hold your hats on: Gemma Marcello.'

'Now we're really getting somewhere,' said Karsten. 'Funny, isn't it? Once the snowball starts to roll . . . it's like a ladder in a silk stocking – or was, when they wore them. Ah, those were the days, my friend,' he added wistfully, giving Gunhild an impish grin. 'But before we make a beeline for Millionaire Row I suggest that the Scout here and I have a few words with Mrs Olesen again. Kristoffersen's not going to decamp, not with us watching his every move.' He looked questioningly at Chief Inspector Albrektsen. 'OK?'

Albrektsen nodded. 'OK,' he said. 'If you think it'll help, go right ahead.'

Karsten thanked him and beckoned to Haraldsen. 'Come on Scout, let's go and see what we can get out of the old vulture this time.'

30

'We've come straight from Victoria Terrasse, Mrs Olesen,'
Karsten said when he and Haraldsen were shown into the room
where the woman lay.

'Oh, so you've found the bank, then.' Her eyes lit up.

'Bank?' For a moment Karsten was genuinely at a loss.

'Where Greta had her numbered account.'

Good God, thought Karsten, that's all she thinks about.
Money, money, money. Her only child's just died and all she's
worried about's her blessed money.

'You didn't give me time to finish what I was going to say,
Mrs Olesen,' he said heavily. 'What I was going to say is that
Albert Linderud – you know the name, I take it –'

The woman frowned. 'No-o.'

'Albert Linderud, who runs a photographic shop near the
East Station has accused Brenner of handing in photographic
equipment and films at his shop. We're holding Brenner at the
moment. You've also made certain allegations. Brenner says
he's not prepared to play games with you, that if you think
you've any proof, then you'd better produce it, otherwise he'll
sue you. That's what *he* says, but *I'd* like to add that if you do
have anything to back up your accusation I'd advise you to
come out with it now.'

'I don't know what you're talking about.'

'Well, in that case,' Karsten replied, as nonchalantly as he
could, 'there's nothing more to be said. And tomorrow you're
going home, I hear.'

'Home? Are they sending me home?'

'Yes, of course. Why not? There's nothing wrong with you
now, is there? You're over the shock and now it's just a matter

of getting your strength back, and you can do that just as well at home as here. Can't stay here for ever, you know,' he said blithely. 'Hospital beds are in short supply.'

'But – home?' She looked fearfully from one policeman to the other.

'Yes, home. What's wrong with home?' As if he were talking to himself, Karsten continued: 'You've no proof, so Brenner will probably go to his lawyer. But that's better than – well, if he's mixed up with some shady international organization and he thought you were a threat . . . Still, never mind all that,' he finished briskly. 'We'll be off.'

'What did you say?' Obviously rattled, Inga Olesen shot upright in the bed and stared at Karsten, breathing heavily. 'What did you say about an international organization?'

'I was just thinking aloud, Mrs Olesen,' said Karsten consolingly. 'Letting my thoughts run away with me. I thought perhaps your life could be in danger. But as you've no proof . . .'

'Wait!' the woman exclaimed, sinking back against the pillow. She sighed deeply. 'And Greta said they were our insurance policy,' she murmured in a voice so low that Karsten barely caught what she said.

'What were?' Karsten asked.

'The pictures. Pictures of her and Brenner and three other couples. All naked, all sort of . . . sort of mixed together. She said she'd pinched them and that I was to take good care of them. Hide them. Could come in handy one day, she said. That's when she called them our insurance policy.'

'And where did you hide them?' Karsten prompted.

'In the corner, under the carpet at the china shop where I clean. It's wall to wall, but there's a loose bit there, under the shelf with glass elephants on it. Near our flat, your know, and Brenner's. Same building.'

'I see. So that's why you felt so secure, was it? If he sued you, you'd threaten to expose him. Stick him for a bit of money too, perhaps?'

'And why not?' said Inga Olesen indignantly. 'You've got to look after Number One in this life. I learnt that when I was a kid, and my word, how true it is! He's as rotten as they come. But go on now, you've got what you came for.' Wearily, she turned her face away into the pillow.

208

31

'Now what is it?' Mrs Moberg demanded irritably when she opened the door to Rudolf, Karsten and Haraldsen. Without waiting for a reply she led them into the television lounge, where, drink in hand, Kristoffersen was watching a television programme on one of the Swedish channels and Gemma and Renee were playing cards.

'Have you found Sonja?' Renee asked excitedly, looking up at Rudolf.

'I'm afraid not, Reneè, not yet. But we shall, you'll see.'

'Go down into the playroom and put one of your cassettes on, there's a good girl,' said Gemma, sweeping up both her daughter's and her own cards. She asked why the policemen had come in such force.

'Raoul Hansen and Jon Valberg have been arrested for stealing the drugs that disappeared from the Surgical Department at Ulleval on the twenty-sixth of February,' said Rudolf. 'The Brenners have also been arrested.'

The woman gave a gasp and put a hand to her throat. Kristoffersen blinked once and stared moodily into his glass. No other reaction was discernible in either of them.

'They say Dr Haakonsen told them to take the container into the Surgical Department as usual. Only instead of leaving it there and bringing back the empty one, as they normally did, they were to take the full one out to their van again. There they put what was in it into two suitcases, which they then placed in the car you hired on the sixth for the twenty-sixth, Mrs Kristoffersen.'

Kristoffersen took his eyes off Rudolf and fixed them on Gemma. 'Did you hire a car? Whatever for? I don't see . . .'

Gemma inclined her head towards the three policemen. '*I* don't see, either. It's true that I hired a car, though – on the sixth for the twenty-sixth. But it was only because I was going to meet a friend who was coming back from . . . America.' She looked a little embarrassed. 'He . . . he . . . well, he was coming back and I didn't want to use one of our cars in case someone recognized it. My, er – husband is terribly jealous, not that he has any reason to be, and I didn't want him to know that I was going to meet this man, this friend.'

'A man?' A look of dismay crossed Kristoffersen's face, to be replaced by a dark frown. 'But if there was nothing between you, why on earth . . .?'

'Well, I did, and that's all there is to be said about it,' Gemma said tartly. 'Maybe it was silly, but it was well-intentioned.'

'There's a lot more to be said, I'm afraid, Mrs Kristoffersen,' Rudolf said. 'But this isn't the place. You'll have plenty of time for explanations when we get to Victoria Terrasse.'

At that moment Anna came in to say that Rudolf was wanted on the phone. He returned shortly afterwards to say that Sonja had been found in Germany in a very poor state. She was in a hospital in Munich and was suffering from withdrawal symptoms. They were going to send her home as soon as she was considered fit to travel. 'She's been on heroin,' said Rudolf bluntly.

'Oh, no!' cried Kristoffersen. 'Not heroin. Oh, my God!'

'Yes, heroin. She's expected to pull through, but only just.'

Kristoffersen buried his face in his hands. A muffled sob escaped him.

'Alf,' said Gemma sharply, 'pull yourself together.'

Kristoffersen looked up. 'What about Harald?'

'He's not been found.'

'So he's dead,' said Kristoffersen with finality. 'They've killed him and destroyed my Sonja. Why didn't they do away with her, too, I wonder?'

'They? Who're "they"?'

'The . . . Organization.'

'What organization?'

'Alf!' said Gemma with a warning frown. 'You're letting your tongue run away with you.'

'Mind if I have a look inside your wardrobe, Mrs Kristoffersen?' Rudolf asked. He rose to indicate that it was a demand, not a request.

'Funny thing to ask, but, yes, certainly, go ahead. Be my guest.'

'Hansen and Valberg have given us a detailed description of what the woman who drove the car had on. The number of the car – they'd noted it down, fortunately – tallied with that of the car you hired. And to cap it all, as you might say, Dr Haakonsen gave them a picture of you, which wasn't very bright of him.'

'Gemma . . . did they force you, too . . .?' Kristoffersen's voice trailed miserably away.

There was no yellow costume among the many garments hanging in the wardrobe.

'It doesn't matter. I didn't expect it, really,' Rudolf said. 'You've got rid of it, I suppose.'

'Got rid of it? I wouldn't put it that way,' Gemma said. 'I did have a yellow two-piece once, but I spilt wine on the skirt, red wine at that, just after Christmas sometime, and when I tried to get it out I made such a mess of it that in the end I just stuffed in into a plastic bag and dumped it in the dustbin.'

'In January?'

'Either early January or at the end of December. You keep on hounding me, but you can't expect me to remember the exact date, surely?'

'Gemma . . . have they . . . got something on you?' Kristoffersen asked piteously. 'But what have *you* done wrong?'

'Alf, I haven't the faintest idea what you're talking about. If I were you, I'd try thinking more and talking less.'

'But Sonja – on heroin. And they only *expect* her to pull through, they don't know for certain that she will. Do you know, I've spent my life working for that girl, worshipped her, in fact. She reminds me so of her mother, even looks like her. If she dies, I shall have nothing more to live for.'

'Oh, yes, you will. You have me, Alf, and you have Renee. I'm not Astrid, I know, and she's not Sonja, but we're both tremendously fond of you, love you, in fact, and that must mean something, surely?'

'I've not had a moment's peace since the Organization started ruling my life, telling me what to do and what not to do. I'm tired, Gemma, tired of the whole damned thing. I can't take any more.'

'You keep on about the Organization,' said Rudolf. 'What organization, that's what I'd like to know.'

'Alf!'

Kristoffersen looked at Gemma. 'I can't sleep, Gemma, I don't enjoy my meals, I don't enjoy anything any longer. All I do, night and day, is to think about the mess I've got myself into. I just can't carry on like this any longer. It's driving me mad. D'you hear that? Mad!'

It was then that the dam broke. Kristoffersen started to talk, and he went on and on despite Gemma's desperate attempts to stop him. He'd been forced into drug trafficking, blackmailed into it, by Dr Haakonsen. The doctor had likewise been compelled to take part in it. How? He'd once performed an illegal abortion on a girl of fifteen, who had died. It was never traced to him, but somehow the Organization had got on to it. And they'd also found out that for years he, Kristoffersen, had been siphoning off money from his foreign business transactions and instead of bringing it into Norway, where it would have been heavily taxed, paying it into a numbered account in Switzerland. He'd no idea how they had got wind of it, but he knew that if it leaked out his secure little business empire would collapse. He had tried to buy the Organization off, but they weren't interested. It was him personally, and his connections, they needed, for their own ends.

He had found himself head of a kind of clearing house for drugs. The doctor had given him a code, changing it every time he made a delivery of drugs, and he had then used it to place a coded ad in an Oslo daily, a different one each time. Not even Dr Haakonsen knew who the top man in Norway was, let alone abroad. He had received all his instructions in writing, but with nothing to indicate where they came from, and it had been impressed upon him that they were to be destroyed once he had carried them out.

Yes, Kristoffersen reluctantly admitted, it had paid – handsomely.

How long had he been in it?

Six or seven years.

Let the Brenners say what they liked if they wanted to defend themselves. He, Alfred Kristoffersen, had had more than enough. He wanted to salve his conscience and to expunge the whole filthy business from his mind. Yes, he admitted that it was filthy. But now it was over, that part of it, anyway. And the Brenners? Oh, yes, Dr Haakonsen had come to him one day and said that the Organization wanted them to remove something from the Brenners' flat. At that time he had not know what the Brenners were up to, and it had come as a nasty jolt when he found out. Kristoffersen was known to everyone in the building, so the doctor had proposed that he should wear a disguise.

'I'd never talked with Harald about Astrid, not in detail, not about her stage-career or anything like that, so I don't know to this day how he found out that she'd once played a part that required her to wear widow's weeds.' Kristoffersen drained his glass and poured himself another drink. 'I thought it was a stupid idea, but I agreed to it because I had no choice. It was as simple as that.'

Oslo's schools had been closed for the annual winter holiday, and they knew that although the Brenners were childless they always took that week for their own holiday. Dr Haakonsen had fetched Kristoffersen early Friday morning, and in a quiet side street the latter had donned his disguise. 'It was more like a blasted chador than widow's weeds,' Kristoffersen said savagely. All the doctor had worn in the way of disguise was a flaming red scarf. 'If anyone sees us,' he'd said, 'afterwards all they'll remember will be a red scarf and a widow.' They'd remembered the widow all right. But the red scarf?

'It's been hell!' Kristoffersen burst out. 'Sheer hell.'

'It will be if you don't keep your mouth shut, Alf,' Gemma admonished him sharply.

'And Brandt?' asked Rudolf, making an effort not to betray the emotion he felt.

'We hadn't counted on a patient turning up at that hour,'

Kristoffersen said in a low voice. 'I should never have started talking to him. I panicked, that's all there was to it.'

'But why kill a completely harmless and innocent man like him?' Rudolf asked. Again he found it difficult to keep his voice steady. His loathing for the abject figure before him was increasing every minute. 'You had a veil. No one in the building knew Haakonsen, you say. That's why he thought all he needed was a red scarf. And Brandt didn't even live round there. And yet . . .'

'I've told you. Panic. I just plain lost my head.'

'What happened, exactly?'

'The only consolation I have is that it was all so sudden that I don't think Brandt had time to be afraid. I closed the door of the waiting-room behind me, turned on the tap, and told Harald – I had to keep my voice down, of course, even though the water was running – that there was a patient there, a man, and that I'd said my "son" would be along soon. Harald said we'd just have to kill him. I couldn't have been thinking, because I never even questioned it, I just asked Brandt to come into the surgery. Harald was behind the door. The sink was full of water by then. It . . . it was all over in no time. I don't think he realized what was happening. He can't have seen a widow like that for years, so his mind must have been in pretty much of a whirl, I should think, and it was dark, too, remember. We hadn't dared to switch the lights on.'

Kristoffersen stopped and took another swig at the drink in his hand. 'You kept on wondering about that towel that was missing, Sergeant. The explanation's quite simple. I had a bout of coughing, I had the flu, you know. In my confusion I'd left my handbag – well, it was more than that, it was bigger – in the waiting-room, not being used to walking around with a handbag, and I just grabbed the first thing that happened to be to hand, and that was Brenner's towel.'

In a flash Rudolf recalled the woman on television. 'Whatever you have to hand,' she'd said. So that was what had been nagging him all this time.

'But why was it necessary to search Brenner's flat and to remove the camera and things?' Rudolf asked curiously.

'Because the Organization had found that the game was up, that he was on the point of being exposed, and they couldn't

214

risk that. He couldn't be got back from Voss in time, I expect, so that's why they picked on us.'

Exposed? By whom? Rudolf wondered. The police had had no idea of what he was up to. It must have been one of the men or women he'd tried to blackmail who had refused to pay. And the Organization that Kristoffersen talked about was probably afraid that one thing might lead to another . . .

Poor Brandt. And poor old Mrs Brandt, who had told him all about her son's sad love affair with an air hostess. A fabrication from start to finish, Rudolf concluded. The old lady had said how wonderful it was to receive a visit from her son three times a week, because he'd always such a lot to tell her. It was pitiful. Rudolf could picture his life, grey, humdrum, unvaried, the same routine day in, day out, week after week. No wonder he'd built up a world of fantasy. It could have been as much for his own sake as for his mother's. They'd both had their interest aroused by all the publicity surrounding drugs, so to add a little spice to his story he'd made his air hostess into a smuggler. The only plane trips she'd ever made had been flights of imagination. He smiled wrily at his own joke and with an effort brought his mind back to what Kristoffersen was saying.

Dr Haakonsen had phoned Greta Olesen and told her that he and Kristoffersen felt like having a party, a good one. He'd told her to dress up a bit – 'doll yourself up' was the expression he'd used, Kristoffersen remembered. 'We had a few drinks at her place and then we drove out to a restaurant on the peninsula.'

Rudolf drew a deep breath. 'You said you were going to, you mean. What you actually did was to get her drunk, fill her up with pep pills and topple her into the fjord.' His lips tightened. 'I suppose it was the good doctor who gave her the final push?'

'Yes,' said Kristoffersen miserably, not daring to look Rudolf in the eye, 'yes, it was.'

'Nurse Anker must have been a bit of a problem. She didn't drink and *she* wasn't on drugs.'

The man slumped in the chair shifted uncomfortably. 'Yes,' he said, his voice so low that Rudolf had to lean forward to catch what he was saying. 'It was – terrible. Terrible. I had to hold her while Harald poured whisky down her throat and . . . and then some pills. He had a drum full of water in the boot of

215

his car and . . . and a bucket.' He buried his face in his hands. 'I don't want to think about it, even.'

'No, I don't suppose you do,' said Rudolf grimly. 'Nor do I, but I have to. Why did you and your precious doctor friend have to dispose of her, anyway? She wasn't involved in any way, surely?'

'She'd been having an affair – well, not an affair, they were genuinely in love, I think – with Raoul Hansen, and – I have all this from Harald, Dr Haakonsen – and when he tried to break it off, because his conscience was pricking him – he was the weak link in the chain, Harald said – she kept pestering him to know why, and in the end he either broke down and confided in her or she wormed it out of him, one or the other. And so Harald said she had to be got rid of.'

'The woman next door saw you come out with her and she was crying. How did you manage to get her to go with you?'

'I had a gun – and I said her brother would be beaten up or worse if she didn't.'

'Alf, do you realize what you're saying?'

'Yes, Gemma. And I realize that this is the end – of everything. Everything I worked for years to build up, you and me, the lot, it's all over.'

'But why go to all the trouble to drive up to Skogen and drown the poor girl in a bucket of water?' Rudolf asked wonderingly.

'You may well ask,' said Kristoffersen. 'Harald made the running, I just did as he said. By that time I was in a kind of daze. He didn't want to kill her in the flat because the body would have been found so quickly. I've asked myself about why he went to all that trouble, getting me to dress up again in those stupid clothes and drowning her in a bucket. I didn't dare ask him, he'd have snapped my head off, but the only thing I can think of – it sounds crazy, I know, but – well, I think I appealed to his sense of the melodramatic. I think it had gone to his head, all these killings and the dressing up, the way the papers splashed the story of the widow. It's an awful thing to say, but I think he actually enjoyed it, the killing and all.'

Rudolf shook his head. 'I think we'll leave the rest till we get to Victoria Terrasse,' he said, getting to his feet.

'No,' Kristoffersen said imploringly, 'let me finish. Please!

Kari, Kari Gundersen, she was a wonderful person. I know the kind of life she led, but she was a wonderful person, a *good* person, even so. You may not believe me, but she wasn't a bit interested in who I was. She liked me – loved me – just for myself, just for, for being me. What about that, eh?' For a brief moment he brightened up. 'We met in Switzerland, and it was Harald who was so insistent on my not telling her who I was. So I bribed the staff. I did everything possible to make sure she didn't get to know anything about my private life. And none of it was necessary. She just wasn't interested.'

The recorder stopped with a sudden click. Karsten inserted a new cassette.

'I was a coward, Sergeant. I ditched her in Montreux, slipped away without saying goodbye. And then we bumped into one another behind the Town Hall, quite by accident. There wasn't a word of recrimination. We agreed to meet at her place that same evening – she invited me. She made no attempt to disguise how she was making a living – though she was working, too, wasn't she? She was quite straightforward about it. That's the way she was. I took a bottle of vodka with me. We . . .' He broke off and cleared his throat. 'Well, that's beside the point. What I was going to say was that I offered to keep her. I wanted to get her off the streets. We got on so well together, you see. We had the same sort of background. We *understood* one another. I'd no idea she was on drugs. If I had, I'd never have encouraged her to drink the way I did. And when I heard that she'd . . . that she'd . . .' Kristoffersen stared glassy-eyed into space. 'Why? That's what I keep asking myself. Why?'

'And the drugs theft on the twenty-sixth?'

'I don't know anything about that. You say Gemma –' He looked helplessly across at the stony-faced woman opposite him. 'Don't tell me you're not in it too,' he said. He shifted his gaze back to Rudolf. 'Harald phoned me late the next day and said he'd put two suitcases in the garage. He didn't say what was in them, but I could guess. He didn't say where it was all from, either, I found that out when I saw the papers. He never told me anything, any of the details. He just said that they were under a tarpaulin and asked me to take them to Brenner's flat as early as I could next day. I realized that he wasn't just asking, of course, that it was an order, so all I could do was

217

say yes.'

'Why didn't he take them up to Brenner's himself? You say no one there knew him.'

'It was better that I should do it, because every now and then I used to go there with cases of clothes and things for Brenner's jumble sales. He was an active member of two charitable organizations.'

Murder, pornography, blackmail, drugs – and charity work. Rudolf shook his head in amazement. 'That's it,' he said resolutely. 'Now we're going.'

Kristoffersen made no move. 'Do you know something, Gemma?' he said. 'It's just struck me. This hold that Harald had on me. There's only one person knows about it, the whole thing, I mean, from this end, and that's you. He said he received his information from the head of the Organization in Norway. And I've been worrying and wondering all these years, looking everywhere – except here at home, right under my nose. Are you . . .?'

'You're letting your imagination run away with you, Alf. All this worry about Sonja – it's driven you distraught.'

'*Are* you Number One in Norway? Are you? Answer me!'

'My husband's not himself,' said Gemma forcefully. 'He doesn't realize what he's saying.'

'Perhaps,' said Rudolf. 'Perhaps not. Anyway, get your things together, please, both of you, we're going now.'

'*I* can't help you,' Gemma said calmly, getting to her feet and going over to the window. 'So why should I go?' Her back to the four men in the room, she stood staring out into the garden. Then, to their surprise, she suddenly lit three candles standing in a decorative holder on the sill.

'What on earth are you doing?' Kristoffersen asked in amazement.

'I love candles,' she said, 'candles and candlelight.' Abruptly, she blew them out, only to relight them a few seconds later.

'Have you gone crazy?' Kristoffersen asked.

'Leave them for a while, Alf,' Gemma said with a wan smile. 'I'd like to say goodbye to Renee. She's so like me. She loves candles, too.' She rang for the maid, who went to fetch the child.

'But where're you going, Mummy?' Renee asked anxiously.

218

'I'm only going to help these policemen with something, dear,' Gemma said. 'It's nothing to worry about. You'll be all right with Anna and Mrs Moberg. Now, run along, back to your cassettes. You'll see, I'll be back before you know it.'

Obedient to her mother's wish, the girl left, but she was plainly unhappy with the situation.

Poor kid, thought Rudolf, another innocent victim. It's like rings in the water.

'Let the candles burn down of their own accord, Anna,' said Gemma. 'Candles in a window, there's something peaceful about a lighted candle.'

Anna looked at her uncomprehendingly. 'Yes, all right, Mrs Kristoffersen, if you say so.'

Rudolf's car stood close to the gate. 'It's colder than I thought,' said Gemma, drawing her mink coat closer about her. Rudolf didn't answer.

Just outside the gate Gemma paused and turned to look back at the house. At that moment a black Mercedes swung out from a drive on the opposite side of the road. As it passed them, the car slowed down. Gemma sprang towards it. Realization came to Rudolf in a flash. The candles! They'd been a signal. As he made to follow her, he saw in his mind's eye the rear door open and a man lean out and haul Gemma in.

He was wrong. Instead, there were two short bursts of automatic fire. Just two. The first caught Gemma. The second, Kristoffersen. Kristoffersen died instantly. Gemma lived long enough to gasp out one word: 'Bastards!'

The car was away before anyone had time to take the number. Not that it would have helped. It would either prove to be stolen or the plates would be false.

Late that same evening Chief Inspector Albrektsen, Rudolf, Karsten, Haraldsen, Arvik, Robotten and several other policemen who had been on the case were still at Victoria Terrasse. All that could be done that day had been done; all that could be said had been said. But still no-one seemed to want to go home.

The house from whose drive the Mercedes had so suddenly appeared turned out to have been empty for the last two months. The owners had a house in Spain where they were accustomed to spend the winter. As a rule they let their Oslo house, but this year they had not done so, not thinking it worthwhile as they planned to remain in Spain for only ten weeks.

Had Gemma been head of the Norwegian branch of the Organization, whatever it was? There was much to suggest that she had. Those candles. Had she thought they would help? Had they been a prearranged signal? Again, all the evidence pointed in that direction. Poor Gemma, Rudolf couldn't help thinking. Caught up in something that had got to be too big for her. A pawn in the game. Expendable.

Was Dr Haakonsen still alive? And if he was, would he ever be found? Interpol were already doing all they could to help, but with plastic surgery, dyed hair, money and good connections the odds were heavily on his side. Perhaps he had been Number One and it was for that reason that he had been able to make a getaway.

It was good that Renee had grandparents in Italy. The gunfire had brought her and Anna and Mrs Moberg running out of the house, and she had been put to bed shortly afterwards under sedation. Thank God for the resilience of childhood, thought Rudolf.

'Binder' Pearson came into the office, weaving his way through the throng. He sniffed, then started to cough. 'A Mrs Jansen's just phoned,' he said. 'Her fourteen-year-old son's missing. She knows he's on drugs, but she doesn't know what. He's not been home for a week, and she didn't dare wait any longer without reporting it.'

The words reached Rudolf as through a fog. My God, he thought, here we go again. Bloody drugs! His thoughts were still on Gemma. There had been something special about her, something . . . No, that wouldn't do, he told himself, he was a married man. He had his Magda.

Magda. A thought struck him. The flowers! He'd forgotten them. Again.